The
Shape Stealer

www.**transworldbooks**.co.uk

Also by Lee Carroll

Black Swan Rising
The Watchtower

The
Shape Stealer

Lee Carroll

BANTAM PRESS

LONDON · TORONTO · SYDNEY · AUCKLAND · JOHANNESBURG

TRANSWORLD PUBLISHERS
61–63 Uxbridge Road, London W5 5SA
A Random House Group Company
www.transworldbooks.co.uk

First published in the United States
in 2013 by Tom Doherty Associates, LLC

First published in Great Britain
in 2013 by Bantam Press
an imprint of Transworld Publishers

A CIP catalogue record for this book is available from the British Library.

ISBN 9780593066294

Addresses for Random House Group Ltd companies outside the UK
can be found at: www.randomhouse.co.uk
The Random House Group Ltd Reg. No. 954009

The Random House Group Limited supports the Forest Stewardship Council
(FSC®), the leading international forest-certification organization. Our books
carrying the FSC label are printed on FSC®-certified paper. FSC is the only
forest-certification scheme endorsed by the leading environmental organizations,
including Greenpeace. Our paper procurement policy can be found at
www.randomhouse.co.uk/environment.

Printed and bound in Great Britain by
CPI Group (UK) Ltd, Croydon, CR0 4YY.

2 4 6 8 10 9 7 5 3 1

For our brothers Bob, Joel, and Larry

Contents

Acknowledgments

We thank once more our most perceptive and helpful U.S. editor, Paul Stevens; our brilliant agent, Robin Rue; and the most energetic and enthusiastic Simon Taylor and Lynsey Dalladay at our UK publisher, Transworld, for all their help and support. Thanks also to the excellent agents Loretta Barrett and Nick Mullendore for their continuing efforts in the realm of foreign rights. And we thank our publishers in the Czech Republic, Poland, Russia, and Turkey, and our fine agent in Belgrade, Serbia, Tamara Vukicevic of the Prava/Prevodi Literary Agency, for finding us new audiences to the east.

Readers who have made immense and ongoing contributions to Lee Carroll's writing include Gary Feinberg, Harry Steven Lazerus, Dow Jones News columnist Al Lewis, Lauren Lipton, Wendy Gold Rossi, Scott Silverman, Nora Slonimsky, and Maggie Vicknair. Special thanks are given to three gifted poets who have contributed their own wonderful poems to this novel: Elizabeth Coleman (www.elizabethjcoleman.com), Katherine Hastings (www.wordtemple.com), and Pui Ying Wong.

Nothing would be possible without our loving and supportive families.

The
Shape Stealer

1

The Little Bridge

Paris in the morning. The streets newly washed by rain. The smells of coffee and fresh baked bread wafting from cafés. Sunlight a glittering promise of the day on the Seine. I'd dreamed of walking like this across the Pont Saint Michel with Will Hughes some day. How after four hundred years of night he would see his first day-break by my side. To win that dawn we'd traveled back in time, faced a conniving alchemist, an evil astrologer, an ancient sorceress, a monster, assorted crocodiles, and Will's own sordid past . . . and won a cure. We'd come back using the Astrologer's Tower and a timepiece I'd fashioned as a time machine, and I'd handed Will the cure—the blood of the shape-shifting creature that had made him a vampire. He had drunk and become human. Descending the Astrologer's Tower we'd learned that the creature, Marduk, had traveled back with us. But I knew that together we could handle even that. When Will looked around him, amazed at the new world at his feet, I thought it was wonder at the new world of daylight after four hundred years of night, but it wasn't. He was amazed because he'd never seen twenty-first-century Paris. The Will I had brought back with me was not the man I had fallen in love with. It was his earlier self. Nineteen-year-old Will Hughes, the callow youth whom I'd found when I traveled back in time to 1602 and inadvertently brought back with me.

"You're not *my* Will," I had told him. "I saved the wrong one."

"Tell me again what he said to you in the alley?"

We were in the Café Le Petit Pont across from Notre Dame. I was on my second café au lait. Will was sipping his, his childish delight at the beverage beginning to grate on my nerves.

"What my dark twin said?"

I sighed with exasperation. "I've explained. He's not your dark twin. He's you—four hundred years later. We came from the future—*now*—to find a cure for him."

Will pouted. My sexy, virile vampire *pouted*. I preferred those lips when they snarled back over fangs. "He said I was his *better self.*"

I snorted. "He was flattering you, probably because he knew it would work. Then what did he say?"

"He told me he knew a way that I could become human again and regain my true love, Marguerite." He made moon eyes at me again, as he had every time he'd mentioned Marguerite. I slapped the table.

"I told you, I am not your Marguerite. I'm a distant descendant."

"Well, he told me you *were*. He said I'd find you at the top of a tower in Catherine de Medici's palace. That I'd have to fight my way there, but when I did I'd find you . . . er . . . Marguerite . . . on top with my cure. And I did fight! There were crocodiles!"

"Yes, you were very brave," I said for the fifth time. "But didn't you ask him *why* he was sending you instead of going himself?"

Will's brow creased. "Why should I question my dark twin's desire to save me?"

I sighed and lowered my head in my hands. "No, I suppose you wouldn't."

"But now that you mention it, he did say one other thing."

"Yes?" I said, picking up my head.

"He said to tell you—well, to tell Marguerite . . ."

I made a circular motion with my hand to urge him to go on.

"Let's see, what were the exact words? He made me memorize them . . . oh yes, that he was sending you his better self because that's what you deserved."

"Then you're both idiots," I said, tossing a euro coin onto the table and getting up. I headed east along the Seine, battling the early morning flow of tourists, not caring if he followed me. But of course he did. He caught up with me in front of the Shakespeare and Company bookstore, where a shopkeeper was setting up the outdoor bins of books in the little square in front of the store.

"I don't know why you're angry with me, good lady. I merely followed the instructions of what appeared to be my dark angel."

"That's why I'm angry with you," I said, wheeling on him. "You followed orders; you didn't think to question him, did you? If you had, he might have told you that he was you four hundred years later and merely because he'd done some questionable things in those four hundred years he didn't think he was good enough for me. Then you might have asked, 'Verily, good sir, have you asked the lady what she thinks?' And he would have been forced to admit that the *lady* had already told him that she didn't care what he'd done, that she loved *him*, the man he was, with all the experiences he'd had, not the silly boy he'd been four hundred years before."

Will, who had grown nearly as pale as his vampire self under my tirade, fidgeted with the frills of his shirt cuff. "I am not silly," he said. "And neither was my older self an idiot. We both did what we did for love. Can we not be friends, you and I? We both want the same thing. You want your beloved Will back and I want my Marguerite. Can that not be arranged? I am willing to go back in time and change places with my dark . . . er . . . my older self."

"That's very gallant of you," I said, "only as I mentioned earlier, the timepiece we used to travel back in time is broken." I held up the watch that hung around my neck. Its glass face had cracked and its gears no longer moved.

I sighed and looked away from him, toward the river and the square in front of Notre Dame where tourists were lining up for morning tours. Time was moving on. Irrationally, I felt it was moving me even further away from Will—the real Will, stuck in 1602. But then something occurred to me. *Time was moving on.* Will wasn't stuck in the past. Without Marduk's blood he had remained a vampire, which meant he would have continued living from then until now. He must exist somewhere in the present . . . but then where was he? The question quickly made my head hurt. I needed to find someone who understood time . . . Of course! Horatio Durant, the watchmaker who had helped me make the timepiece. He hadn't admitted to any supernatural knowledge, but that didn't mean he didn't have any. I would start with him. Relieved to have come up with a plan of sorts, I turned to share it with Will . . . but Will was gone. I spun around in a circle, searching for him, but didn't see him anywhere. He'd vanished into the crowds of tourists streaming along the Seine as completely as his older self had vanished into the river of time.

2

Tender Like a Rose

Despondent over Garet's iciness, Will had turned away from her in front of the bookstore named for his long-lost mentor and love rival, its presence another unfriendly rebuke to his spirit. His eyes had wandered across the faces in the crowd, searching for a friendlier mien, when suddenly he had spied a familiar façade. Not of a person, but of a building. It was the Church of Saint-Julien-le-Pauvre, where he had kept his Paris vigil over Marguerite four centuries earlier after they had parted in London in a conflict over his desire to join her in immortality. A sign at her previous lodgings in London had directed him to wait for her at this church. She never arrived, but another sign he encountered there eventually guided him toward Paimpont in Brittany, where he had found her. Perhaps even now there would be a sign there that would lead him to her. He'd headed toward it, leaving Garet behind him in the crowd.

A distinctive tree near the church's north wall, which

he recalled clearly from 1602, was still here, now with a
plaque on its trunk labeling it "the oldest tree in Paris."
It was, indeed, an ancient-looking specimen. Poor thing,
it had weathered the centuries badly. At some point in its
long life it had leaned so far to one side that it had been
propped up by a metal girder and its trunk had split in
two and been filled with stone. Will sank down onto a
bench in front of the tree, feeling at this evidence of the
centuries that had passed for him and the tree as if he,
too, needed support and as if his heart, too, had been
filled with stone. He was still staring morosely at the
tree when an odd little man approached him. The man
was no more than five feet tall and gave the impression
of a human egg, waddling about rotundly on two short
legs: of a robin's egg in particular, given the pale blue
tint of his summer attire, shorts and a tennis shirt. Dis-
pensing with any social niceties, the man approached
Will, closely observed him with deep-set blue eyes, and
told him that he happened to know that Will was in
need of a time portal. The man knew where Will might
find such a portal, or where rumors among the fey suggested he might find one.

"How on earth do you know my plight?" Will asked,
astonished.

The man allowed himself the smallest crease of a grin.
"It's not on earth that I know your plight. It's in earth."

"How so?"

"I have familiarity with subterranean circles where
certain fey wander. Word travels there. I happen to be

Paul Robin, descendent of the great royal botanist Jean Robin, who remains somewhat alive below ground in this very locale, amidst and part of the roots of the tree you see before you. Indeed, my great-great-etc. grandfather has heard of your arrival here from his sources, and he has sent me to help you."

"Arrival at the church? Or arrival in 2009?"

Paul smiled. "Both. Sources tell me that there's a certain bookstore along the banks of the Seine, Kepler and Dee's, where—assuming you were to find it—if you browse along its shelves long enough, a time portal might open. At least, this is an experience some fey have had. It's through a method called transmigration of atoms, though I have no idea what that is . . ."

But Will did. He had learned of it in London this past unforgettable summer in which he'd fallen in love with Marguerite, and he had some brief experience with it too. Hope flared at hearing the term again.

"Unfortunately I do not have the address of Kepler and Dee's," Paul Robin went on. "But I'm sure that if you walk along the Seine long enough, you will find it. I hope so, anyway."

Paul Robin wheeled around like an egg spinning on its axis and walked swiftly away, without another word. Will was left staring after him, amidst the fading red and gold sunlight, the burgeoning shadows cast by the church and the trees in the park, wondering if he should take him seriously or not. But the man had known his name and his problem. It was worth a try. If he found the portal he'd not only solve his problem, but he'd prove to Garet James that he was not an idiot, as she had so rudely called him.

But after Will had been strolling along the banks of the Seine for nearly two hours, he still hadn't found the store. He'd found a few bookstores, but none with a name like Kepler and Dee's, and the one whose name had rung a bell, Shakespeare and Company, rang it in a somewhat inflammatory way. Nonetheless, he'd been moved to go inside and ask if the store had previously been named Kepler and Dee's, but the clerk only shook a head for no and looked at him as if he were drunk. As had the half dozen people he'd stopped along the way to ask, in his best court French, if they knew the establishment.

Some had stared, a few had laughed. But on the other hand, they all seemed a very civilized bunch, nothing like the rough street crowds of Elizabethan London who could jostle you in the interests of pickpocketing, or out of meanness. Still, he was becoming tired—he'd like another cup of that excellent beverage Garet had procured for him earlier.

That had been kind of her. Even when she was angry— which he could hardly blame her for, after so keen a disappointment as she had suffered—she'd bought him breakfast. And she would have taken him back to her lodgings if he hadn't wandered off. In truth, her coldness hadn't been any more dismissive than Marguerite's final walk away from him in Paris had been, when he'd revealed to her that he had become immortal, and she'd told him that she had simultaneously had herself turned into a mortal, under the cruel illusion that she and Will could now be together in harmony. How hopeful a situation was that?

The more he walked on, the more Garet came to mind. Maybe it was the irrepressible nature of youth, which needed someone to love close at hand. But a wave of feeling came over him, and, poet at the core that he was, he felt the urge to compose a sonnet. It could begin with a recitation of his lover's quandary, but he wanted it to end with a fervent expression of his new feeling. He sat on a bench on the Pont Saint Michel and wrote feverishly, in a tumult, scarcely noticing the crowds or the waning daylight. When Will was done he stared down at the lines he had written as though startled by them, as if he had learned something about himself and his situation he couldn't have learned otherwise, as if a hand other than his own had written the poem.

Love Garet?—Marguerite?—I'm so confused:
whichever way I turn, I seem to lose.
My true beloved's buried in the past
and yet Time's twin of hers perhaps could last
as my great love, if she would only see
that I can love her deeply, as truly
as sunlight loves a gnarled and ancient tree,
as wind's enamored of the clouds that flee

its western onrush; wind pursues them for
as long as there is weather, and birds soar.

I pledge that I am yours forevermore,
fixated like Othello, jealous Moor,
yet tender like a rose embracing spring.
Please understand my plight! Let love take wing!

After reading the poem over, Will went to the nearby railing and stared down at the Seine as if he pondered his own fate there, inside a mirror of water tinged with the red light of the setting sun. And it was Garet's face he saw in the mirror, not Marguerite's. They were similar faces but now, for Will, they were so very different. He recited the poem aloud to himself one more time, and then decided it should be entitled "Tender like a Rose."

Yes, he could . . . perchance he already did . . . love Garet! He'd go find her and show her the poem . . . but find her where? When he'd left her standing in front of the bookstore he hadn't stopped to wonder where they would meet again. Now he rushed back to the store, but of course Garet wasn't there. And he didn't know the name or address of her lodgings. He turned in a circle twice, searching the crowds for her face, but now that night was approaching, the cafés and streets were even more packed. These crowds might be more polite than the 1602 mobs he was familiar with, but they were larger than any he had ever seen. The wall of people seemed to go on and on . . . forever. He turned around and around again . . . and found himself facing a man who was staring at him curiously.

"Are you the man who has been asking everyone for Kepler and Dee's Bookshop?" the man asked.

"Yes!" Will exclaimed. "Do you know where it is?"

"I ought to," the man replied. "I am Johannes Kepler."

3

The hall of Time

I searched the streets and cafés for Will and then, thinking he might have been drawn to the familiar name of his
former tutor, the bookstore. At first I was angry that he'd
caused me this delay in going to Monsieur Durant, but
slowly I became worried. He was such a hapless innocent! What would become of him wandering twenty-first-
century Paris? Then I became regretful that I'd been so
hard on him. He was right that the situation wasn't his
fault. It had been his older self who'd made the decision
to stay in 1602—a decision I should have seen coming.
Older Will had habitually expressed regret about his
past conduct and professed a romantic idealization of his
younger self. I'd tried to reassure him that it was *him* that
I wanted, but maybe I hadn't tried hard enough. Now
I'd lost both of them. I could only hope that young Will
would eventually come back here to the store because it
was the last place we'd been together. I'd leave a note.

Recalling that there was a manual typewriter where
lingering expats typed notes—and poems and unfinished

novels, for all I knew—to each other, I climbed the stairs to the second story and slid into the snug alcove that housed the typewriter. I grabbed a piece of paper, but then glanced at the pages thumbtacked to the walls of the cubby. *Michele, je t'aime, Nicole. Zeke, meet me at the Musee D'Orsay beside our favorite Cezanne. You know the one. Yours evermore, Twink. Elsa, we'll always have Paris. Rick.* And then, *Garet, go to the Institut Chronologique, 193½ rue Saint-Jacques. All your questions will be answered there.*

I yanked the page off the wall and studied it for a signature, but there was none. Could Will have left it for me? But I wasn't sure how he would know about an Institut Chronologique in Paris.

And what the hell *was* the Institut Chronologique? I'd never heard of it. But if it had to do with time, then it was probably a good place to start.

I rolled the paper into the typewriter and typed a reply beneath the enigmatic note: *I'm on my way, Garet.*

The northern end of the rue Saint-Jacques was right around the corner from Shakespeare and Company. Checking my notebook, I saw that the Institut Océanographique, where just a few days ago I'd met Madame La Pieuvre, was at 195 rue Saint-Jacques. I didn't recall an Institut Chronologique on that block, but I must have missed it.

As I walked south past the great marble façades of the Sorbonne I wondered where Octavia La Pieuvre was now. She had traveled with me to the Val sans Retour in Brittany to find passage to the mythical forest of Brocéliande, there to ask to be made a mortal so she could live out a mortal life with her beloved, Adele Weiss. She had told me about the curse of the Val sans Retour, which condemned all faithless lovers to wander there forever. Part sea creature that she was, Madame La Pieuvre had been dehydrated by the hike. When I'd left her to find shade she'd been reminiscing about a past lover. Did that make her unfaithful? I'd lost her during my own trials in the Val, but eventually I'd found Will and together we'd found our way out—albeit that way had led through 1602. Had Octavia la Pieuvre found her own way out? I would have to find Adele Weiss (she was the concierge at my hotel, so that shouldn't be hard) and, if Octavia was still missing, tell her what had happened. I didn't look forward to *that* conversation. Far better to follow an anonymous note to an unknown institute . . . which I should be arriving at soon.

I had come to the Institut de Géographie with its twin globes above its doors, and I could see beyond it the square tower of the Institut Océanographique. The Institut de Géographie was number 191. So the Institut Chronologique must be next door . . . but the next building appeared to be the Oceanography Institute. I checked the numbers again. 191, 195. No 193, let alone a 193½. Had my anonymous note writer gotten the number wrong? Or was it simply a ploy to send me wandering aimlessly around Paris? After all, there were half a dozen things I should be doing—finding Monsieur

Durant, looking for Marduk, telling Adele Weiss about Octavia . . . the list grew as I paced between the two buildings under the baleful glare of the cast-iron octopus above the door of the Institut Océanographique. I was so tired and overwrought I could hear a humming in my head and something ticking . . .

I paused directly in between the two institutes and, peering down the alley between them, recalled something that Octavia La Pieuvre had said to me on the drive to Brittany.

"The mythical forest of Brocéliande is not a place of this world. It can't be found on a map of France. You can't reach it on the E50 or take a TGV from Montparnasse and expect to find the door open to Brocéliande."

Perhaps the Institut Chronologique was not on the map of Paris. Perhaps to find it one had to look hard, or listen . . .

The ticking was coming from the depths of the narrow alley between the two buildings, which ended in a wall covered with vines and ivy. As I stared down the alley, a breeze wafted through it and disturbed the greenery, revealing a marble caryatid flanking a doorway. In the brief glimpse I had of the statue I thought she might be holding an hourglass.

As I walked down the alley the ticking became louder. When I reached the door the breeze stirred the ivy, revealing a huge clock above the doorway, half-hidden by vines—a huge and complicated-looking clock made of three revolving disks filled with celestial symbols, which were transversed by four sweeping hands. The whole contraption was encircled by a dragon biting its own tail, and every inch was inlaid with gleaming enamel.

I immediately wanted to make a reproduction of it for the line of watches I'd been thinking of launching. I took out my sketchbook and began to draw it, losing myself in the myriad details of the complicated mechanism. I hadn't drawn like this since the week before I'd left Paris, when I'd given up on finding Will and thrown myself into sketching in the museums. On this very page I was drawing on were the sketches I'd made in the Musée des Arts et Métiers of timepieces and astrolabes. From them I'd come up with the timepiece I was wearing now. On the night that I'd finished making the timepiece I'd gone to Saint-Julien-le-Pauvre to say my final good-bye to Will and my quest for him. But as I'd sat outside in the Square Viviani, the bells of Notre Dame had chimed midnight and the oldest tree in Paris had split open to admit me into the earth where I'd met Jean Robin, my first guide toward finding Will. Would this door lead me into another adventure? Would it help me find Will again? I looked down for a knob . . . but there wasn't one. Nor was there a door knocker or . . . when I searched through the vines at either side of the door . . . a doorbell. I'd come to a closed door at the end of a narrow dead-end alley where an extraordinarily complicated clock ticked away the seconds. Was this the beginning of an adventure, or the end? As I pondered that question the gears of the clock moved and three of the hands met at the top. Bells began to chime. One . . . two . . . seven . . . eight . . . twelve . . . thirteen . . .

Thirteen?

Two little windows flanking the clock slid open. I waited to see what sort of mechanical figures would pop out, but instead an elderly man's face framed with white fluffy hair appeared in one of them.

"Ah, Garet James," Horatio Durant said. "It's about time."

From its half-hidden door and narrow alleyway entrance I expected a tiny atelier similar to Monsieur Durant's watch shop in the Marais; instead, I walked into a lofty atrium at the center of which was suspended a gigantic pendulum swinging above a black granite basin filled with sand. As the pendulum swung, it described arcs in the sand. Looking up, I saw that the roof soared so high above us I could barely make it out.

"How . . . ?" I began, turning to Monsieur Durant.

"Is it bigger on the inside than the outside?" he finished the question for me. "The institute lies outside the restrictions of time and space," he intoned rather formally. Then he shrugged, threw up his hands, and lifted his white bushy eyebrows at me. "At least, that's what it says in our brochure. As far as I'm concerned, it's a big nuisance. Do you know what it costs to heat this place in the winter? And forget about keeping it clean! The last cleaning crew we hired got lost in the archives and we haven't seen them since."

"I was going to ask how you knew I was coming."

"Ah." Monsieur Durant tapped the side of his nose.

"The pendulum always knows. Look." He pointed to the lines drawn in the sand, all smooth uninterrupted arcs except for one that had an intricate knot in it. I tried to imagine the motion the pendulum would have had to perform to describe such a design—and failed.

"That knot indicates an anomaly in the time line. It told me that someone had traveled through time today. I assumed it was you, since you used my workshop to fashion your timepiece." He tapped the watch that was hanging around my neck and then moved closer. "May I?"

I took the timepiece off and handed it to him. He dug a jeweler's loupe out of the pocket of his baggy trousers and fitted it over his right eye.

"It broke when we came back. Can you fix it?"

He opened the case and studied the gears. His lips moved as though he were counting—or saying a prayer—but he made no sound for several moments. Then he looked up, one eye made giant by the jeweler's loupe. "Did you adjust the settings at any time while you were in the past?"

I shook my head. "I don't think I've adjusted anything on it since it left your workshop."

"Hmph. I'll have to see. It'll take . . ."—He grinned—"*time*. But we've got a bigger problem than your watch. The time line. Ever since we saw the anomaly this morning we've been charting the changes in the archives. Come . . ." He motioned for me to follow him through an arched doorway. As we walked around the pendulum I paused to listen to the soft whooshing of its progress through the sand.

Whooosh, whoosh, Will, it seemed to whisper. *Whoosh, whoosh, why?*

I shook my head. I was just tired, I thought, following Monsieur Durant through the arched doorway and into an even loftier domed space.

"Voilà la Salle du Temps!" Monsieur Durant announced with obvious pride. The Hall of Time was as vast as the Gare de l'Est, only instead of trains standing in their tracks, stacks of books soared up to the domed ceiling. The stacks were fashioned of curving black cast iron and looked as though they had been made by Hector Guimard, the designer of the Paris Metro entrances. The ceiling, too, was spanned by cast-iron ribs that came together in a giant oculus and supported panes of brightly colored and intricately patterned stained glass. The effect was that of being inside a brilliantly painted hot-air balloon that was soaring through the air. A steady breeze wafting down through the oculus added to that impression and filled the hall with a fluttering that sounded like flocks of pigeons but that came, I saw, from rows of old-fashioned newspaper racks—the kind that libraries or some cafés used to have. I recalled an old Italian café on Bleecker Street in New York City where my father liked to have a morning espresso and pastry and read the selection of European papers that hung from racks like these.

Another source of the fluttering came from long wooden tables that stretched between the racks, where men and women sat gazing into large tomes, whose pages turned by themselves while the readers hurriedly took notes in composition books.

"What are they doing?" I asked Monsieur Durant.

"The *chronologistes* are recording the changes in the archives," he replied. "When the anomaly appeared this morning, a number of books were disturbed . . . There goes another one."

He pointed to a shelf about thirty feet above the floor where a book was protruding over the ledge. As we watched it slid even further out. One of the *chronologistes*—a young woman with crimped tea-colored hair and thick square rimmed glasses—ran toward the shelf, her rather impractical green suede heels clicking on the marble floor. She reached the shelf just in time to catch the book.

A thunderous pounding greeted her successful catch as the *chronologistes* applauded their comrade by stamping their feet.

"Brava, Annick!" Monsieur Durant exclaimed. "What have you got?"

Annick, blushing beneath her freckles at Monsieur Durant's praise, laid the book down on the table and gently opened its cover—I noticed she was wearing white cotton gloves—to the title page. "A *History of the Dutch Stock Market*," she read aloud in proper, only slightly accented English. "*From 1602 to the Present*."

"Ah, it looks like your friend Will has been busy."

"Will? Which Will?"

Annick covered her mouth and giggled.

"The one you left behind in 1602," Monsieur Durant said, shaking his head. "He's been changing things—nothing big, nothing that would threaten the world's existence—but little things. Here, let me show you."

We left Annick poring over the Dutch stock market and walked to a table where a balding middle-aged man in a pin-striped suit and yellow bow tie was bent so far over an ancient-looking tome that his sharp nose nearly touched the page.

"Anything more in the folio, Jean-Luc?"

Jean-Luc's head jerked up, his round spectacles fogging as he let out an excited gasp. "*Love's Labour's Won* is no longer lost and *Cardenio* is appearing!"

"There are some more sonnets," a white-haired woman sitting on the other side of the table said. "Granted, some have fifteen lines and/or titles, not characteristic of the famed 154. But there are other signs of the same authorship, and they all laud your friend Will."

"But Shakespeare hated Will for stealing Marguerite," I said.

"That was BA—Before the Anomaly. The Will who stayed behind in 1602 made it up with his mentor. Here, listen to this . . ." She read a sonnet aloud:

"Unmasked"

Come here, dear Will, and let us pluck a rose,
One petal Marguerite and one your Garet James;
We'll know their scarlet hues without their names,

Rare tints a match for both our bloods. Wind
  blows,
Rain falls, or sun burns bright—it's all the
  same—
When love exceeds both of our growing fames,
And all the theories, facts we'll ever know.
A bond outlasting eons, drifting snow,
And all the seasons calendars can grow.
Our friendship now restored, we're London-kin,
As well as colleagues in the sonnet. Let's
Walk slowly on down Lyme Street, close to dusk,
Envision our beloveds in the mists
The river conjures, cleansing love of sin.
Feel jealousy no more. Our loves unmasked.

Friendship now restored? Could that mean . . . ?

"Wait," I said. "I don't understand. Where is all this coming from?" I looked around the great hall. Books were falling, pages were fluttering. "What *is* this place?"

"I told you," Monsieur Durant replied, smiling impishly. "La Salle du Temps of the Institut Chronologique. The great Hall of Time. We keep track of changes in the time line here. When the oculus is closed, the hall is impervious to changes in the time line. There is at all times . . ." His lips quirked into another smile and Jean-Luc smirked, leading me to believe that the *chronologistes* were prone to punning on the word *time*. ". . . a corps of archivists on the premises who are also impervious to the anomaly, as is our library." He waved to the

stacks of books. "We've assembled a collection representing the world's literature, history, science, financial
records, and assorted ephemera. As soon as we open the
oculus the books in the archives begin to rewrite themselves. The *chronologistes* take notes on the changes
they observe and assemble a report. We confer with our
brethren institutes—"

"There are more places like this?" I asked, gaping at
the enormity of the place.

Monsieur Durant sighed. "Fewer than there used to
be. As you can imagine, this is a very expensive enter-
prise to maintain. And it is always vulnerable to corrup-
tion . . ." A pained look flitted across Monsieur Durant's
face. "And the vagaries of social unrest, or worse. We
lost the Warsaw office in the Second World War. But
there are still two great monasteries—one in the Pyre-
nees and one in the Himalayas—as well as institutes in
New York City, Edinburgh, and San Francisco. We've
been getting some very interesting communications from
New York this morning. Your friend Will has been a
busy fellow."

"So let me see if I've got this straight. Because Will
stayed behind in 1602, he has changed time, and you
are able to see those changes here?"

"See and record. Once any one of us leaves the institute our own memories will assimilate to the new time
line. Jean-Luc here will not remember that *Love's Labour's Won* was ever lost. Claudine . . ."—he gestured to
the white-haired woman who had read the sonnet—"will

think she has known those poems all her life. Because she *will have*. Only here in the institute are we granted a brief window of . . . er . . . *time* . . . to record that the world was ever different and to evaluate the nature of the changes made."

"Why?" I asked.

Monsieur Durant looked perplexed.

"I mean, sure, I can imagine you do this for knowledge's sake—"

He shook his head so vigorously that his fluff of white hair moved like a storm cloud. "*Non, non, non!* Not merely for the sake of knowledge, but to guard against those who would change the time line for their own nefarious purposes. If we find such a change, we send our operatives back in time to prevent the change."

"Oh," I said, abashed at my assumption and looking with new eyes at the bookish crew assembled in the hall. "Will you be sending anyone back this time?"

Although they didn't raise their eyes from their books I knew by the cessation of pen scratchings that the *chronologistes* were listening.

"That assessment is made by the head office when all the data is in, but I would gather from what we've seen so far that the answer will be no. Mr. Hughes has, on the whole, been making harmless and even beneficial changes. I can see no pattern of attempting to gain unfair advantage over the world. Even his dealings in the world's financial markets have been to shield and protect the victims of precipitous crashes, and defenseless animals from cruelty, instead of profiting from any foreknowledge he had. The changes we have seen in the police blotters . . . well, Jules can tell you about them."

A thin young man with fair hair parted in the middle lifted his head from a ledger and pushed his eyeglasses up the bridge of his nose. *"Mais oui,"* he began in French, then cleared his throat and reverted to English. "So far I have recorded twenty-eight fewer suspicious deaths from the years 1602 to 1689."

"What kinds of deaths?" I asked, my mouth suddenly dry.

"Murders of prostitutes and street beggars, some bearing the earmarks of a vampire attack such as wounds about the neck, and great loss of blood. A few murders of this sort each year have been *rewritten*."

"You see," Monsieur Durant looked at me with eyes that were no stranger to pain. "A new vampire would have preyed on such victims. It is not surprising that he would have inadvertently killed many in his blood lust. But when Will went back he chose *not* to kill these people. Of course, there is always the possibility that one of the people he has chosen to spare will change the time line adversely, but so far . . ." Monsieur Durant shrugged. "When you walked through the streets of Paris this morning, you did not observe any cataclysmic changes, did you? The sky was still blue, the sun was still in the sky, *n'est-ce pas*? It seems to me that Mr. Hughes is on a mission of repentance. And, I think, my dear, it's clear what his inspiration is. All of this . . ." He waved his hand at the tables of fluttering pages that sounded in the vast hall like flocks of pigeons wheeling through the sky. ". . . is Will Hughes's four-hundred-year-long love letter to you."

4

Impressing the Lady

"Johannes Kepler! How is that possible? You were alive . . . well, when *I* was alive!"

The man beamed, as if pleased that Will had heard of him. "Let's be blunt here, man," he said. "If you're looking for Kepler and Dee's, likely that's because of its time travel reputation. It doesn't attract much retail traffic. So surely you have sufficient intellect to conjure up reasons as to how I could be here, in 2009!"

"You've traveled in time as well?"

The gentleman tapped his forehead to indicate that Will had guessed correctly. "The problem is, I don't want to be exactly here. I was looking for a different year and must have made some small error in calculation regarding the portal. And now I find that my own store is missing to boot, making it extraordinarily difficult to reenter the portal. Pardon the blasphemy, but this has been a hell of a day for me so far!"

Will saw the man grimace, but Will was feeling a small bit of relief. Maybe this possible Kepler was a colleague in Will's predicament, lost in the wrong year as he was. Kepler was known as one of the scientific geniuses of history. He could figure out a solution to their joint quandary if anyone could—and Garet would certainly have to be impressed when he delivered Kepler to her.

"I believe you!" Will said. "What's more, I think we can help each other."

The man began to eye him with curiosity. "And who would you be, lad, now that you've learned who I am?"

"Will Hughes." He stepped forward and shook the man's hand. His grip seemed stronger than his physique suggested. But this was a person who had figured out the orbits of the planets and maybe time travel too. It should be stronger, Will reflected.

"And why are you searching for my store, Mr. Hughes?"

"I was told that it might contain a time portal. I am, as you surmised, from a different time. The year 1602, to be precise."

"Ah, the year of which you speak, 1602, happens to be a year of special significance to me. I long ago calculated that there is a cycle 801 years in length attached to the spiritual dominion, irrespective of calendar conflicts, uncertainties, even the wars that have tragically taken place over such issues. So 801, 1602, and the 2403 to come should be years of special holy significance. I'll confess that I'm so far at a loss to find anything in historical accounts to make sense of this idea. I've tried to get on the ground in 801, in both Europe and the Holy Land, but access has so far eluded me. The same for 1602, even though I once upon a time lived through it. So, your need is also one of my own, and thus I can't rule out that I might try to accompany you back to 1602 for this purpose. If, I might add, you'd be so kind as to allow me the honor of accompanying you!"

"I'd be honored to have *you* accompany *me*," Will assured the scientist. "Are you able to travel through time so freely?"

"Alas, if it were as easy as that I'd have arrived at my proper destination: 2403. My method is not, unfortunately, a precise one. You see, contrary to what we perceive with the senses, the universe is not three- or multi-dimensional but actually structured from many polygons, adhering together. Sometimes their surfaces do not align perfectly with each other. Think of time, symbolically, as water moving over a streambed with many cracks in its polygonal surface. I have accessed time travel by finding such cracks and other obstacles where time pools up against them, and then entering there and riding along. The trick is to find the cracks. There is one inside the bookshop that bears my name— and the name of my former colleague John Dee."

Will scowled. "I am glad to hear you say *former*. John Dee is my avowed enemy. It is because of him that I find myself in this predicament."

"The man's infamy knows no bounds. I would very much like to hear what he did to you, but first, let us repair to this establishment right here and refresh ourselves with wine while you tell your tale."

Will's new friend led him to a small table at the very same café where he had sat earlier in the day with Garet.

As soon as he sat he realized how tired he was from walking all day—and how thirsty. But he was even more grateful for a chance to unburden his heart of his story. It all came pouring out, over a bottle of excellent red wine. Will told Kepler all that had happened to him from the time he had followed his tutor to London: his first glimpse of Marguerite, his immediate and over-powering love for her, their brief, happy time together, the painful revelation that she was immortal, his decision to seek immortality himself, how he sought Dee out and made a pact with him to gain that immortality, and how Dee had tricked him into becoming a vampire. Kepler, who had remained silent through this long recitation—and barely sipping the wine himself—swore when he heard how Dee had tricked Will.

"That behavior is typical of the man. He tricked me as well. When I first discovered the laws of planetary motion, Dee contacted me on the continent by messenger, with a proposal to publish a book introducing my work in detail in England, to be called *Johannes Kepler: Reaching for the Heavens*. It would have had a lot of beautifully engraved charts of the planets and stars, and he was to write an introduction comparable to the one he had written for a famous Euclidean textbook in England in the 1580s. It sounded like a great idea to me, especially as London was a hotbed of scientific experimentation and discovery at the time. To top it off, Dee offered to donate half of his share of the profits, which he assured me would be plenteous, to orphanages all across England. I was so moved by this great Christian gesture that I agreed to donate half of my own profits to the orphanages.

"I didn't find out until many years later that he had actually stolen all of the profits including mine, which he inaccurately reported to me as 'disappointing,' and had given nothing away to orphans. Worse, he had embedded signals in the planetary and star charts that summoned demons from all over the universe to join him in his damnable efforts at world dominion.

"Only with great difficulty and the help of others have I been able to erase this misbegotten book from recorded history. But ending this terrible bookstore partnership has proven a more difficult matter. Unfortunately I have signed legally binding documents regarding the store, originally conceived of primarily to sell a French edition of *Reaching for the Heavens*, and have not been able to prove to a legal certainty Dee's maleficent intent in the venture. But I will try forever if I have to; now it seems the man has stolen the very physical premises of said store right out from under my nose. That theft should help my cause, at least in a saner world, but the concern of these new economic courts in the European Economic Union for the defendant, always the defendant, only the defendant, has been incomprehensible and disturbing, believe me.

"But as egregious as his mistreatment of me was, his sins against you are greater. To expose a young man to such a hideous monster as Marduk . . ."

"You know of Marduk?" Will asked, shivering at the name.

"Yes, I encountered him in London as Dee's 'aide' when I traveled there to finalize arrangements for the book. He was one of the first things about Dee that made me suspicious. He is the foulest, most evil creature in the world. Thank God you left him behind in 1602."

"But we didn't," Will reluctantly admitted. "He came back with us."

His companion turned so pale that for a moment Will thought he might faint. "Marduk is here? In Paris? Now?"

"Yes, he was in the tower when we traveled through time." Will explained how his "dark angel" had appeared to him in Paris and instructed him to go to the Astrologer's Tower in Catherine de Medici's palace. How he had found Garet—whom he'd believed to be Marguerite—on top of the tower confronted by the foul beast in his own form.

"That was the most horrible aspect of all—that he had stolen my face."

"But you had just recently encountered another with your face—your dark angel. How did you know that the creature on the tower was not he?" Kepler asked with evident puzzlement.

It was not a question that Will had considered up until now. "I don't know," he said at last, "I just knew. Such evil . . . it has an aura."

"And so you fought the creature?"

"Yes, and thought I'd destroyed it. I cast it over the edge of the tower and then Garet used her timepiece to transport us through time to this present."

"And does she not still have this timepiece now?" Kepler asked.

Will shook his head. "When we arrived here she found it was broken. Then, as we were going down the stairs of the tower, we saw Marduk's bloody footsteps going *up* and we knew he'd been in the tower when we traveled in time. I hurried after him, following his footsteps out of the tower, and found them leading into an underground cavern which Garet calls 'the Metro.'"

"An underground transportation system," Kepler replied. "I used it today—quite ingenious. Marduk is a creature of the dark, perhaps he has hidden underground while he recoups his strength. From what you have told me he is still weak from his centuries spent imprisoned by the fey. It is imperative that we find him before he regains all his strength. I must confess that I am surprised that you have been frittering away your time looking for an escape back in time while a monster is on the loose."

"But I have no idea how to find him," Will objected, the blood rushing to his cheeks in shame.

"And your friend, Garet? Is she out looking for this monster?"

"I don't know," Will reluctantly admitted. "I've . . . misplaced her. The last place I saw her was at the bookstore next door."

"Ah," Kepler said, "then we are in luck. I happen to know that this store is a message post for the fey community. No doubt your Garet has left a message for you."

Will looked downcast. "I already asked the clerk. There was no message. I'm afraid that Garet James has little use for me. She tells me that she is in love with my older self. She called me *silly*."

Kepler clapped him on the shoulder. "Cheer up. The messages are not left with the clerk, but upstairs on a most ingenious contraption . . . come, let us go look there now." Kepler left a stack of coins on the table to settle their bill. Will was so overjoyed at the prospect of finding a note from Garet that he didn't ask him how he had come by modern currency—but he made a note to ask him later as he followed him to the store. Inside they climbed a narrow stairway to the second floor to a small cubby that contained a red and white metal contraption that bore the alphabet printed on small round disks. It reminded Will vaguely of a machine he had once seen in a typesetter's shop in London, but it was much smaller. On the wall above were an assortment of printed pages. His eyes were immediately drawn to Garet's name.

"You were right!" Will exclaimed. "She did leave me a note!" Strictly speaking the note was not addressed to him, but that must have been an oversight. "She's gone to a place called the Institut Chronologique on the rue Saint-Jacques. I recall the street from my previous visit to Paris. It's not far." Will was already edging out of the narrow cubby, eager to find Garet, but Kepler placed a restraining hand on his shoulder.

"Although I have known you only briefly, I wonder if you would not find it too forward of me to offer some advice."

"Certainly not," Will readily exclaimed. "Your advice has already led me to Garet."

"Well then, if you find Garet now, how is your situation with her altered? As you described your interaction with her, it appears that she is . . . er . . . not entirely well disposed toward you."

Will had to admit that this was true.

"But imagine how her opinion of you would be improved if you went to her able to tell her that you have destroyed Marduk."

"She certainly wouldn't be able to call me silly then!"

"No, she certainly wouldn't."

"But how will I destroy Marduk if I don't know where he is?"

Kepler grinned, showing so many teeth that Will almost shivered at his glee. "Because I am almost certain where he is. In my previous encounter with him, he hid in the catacombs. He is a creature of habit. I assure you that is where he is now—and I can lead you to him."

Will considered, his desire to see Garet again warring with his wish to see the light of admiration in her eyes when he told her that he had vanquished Marduk. "I'll do it!" he answered. "Let us go!"

Once again Kepler lay a restraining hand on Will's arm. "I admire your spirit, young man, but don't you think you should let your lady know where you are going? A note never goes amiss."

"Yes, you are absolutely right." Will patted his pockets for a pen, but Kepler suggested he use the printing contraption instead. Kepler showed him how to press down on each letter to form an image of that letter on the page. At first it was laborious, but soon Will found that he liked the brisk clatter of metal striking paper and longed to compose something more substantial in this new medium. But he constrained himself to brevity.

Garet, he wrote, *I have gone to find Marduk in the catacombs. If I survive the encounter I will meet you on the Pont Saint Michel at dawn. Yours (I hope), Will Hughes.*

"Excellent," Kepler said, smiling over Will's shoulder as they pinned the note to the wall. "I have no doubt that this note will have the desired effect upon your lady."

5

The Grim Book

"A love letter . . . to me?" I repeated, dumbstruck—and not a little embarrassed. A number of the *chronologistes* were smiling at their books in a way that I suspected didn't come from the contents of those books. Annick was frankly studying me through her horn-rimmed glasses as if trying to assess my worthiness for a four-hundred-year-long love letter. "I hardly think . . . I mean, you don't really know *that*. I'm sure Will had other things to think about in four hundred years."

"Not that I can see," Claudine said, looking up from a handsomely bound volume entitled *The World's Greatest Love Poems*. "Here's something he wrote to you in 1823:"

These trees adore each other endlessly;
The way they've grown together lulls the mind
With thoughts of Paradise, sweetens the eye.
And yet their love's nothing to what we've found.
Their branches have eloped for centuries;
A mingling of two crowns and many leaves

That just this moment's blessed by a mild breeze,
But leaves could never love like you and me. I
        weave
This sonnet for you just as trees have spun
Their interlocking branchery. Which lasts
For eons but will someday join the past,
Unlike these words immortal as the sun.
And even if the sun shall one day die,
we Will go on forever, you and I.

"And here's a haiku he wrote while traveling through Japan in 1959," Jean-Luc said, "called 'In the Distance':"

No beauty great as
snow on mountaintop, sunset
except Garet's eyes.

"And here is a song he wrote to you in the twenties," Annick added, turning on a phonograph, "called 'You're the Art of Art.'" A rich, smoky man's voice sang,

You're made by Michelangelo, I know,
allure so bright that even V. Van Gogh
took off his smock, breathless, and could not
        paint:
Picasso froze, had no choice but to faint.

"Hey, that sounds like Cole Porter," I said.

"It is," Annick confirmed, "but the jacket notes credit the composition of the song to 'my dear friend W. H.'

and clearly it's Will talking about you." Annick beamed at me. *"C'est très romantique, n'est-ce pas?"* Her bottom lip trembled and she removed a handkerchief from the pocket of her snug peplum jacket.

Monsieur Durant crossed over to the young woman and put his arm around her shoulders. "You'll have to excuse my granddaughter. Since she has joined us she has seen many painful things. Observing the fluctuations of time is a sobering business. It is not often that we get any good news."

"I'm afraid it's not *all* good news."

The pronouncement came from the serious looking young man with fair hair—Jules, I recalled, was his name. He was flipping through a newspaper.

"Ah, Jules, you are always the pessimist," Annick scolded, stamping a green suede heel. "You spend too much time reading your crime blotters. I know you do not believe in romantic love."

"My feelings on romantic love are not at issue here," Jules said primly, only the rising color in his cheeks betraying that Annick's comment had stung him. "And I'm not reading the crime blotters. I'm reading today's *Le Monde*. There's been another vampire murder."

"A vampire murder!" I cried. "That can't be Will. The Will I brought back with me is not a vampire and the other Will—*my* Will—has just spent the last four hundred years reforming himself. Why would he kill now?" And, I thought to myself, if he was in Paris, why wouldn't he reveal himself to me? Despite my horror at the thought of Will Hughes killing someone, I felt a flicker of hope. Perhaps my Will was here in Paris.

"People never change," Jules said with a sniff. "Not really."

Annick clucked her tongue impatiently and pulled the paper away from Jules. She scanned the pages quickly, her amber eyes flicking back and forth. Her face paled as she read, making the freckles on her nose stand out sharply. *Quelle horreur,* she whispered, handing the paper to her grandfather.

I read the story over Monsieur Durant's shoulder, translating the French. I caught the phrases "drained of blood" and "homeless woman" and "found in the Cemetery of Montparnasse." The details sounded familiar.

"But these types of murders were occurring *before* I left Paris for Brittany," I said. "And Will was trapped in the Val sans Retour then. Besides, Will would never kill a poor defenseless homeless woman."

"Nor would he drain his victims of blood as these have been drained," Annick added. "It says that the bodies had marks around their ankles as if they had been hung upside down." Annick shuddered. "Your Will would never do that."

Annick squeezed my hand and I gave her a grateful smile . . . that faded as a gruesome image appeared in my head—an image of bodies hanging upside down in a dank cellar, blood dripping into buckets. I had come across just such a scene in 1602 as Madame la Pieuvre and I had made our way through the dungeons of

Catherine de Medici's palace to reach the Astronomer's Tower. We'd then come across an unconscious Marduk, looking eerily like Will, being intravenously fed the blood, and had deduced that Marduk only assumed the features of those victims he fed on directly. For some reason, Dee and Ruggieri, Catherine de Medici's astronomer and Dee's partner in crime, had wanted Marduk to retain Will's features.

"Someone is collecting blood to feed Marduk," I said aloud. "Someone who knew that Marduk would be arriving from the past and who wanted him to remain looking like Will." I explained what I'd seen in the palace dungeons and what part John Dee and Cosimo Ruggieri had played in Marduk's resurrection.

Monsieur Durant's brow furrowed. "Did Dee and Ruggieri follow you back to this time too?"

"No . . . at least, I hope not, but Ruggieri was already here. I recognized him in 1602 because he looked exactly like a man I'd met here—Roger Elden. He said he was an astronomer. He was staying at my hotel, and then I also ran into him outside the observatory—"

I stopped, noticing a look pass between Monsieur Durant and Claudine. At a nod from him she got up and moved to a table that was bare save for one closed book. No one sat at this table. Claudine sat down in front of the book and then Jean-Luc sat down beside her. They each laid a gloved hand on the cover and together opened it slowly as if the cover weighed a hundred pounds or they were afraid that something might fly out of it.

"The *Grimoire of Aberatti*—or the *Grim Book*, as

some call it. It contains the history of dark magic from the fourteenth century to the present. If Ruggieri has been active since 1602 there're sure to be signs of it there."

Claudine and Jean-Luc bent their heads solemnly over the book, carefully turning the pages, their faces grim.

"Why doesn't it turn by itself like the other books?" I asked.

"Because the *Grimoire* is not like other books," Monsieur Durant said in a hushed whisper. "Some believe it has a will of its own." He shuddered. "It is rumored that the pages were made from the skin of murdered witches and the ink from their blood and that the power of those witches resides in its pages. It is very dangerous to look at, so we don't open it unless we have good reason and never alone. There is always the risk that the spirit of one of the departed witches will enter the body of the reader."

I looked back at Claudine and Jean-Luc. Claudine was noticeably paler; Jean-Luc's jaw was clenched so tightly I could hear his teeth grinding.

"What have you found?" Monsieur Durant asked.

"Unspeakable things," Claudine whispered, her lips white. "It looks as though Cosimo Ruggieri made a bargain with John Dee to gain perpetual life, much as Will Hughes did, but the immortality Ruggieri received was even worse than the kind Will got. He is cursed to grow old and die brutally but then to be reborn."

"That sounds like what Roger Elden told me," I said. "He said that when Ruggieri was dying, priests were sent to his rooms to hear his last confession, but he threw them out, screaming that they were mad and that there were no other demons than the enemies who torment us in this world. The priests were so offended at this treatment that they denied Ruggieri a Christian burial. When he died, the people dragged him through the streets of Paris and left his remains in the gutters. Elden said that some believed he had crawled into the catacombs beneath the streets of Paris and there, maimed and dying, found a way to restore his life, but instead of existing in ageless immortality he must grow old repeatedly and experience the same pains of death that he experienced being dragged through the streets of Paris—only *then* can he be reborn each time as a young man."

"What a brutal sort of immortality," Monsieur Durant said. "It is no wonder that the man is a monster."

"Or that he would do anything to escape his curse," Jean-Luc said, looking up from the book. "From his travels I suspect he has been looking for a cure for centuries. He began researching blood in the eighteenth century, and in the nineteenth century he became interested in time travel. If he knew that Marduk was going to appear in twenty-first-century Paris . . ."

"He'd want to be ready for him by collecting blood," Claudine finished the sentence, looking up from the book grimly.

"So you think Roger Elden is responsible for killing these people and draining their blood?" I shuddered, recalling that I'd spent an evening drinking wine with Elden on top of the Astronomer's Tower, never guessing that he was the man who had built the tower, or that he was a cold-blooded killer.

"I'm afraid so," Monsieur Durant replied. "It sounds to me as if Cosimo Ruggieri has been waiting for centuries to find Marduk again and use his blood to gain a more palatable immortality for himself. But the question is, where is he keeping Marduk while he supplies him with this blood?"

"I think I know," Jules said, looking up from the newspapers. "The murders have all taken place in Montparnasse in the vicinity of the catacombs."

"That's where Elden said Ruggieri escaped to after his first 'death,'" I said.

"And," Monsieur Durant added, "the catacombs are built beneath the former Chateau de Vauvert, the site of unspeakable evils."

"And they're near the observatory where I ran into Roger Elden. But how can we be sure—"

We were interrupted by the sound of an old-fashioned typewriter. I might not have remarked on it, but Annick, Jules, Claudine, and Monsieur Durant immediately turned toward the sound. A red manual typewriter, identical to the one from Shakespeare and Company, sat in the middle of one of the library tables, its keys clacking away now by themselves.

"How . . . ?" I began, but the four *chronologistes* were already rushing to the typewriter to read the words appearing on the page inside its roller. When I reached them I saw that there was already a message typed on the top of the sheet.

Garet, go to the Institut Chronologique, 193½ rue Saint-Jacques. All your questions will be answered there.

And below those, *I'm on my way, Garet.*

"That's the message I found in the bookstore!" I said, and then pointing below it, "And that's my reply. How . . . ?"

"It's a little message system we have rigged up," Monsieur Durant explained. "Anything typed at the typewriter in Shakespeare and Company appears here, and vice versa. Look, Will found your message."

I read the lines that had just typed themselves on the page: *Garet, I have gone to find Marduk in the catacombs. If I survive the encounter I will meet you on the Pont Saint Michel at dawn. Yours (I hope), Will Hughes.*

"Crap, that's young Will," I said, "But how did *he* figure out that Marduk is in the catacombs?"

Monsieur Durant shook his head. "I'm afraid it's likely that he's walking into a trap."

a Day's Work for Death

During the fifteen-minute cab ride to the entrance to the catacombs, Will Hughes began to get a little nervous. He'd been impressed with the way Johannes Kepler, refugee in time like himself, had hailed a cab in this era alien to him, stepping aggressively up to an empty one stopped at a red light. Kepler had pleaded with the driver that they were desperate for a ride, and it had worked, even though Garet (while introducing Will to the invention of the car that afternoon) had explained that a person had to wait on line at a taxi stand. Kepler, if he knew of this rule, paid it no heed. And after pleading desperation, he had swashbuckled them both into the rear seat, as if Will were a dignitary and he was escorting him. Will was impressed.

But on the drive Kepler lapsed into a discomforting silence. He had initially been the garrulous sort, though of course Will didn't know him well. But now he turned gloomy. Maybe, for all his bold talk, he found Marduk fearsome and was trying to think of a way to extricate himself from their mission. Even more disturbingly, Will thought he detected a faint odor coming from Kepler now, one that had perhaps gone unnoticed in the sweep of the street and the bustle of café and bookstore. The odor was mildly rank, suggesting mold or decay. Perhaps it was some lingering effect from time travel, common to all travelers. But when Will furtively sniffed his own sleeve, pretending to wipe a speck of lint off it with his chin, he smelled nothing.

He asked himself how well he knew this man. What—for all of a half hour? The smell, dank and now vaguely sulfurous, grew stronger. Did Kepler, a genius revered for centuries, previously work as a laborer in a sulfur mine? Not to condescend to manual labor, but . . . Will scrutinized Kepler's attire, but the man's clothes were spotless. Fighting a hint of nausea, he rolled his window down as far as it would go, and then at last the cab pulled up in front of the entrance to the catacombs. Kepler seemed jarred out of his gloom by the cessation of motion. He paid the driver—with a generous tip, judging by the latter's reaction—and then bounded enthusiastically out of the car, Will following.

Without as much as a glance at the apparently locked entrance to the catacombs, Kepler turned to the south and gazed up at the night sky. He made a grand sweep with one arm that seemed to include all of the universe, and then pointed in particular at a bright red star, which Will suspected was Mars. Lord, is this fellow volatile in mood, Will reflected. It doesn't take much to excite him! He could have moved his neck a little and seen the night sky all throughout the car ride, if his bleak-eyed gaze hadn't been sunk in his lap.

"Look!" Kepler exclaimed.

"I know, Mars," Will replied impatiently. He was anxious to bring home—if home were Garet—the trophy of Marduk.

"My dear lad," Kepler said, clapping Will on his shoulder, "that's not the point. It's Mars at the twenty-second celestial latitude at exactly eleven p.m. on this date, just as my theory predicted in 1602. Not bad, huh?"

"You are able to gauge celestial positions with your eyes like this?" Will asked wonderingly. "Without maps or charts? Or a telescope?"

"I have lived with celestial positions like the most romantic of lovers lives with the face of his beloved, moment after moment, for so many years. In my thoughts always. So yes, I can gauge them." His face was flushed with excitement. But then he suddenly grew subdued again, as if turning his thoughts toward the matter at hand.

The entrance to the catacombs was a small stone building with an iron door that was shut. No doubt there was some stairway or (another invention he had just learned of) elevator within, Will thought. A sign above the door, one with much larger lettering in French than in English, advertised daytime hours as posted and "tours by appointment," but there was no sign of activity of any sort. A mild breeze blew a few scattered papers across the concrete path leading up to the door, as if to emphasize the desolation of the place.

Kepler walked up to the door and rattled its knob to no avail. Will observed him gaze disappointedly at the knob, but what else could the man have expected? Though Marduk might well be hiding down there, the place was also a tourist attraction, and Will had noted all evening that the city's many attractions seemed to be gradually shutting down for the night.

"I guess Marduk will have to wait for daylight . . . ," Will said tentatively. He would not admit to himself that he might be feeling any sense of relief. Then Kepler's defeated expression relaxed, became almost cheerful.

"Mathematics can do many things, even this late at night," Kepler told Will wryly. "Opening a locked door not the least of them. But a wizard cannot reveal his tricks. Please turn away from me for the moment . . ."

Will did not grasp the need for physical secrecy with a mental process like math, so he didn't move at first.

"Turn away lad!" Kepler boomed.

The volume of his voice took Will aback; it was almost as if a different person had spoken. Someone with a hoarser, deeper voice than the man he had just met. A whiff of the rancid odor from inside the cab drifted across the breezy air to him. He turned away. The next thing he knew, there was a loud crunching sound, as if a rough piece of metal were being flattened. Then Will saw a brilliant flash of light from the corner of his eye. Startled, he could not help but turn back to Kepler immediately. What sort of math made this kind of noise? he wondered.

Where the doorknob had been, there was a jagged, smoldering hole, a trail of white smoke rising from it. Kepler grinned at the hole, beaming as if proud of his handiwork, and then began to push the door open. This was a conjurer's math, a sorcerer's, Will told himself. But he followed Kepler through the doorway. He wanted Marduk badly, and he did not want to appear ignorant of the powers of "math" before Kepler. And if Kepler found him querulous . . . no doubt flesh could be flattened and made to smolder just like this metal had been! Let that be a problem for Marduk, not him.

They took the elevator from the aboveground lobby straight down to its only other floor, "C." That was a long ride, and Will thought he detected the air getting chillier and damper as they descended. They emerged into a subterranean lobby with fluorescent lighting and an array of photographs with descriptive French captions in white ink on glossy black plaques next to them. The lobby narrowed in one corner into the entrance to a dimly lit tunnel. Will did not linger before any of the photographs, but he could see at a glance that most of them were of excavation sites or grim piles of skulls and bones. An inner voice whimpered to him for a moment at these ghastly vistas, and he wondered if he was made of sufficiently tough stuff to grapple with the likes of Marduk in such an environ. But, on the other hand . . . he had Kepler to assist him.

Kepler walked into the narrow tunnel as blithely as if he strolled along the Seine on a sunny morning in May.

Will followed him, his heart beating a little louder. They walked for quite a while down a gloomy corridor, the tunnel walls varying between grime-encrusted bricks and densely packed black earth; the air, though, seemed oddly antiseptic and free of odors of decay, as if filtered through a powerful ventilating system. Then they came to the first burial pit.

Will had tried to steel himself preemptively for this sight, but when he saw such an ample compilation of bones, with skulls placed here and there like grinning sentinels, his breath caught in his throat and his knees weakened. Dizzily he planted his feet as far apart as possible to keep from falling. He knew rationally that this was simply an underground graveyard, where many of the citizens of Paris had once been buried, but the visceral impact of so many full and partial skeletons was still overwhelming. How much death there must be in this world, he reflected, gloomily. And then Kepler interrupted Will's thoughts with his own.

"You seem stunned, my boy," he said, coming close to Will and facing him. "But what you see here is a tiny fraction of a day's work for Death. For true perspective, think of all the millions of beings who have come and gone, vanished, during all prehistory while the human race was evolving. A process I hadn't dreamed of in 1602, until I came forward into the future and learned of it. Evolution! Those millions of human and near human and prehuman beings: all we have of them now are a few slivers of fossilized bone. The rest are grass and dust, and yet they were far more numerous than what you behold in this revolting pit. Darwin, though he found the truth, failed to mention that this truth adores death: the individual means nothing to it, the species everything. And yet life is entirely experienced by individuals. What a sadistic conflict! We don't even know what our own ancestors and their thoughts were like—countless millions—let alone have their bones. That's sobering, not this! Buck up, lad! Death, sadly, rules."

"Sobering, yes," Will mumbled in agreement, rolling the strange term "evolution" over in his thoughts and wondering who this fellow Darwin might be. But he didn't find Kepler's expression to be sober during his dark speech. No, there seemed to be a glint of . . . almost . . . triumph—or maybe even amusement—in his eyes. Such dissonance added further unease to the turmoil in Will's gut. Had time travel made the man a little odd—or mad? Distracted by this concern, he shuffled forward again, following Kepler's unaccountably brisk, even bouncing strides.

They passed other pits in silence. And it struck Will that there was no conclusion to their path in sight, no circular or other logic apparent to the catacombs' meanderings. He stopped and asked Kepler in a loud voice, "See here, man! Do you have any idea where we are going? We don't exactly seem to be creeping up on Marduk in a stealthy way!"

"I know exactly where we are going," Kepler responded coldly. "I know these paths like I know the paths of the planets. It won't be long now, and stealth will not be a requirement. You'll see."

Will wondered how that could be so, but followed meekly. This was Kepler, savant of the ages.

A whiff of that bad odor from the inside of the cab came to him again. But he shrugged it away and plodded on. A moment or two later, he heard the faintest of cries, a thin and pleading moan, possibly human, and low-pitched enough to probably be from a man. It chilled him. It might have come from the pits of bones to either side at that moment, but Will suspected it came from a little farther ahead in the tunnel. For all his trepidation, he knew right away it was from a living being, not from another world. Frail—as if its source had been weakened—but very much alive. He could feel that in his own bones.

Kepler suddenly stopped a few paces beyond him and tapped a bricked-up section of the passageway to their right with his balled right fist. Will caught up to him and observed that Kepler seemed to have stopped near the source of the cries, which were continuing. He was gazing through an opening in the center of the bricks, one where a few had been removed. Kepler took a step back and gestured at it to indicate that Will should look through it. Indeed, the sound of whimpering, plaintive as a fawn's, was coming straight through the opening. A human fawn.

The aperture opened on a small room about six foot square, eight feet in height, lit by a flickering candle on a plate set in one corner. The brick walls were grimed over everywhere, remarkably dingy, as if charcoal fires had burned here for decades. A man in a dirt-streaked gray shirt, black pants, and black shoes was chained to the wall near the candle. His head was tilted down so that his chin touched his chest, obscuring his features from Will's view. He was the source of the moans. Blood dripped from his mouth, and one arm hung at an angle, as if it had been broken. When he picked his head up with a great effort, as if he sensed someone at the aperture, or maybe heard Will's breathing, Will gasped.

This man was Kepler too, identical twin to the man he had met by the Seine.

Will's knees buckled again, and he did the best he could to stay upright by flattening the palms of his hands against the bricks and clinging to them. He heard a low, menacing chuckle behind him. Before he realized what was happening, powerful hands jerked his wrists away from the wall and pinned them together behind his back; cold metal curves like those of manacles were slipped around his wrists and put them in a vise.

"Fool!" the first Kepler said to Will in an excited whisper. "You won't be bringing news of Marduk's demise to Garet. Marduk will be bringing Garet's severed head to you! No one should ever trifle with Lord Marduk. The time it will take me to leave you here and kill her will also give me sufficient time for planning infernal ends for you and your mathematician friend. Kepler, traitor to John Dee!" He spat out the words. He proceeded to remove bricks with superhuman strength and speed and then to manhandle the manacled Will through the larger opening as though he were moving an unruly child. He chained Will to the wall, which Will could now see crawled with vile-looking insects, next to the real Johannes Kepler. Marduk moaned, but with an otherworldly pleasure, as he chained Will up.

Then he departed without another word, bricking the chamber back up.

7

Knights Temporal

"I should never have let him out of my sight," I said. "I'll have to go get him."

"You'll be blundering into a trap," Jules said. "That's what Marduk and Ruggieri want. In all likelihood, they've set one."

"We can't just let Marduk kill him!" Annick objected. "Besides, it's our best opportunity to catch Marduk."

"Annick is right," Monsieur Durant said, smiling proudly at his granddaughter. "Of course, we won't let Garet go alone. We'll mount an offensive team."

"I know the catacombs," Jules said with a quick glance at Annick. I had the feeling he was trying to impress her, but then he ruined the effect by adding, "I'll take two armed men with me. You'd better wait here with Annick, Miss James; a battle in the catacombs is no place for a woman."

Annick stamped her shoe with annoyance. "We have no time for your male-chauvinist posturing, Jules! I am just as well trained in armed combat as you. In fact, I believe I beat you in our last fencing competition."

"And I'm certainly going," I said, forestalling Jules's stuttering objections to Annick's statement. "If Marduk still looks like Will, then someone will have to ask the right questions to determine who is the real Will."

"Don't assume Marduk will be in Will's shape," Claudine said. She was still sitting in front of the grimoire. "I've been reading the section on shape stealers. They need to maintain the shape of their most recent victim for thirty-six hours before drinking blood directly from another victim. But once they have, they can revert to that earlier shape whenever they choose. Who knows how many other victims Marduk has drunk from since he arrived in Paris? He could look like anyone. Nor should you trust Will's—or anybody else's—ability to answer questions or engage in conversations. According to this, a shape stealer absorbs many of the memories of his victims along with their blood, enough to impersonate them. You must not let each other out of your sight once you are in the catacombs, and trust no one but each other."

"I never do," Jules said, giving Annick a meaningful glance. Then switching his gaze to me he asked, "How do we know *she's* not Marduk?"

All the *chronologistes* looked at me. I started to sputter out a defense, but Monsieur Durant forestalled me by grasping my hand in his. "This is how you unmask a shape stealer," he said in a loud booming voice. Moving more quickly than I would have thought possible for a man his age, he withdrew a dagger from a sheath at his waist and drew it across the palm of my hand. I gasped at the pain.

"My apologies, dear, but it is necessary that they trust you." He held up my hand for all to see. "Notice that the blood is red. If this were Marduk, it would be black. If you have any doubt, this is how you can unmask the monster."

"Good to know," Jules said, fingering a sheath at his waist. Looking around, I noticed that all the *chronologistes* wore long leather sheaths at their waists.

"You're not just archivists," I said.

Monsieur Durant smiled as he resheathed his dagger. "No, my dear. We are the Knights Temporal. Sworn enemies of the Malefactors, and grand protectors of time."

"What *are* the Knights Temporal?" I asked Annick as we repaired to a dressing room to bandage my hand and "gear up" for our raid on the catacombs. I didn't know who the Malefactors were, either, but I figured I'd take them up one term at a time.

"We're an ancient order pledged to preserve the integrity of time." She withdrew the blade from her own leather sheath and showed me its hilt. Etched into the metal was the same symbol I'd seen above the door—a snake eating its own tail. Inscribed within the circle were the words *Tempus fugit, sed manemus*.

"I know what *Tempus fugit* means, but *sed manemus*?"

"But we remain," Annick said with a small, proud smile. "Our family has belonged to the order for hundreds of years. Here . . ." She removed a bundle of clothing from a cabinet and handed it to me. On top was a sheath like hers. "These belonged to one of our knights, Lea. I think you're about her size, and I'm sure she would want you to have her dagger."

"What happened to her?" I asked, taking the clothes and the knife.

"We don't really know," Annick said, turning away from me to take off her smart suit and pull on slim black pants. "She went on a mission to the thirteenth century and never came back. She is probably dead, but I like to think she met someone she liked and stayed behind. We call it 'going temporal.' It happens sometimes. No one likes to talk about it, because we are sworn to preserve the time line and falling in love with a 'local' might change the course of history, but if one is in love . . ." She shrugged and pulled on a black turtleneck, shaking her curls out when the top was over her head. "Would you have stayed in 1602 with Will if that was the only way you could be together?"

"With *my* Will?" I asked.

She nodded.

"Yes," I said, without hesitation. I looked away and busied myself putting on black jeans and turtleneck, glad to get out of the antiquated dress I'd been wearing. I removed from its bodice, though, the swan-shaped brooch I had inherited from Marguerite and had used to blind Marduk when he was attacking Will on the beach at Paimpont. I hadn't hesitated to protect Will then, but I wasn't sure how I'd react if young Will were in danger. I pinned the brooch to my turtleneck. "But I wouldn't have stayed in 1602 for *this* Will."

"Are they really so different?" Annick asked.

"Completely," I replied, pulling on the black boots Annick gave me. "This Will is a silly boy—selfish, vain, and foolish."

"But also innocent, yes? His illusions have not been shattered."

"I'd rather be with a man who has faced the worst in the world and still has the courage to believe in doing good."

"Ah," Annick sighed, "but how many accomplish that? Too many lose their optimism through the experience of evil."

"Like Jules?" I asked.

Annick blushed and turned to the mirror to adjust a black beret on her head, tucking her springy curls beneath it. "Yes, like Jules. We grew up together. His family, too, have been in the Knights Temporal for centuries. We used to play at dragon hunting and time questing together. He quoted Malory and Sir Walter Scott to me." She smiled at herself in the mirror. "But then . . ." Her smile faded and she shoved an errant curl beneath the brim of her beret. "He went on his first mission. He came back . . . changed. He will tell no one what happened." She turned to me and adjusted the beret I'd put on. "If I could have back the boy I grew up with—with all his innocence and illusions intact—I would take *him*."

"Perhaps that boy will come back to you," I said. "Remember, it took Will Hughes four hundred years to become the man I fell in love with. Give Jules some time."

By the time we left the institute the one thing I was not inclined to give Jules more of was time. I wanted to get to the catacombs as quickly as possible to keep young Will from falling into a trap, but Jules had been named leader of the catacombs mission—even though Jean-Luc was also accompanying us and was older—and he took his role very, *very* seriously. He had us check our equipment three times (in addition to the daggers we were each given a rope, compass, water bottle, flashlight, and map) and went over the "safety protocols" four times. He made Jean-Luc take off his bow tie and fussed over Annick's hair. He paid particular attention to making us swear to never let each other out of sight. I began to suspect that whatever had gone wrong on Jules's first mission, he held himself accountable and was determined not to make the same mistake again.

Before we left, one of the *chronologistes* made another discovery. One of the late-edition newspapers had a story in it about rumors of an as-yet-unnamed hedge fund manager setting up a new fund that would "sell overly leveraged currencies like the euro short, and try to trade gold at its 'true intrinsic value,'" whatever that meant.

"This might be why Marduk wants to do away with the young Will Hughes," Monsieur Durant said speculatively, looking up from the paper with a somewhat impish smile, but one belied by a worried look in his eyes.

"He might be planning to use Will Hughes's identity to complete some nefarious scheme, and he can't risk having another Will Hughes on the loose. Please, stop him."

"*Je suis prest*," Jules said, repeating a motto I recognized from heraldry as "I am ready." He strode out the door of the institute without a backward glance. Annick rolled her eyes and paused on the threshold to kiss her grandfather's cheek and assure him that we would all be fine and back before breakfast. Monsieur Durant's eyes were gleaming in the dark alleyway. Claudine, who had accompanied us to the doorway, put her arm around his shoulders and drew him back inside, "out of the drafts of time," she said. "I'm already forgetting that I've discovered a new Shakespeare sonnet. Come, let us read it and others together while we wait for the young people to return."

It was comforting, somehow, to think of Claudine and Monsieur Durant reading poetry together in the Hall of Time while we ventured forth to the catacombs. Whatever happened to us they would bear witness—and if we failed, there would be someone left behind to pursue Marduk.

8

Beast Without a Soul

The desolation Will felt when he heard Marduk slam the last brick into place was unlike any sensation he had ever felt before. He was still breathing, and he could hear himself thinking, but he felt as if he were otherwise dead. A clammy dread penetrated him as if his flesh had turned to sodden clay.

"Kepler!" Will shouted at the chained man next to him, so loudly he hoped he loosened the mortar between the bricks. Marduk had pretended to be Kepler, and this man appeared to be Marduk's twin, thus he had to be Kepler. Logic had its place, even in this mire-bound world lit only by a candle on a plate in one corner.

But the man did not stir. Had he died? Will thought he could make out the faintest signs of shallow breathing in the man's throat. Maybe another shout could revive him. But several failed to. Then Will looked around himself uneasily, trying not to panic, trying to formulate some sort of escape plan he could carry out before that awful man—that thing—returned.

He could barely see in the thick gloom, and from the glimpses he managed of crawling insect motion on the bricks, he was glad of it. But that made planning for an escape nearly impossible. Even if he could get his chains off—and Kepler, a genius, hadn't been able to—where was he going to go? But he needed to keep his thoughts steady and calm. Instead of formulating a plan, he found himself composing a poem. A despondent plea of a poem, but a better use of his time, he thought, than breathing madly or panicking his own heart into stopping. Will had neither paper nor free hands, but he came up with a sonnet anyway and memorized it with an ease that surprised him, reciting it softly to himself at first, and then to the seemingly unconscious Kepler.

"Kepler!" he shouted after each recitation. "Johannes Kepler!" As if the man might respond better to this poetic oration than his earlier shouts:

The dank and murk of these four walls appall,
No matter if a jail, or woe-soaked tomb:
Time's dreadful to me as it slowly crawls,
Just like the mites on blackened walls. This womb
Belongs to Satan's corpus; we must flee
Or we'll be born again as something foul,
And Garet, suffer Marduk. I can see
In mind's eye how that beast without a soul
Craves vipering her blood to make him whole.
A thing of such malevolence that Dee,
Though sinister himself, will shriek and flee.
Yet now, if only Kepler might awake,

And use his genius for poor mankind's sake,
We might be saved. And Marduk take a Fall.

There was still no response. But then Will heard a rustling sound, very near the aperture Marduk had bricked over, as if a moth were fluttering out in the hallway, loudly enough for Will to hear. (Or as if he were in woods instead of this makeshift morgue, and a breeze was moving leaves.) The rustling was followed by a high-pitched whistling sound. Shadows were gloomy, and despite how intently Will peered through the meager candlelight he could see very little, but then he thought he could detect one of the bricks moving slightly. Suddenly dust seemed to billow everywhere, and there was a harsh screeching noise of brick and cement being separated. Then a loud clattering sound, of several bricks falling heavily to the floor.

When the dust started to clear, Will was startled to see a tiny, winged, green creature with a recognizably human face come flying through the revived aperture with a whoosh. She was no more than eight or nine inches from head to toe, longish golden hair suggesting a female; she wore a tiny blue satchel on her back, in between where her wings sprouted. Without a glance at Will, the creature hovered in the air near Kepler's face, gossamer wings beating so fast they were a blur.

She gazed with concern at Kepler's bedraggled features, took what looked to Will like a miniature cylinder from her satchel, and, as she continued to hover, deftly sprayed a fine mist onto Kepler's eyelids (pressing her finger to the cylinder), then onto his parched lips. Kepler's eyelids immediately began to flutter, and he seemed to be regaining consciousness. He licked his lips eagerly, as if thirsty for more spray.

"Who are you?" Will asked the creature, but she ignored him.

"This is Lol, a fire sprite, distant cousin of the lumignon," the man said to him in an audible, though feeble, voice. "An old friend, who has most fortuitously had the good grace to show up." With each successive word of his statement, his strength seemed to acquire momentum. Lol chirped delightedly at his comment, though she ignored Will.

"Are you Johannes Kepler?" Will asked the man.

"That I am, lad. The one and only."

"And how have you stumbled into this grotesqueness?"

"John Dee is the greatest scoundrel in history," Kepler explained. "I thought he was my business partner, and my friend. But it was all his ruse to obtain profits from a book about my work that has turned out to be an exercise in thievery. Even after I confronted him about that, and taken the necessary legal action, he has still tried to elicit more services from me, ones that no human being can provide—for example, stable rules predicting stock market performance similar to those that govern the movements of celestial bodies. When he was disappointed recently in this foolish request, he delivered me to a blood-gorging fiend in retaliation. Ugh!" Kepler paused to spit on the ground before him. "And how about you, lad? Who are you, and how do you find yourself in this dungeon?"

"I am Will Hughes of Somerset, England, more lately of London," Will replied formally. "I am the suitor of a Watchtower, and apparently that has ensnared me in this malevolence. As you can see." Will made as if to extend his right hand to Kepler, then demonstrated how it was restricted by his chains. He wasn't sure if he'd given an accurate reason for his captivity, but it seemed as good a guess as any.

"See here, my lady," Kepler said, turning his attention to the still-hovering Lol, "you've been astonishingly helpful already, but can't you assist us with our chains?"

Lol retrieved a tiny file from her satchel, one that gleamed in the morbid air like a sliver of silver. She set to work sawing away at the first of Kepler's links. She made quite the high-pitched scraping sound with her implement, but it appeared her work would be slow going. Kepler fixed his gaze on Will again and rolled his eyes with impatience.

"If you don't mind my offering a suggestion, sir," Will said hesitantly.

"Go ahead."

"I know he's the darkest of counterparts, so to speak, a trick of evil flesh made up to look like you in surface only. But Lord Marduk did make mention, when we first entered the catacombs, of the power of math to perform miracles. He seemed to blow open a lock with mental powers. I know you are a great genius; might you not have some explosive skill like that in your repertoire?"

"Ah, you are so very young, lad, so I forgive you your little venture into insane thinking. Lord Marduk was babbling. Assuming he opened a lock in the nonmaterial manner you mention, he did it with the wickedest act of sorcery. True mathematics is a gentle art only. It is suitable for comprehending the planets and the stars, not for implementing mayhem!"

Lol's scraping seemed to have achieved a greater intensity now, so she was making progress, if at a still sluggish pace. She was more than halfway through the first chain link. Several would have to be severed to even partially free Kepler.

"I understand, sir. Marduk is a complete deceiver, then."

"Right you are. Indeed, he's far worse than that." Slowly, Kepler removed his clenched left hand from his left side, where it had been hidden from Will's view, and extended it to the limit his chains allowed. The links clanked drearily as he moved. Even more slowly, having attracted Will's gaze, he unclenched his hand.

Will gasped. The middle and ring fingers were blackened stumps, the blackness redly tinged as if from dried blood. "What happened?" He could see tears glimmering in Kepler's eyes.

"Marduk toyed with me first, saying he had a voracious pet who liked fingers. 'Fingers of the famous.' He warned me that he'd provide him—it—with a further meal the next time he saw me, stuffing my fingers meanwhile in his pocket as if they were a couple of used napkins. And then he emitted an awful cackling laugh, one that sounded like hell with a personality.

"But"—Kepler's features brightened—"if I can get back to the lost time portal and travel to a happier moment, before this encounter, my anatomy will be restored. Something that sadist may not have reckoned with. I am not a violent man, lad. But I can't deny reflecting, in this last hideous hour or so, just how my fully fingered hand might feel sliding around a lethal weapon, the handle of a knife, the trigger of a revolver for two examples."

"I do admire your pluck, sir. And in the meantime, sorry about your loss."

Then Will thought he heard a murmur of voices in the hallway, through the aperture Lol had reopened, faint but seeming closer with each passing moment. He was tempted to shout out but decided to wait. As the voices drew closer, he could distinguish three, a woman's and two men's, though they were still too distant to be identified other than by gender. Finally they were close enough that Will had to presume that, if he could hear them, they would hear him. "Helloooooo," he called out. "Heeeeelp!"

"What are you doing?" Kepler asked.

"I hear voices outside. Don't you?"

"Maybe. But I don't know if they would be friend's or foe's. Marduk could have sent spies around in his absence. Best not to call attention to the progress Lol is making. Patience, lad. Our little helper may get us out of here before you know it."

But Will could see that Lol still had a ways to go even on the first link. Then, for a thrilling millisecond that lit him up like lightning, Will recognized the approaching woman's voice. It sounded like that of Garet James. Could it be?

"Gaaaaret," Will called out, thrusting Kepler's cautionary words aside. There was no immediate response, but the pace of the speakers seemed to quicken as they neared him and Kepler, their voices to each other louder and more excited-sounding. "Gaaaaret," Will repeated.

"Who is that?" Kepler asked.

"Garet James is the Watchtower I spoke to you of. And here she comes now," he added triumphantly. "She must have been watching over us!"

"Is that you, Will Hughes?" Garet asked, seemingly only a few feet away now. Will felt a burst of energy so intense he thought he could rip his chains right out of the wall. But he remained levelheaded enough not to try that.

"Yes, yes it's me. Imprisoned, all chained up. And none other than the famed Johannes Kepler is imprisoned right alongside me."

"Kepler? The astronomer?" Garet asked. Will heard a murmured colloquy between Garet and an unknown male's voice; the only word of it Will could make out was "hallucination." Will bristled at the thought of Garet discussing his sanity with another man.

"I assure you I am *not* mad!" Will yelled.

"Don't worry," Garet said in a soothing voice. "I've got others with me—two sturdy men, *chronologistes*—we'll have you out in no time."

Then Will heard her shriek, and another loud cry from her unseen companions. There were some guttural noises, all male, like those in a struggle, the sound of something crashing, then a long, penetrating scream, also male. Silence. Then a fresh voice.

"Don't you fuss, Will Hughes. You'll be reunited with your love in no time."

Marduk. As bone-chilling a voice as Will could imagine. He felt as if the temperature in their miserable cell had plunged to absolute zero.

The voice was like a serrated blade of steel, tickling his throat in the candlelit gloom.

9

Unexpected Blood

Will beheld the awful spectacle of Garet being thrust through a new opening in the corridor wall, arms pinned behind her back in Marduk's crushing left-handed grip. She seemed to be trying to shout, perhaps to him, but Marduk's other massive hand—Will wondered why he hadn't noted their bestial contours before, huge, hairy and unnaturally muscular—was clamped over her mouth. Kepler hadn't told him exactly how he'd lost his fingers, but Marduk's looked like hands brutish enough to have ripped them off; Will sickened a little at their appearance.

Out of the corner of his eye, Will observed Lol cease and desist from her link sawing and flit unobtrusively to the darkest corner of the chamber, where she made herself as inconspicuous as possible.

Will was even more enraged by the second pair of people to come into view. He did not know the young fair-haired man bound up in spirals of what seemed to be gossamer thread. But he knew the sorcerer behind him, prodding him along with a wand, from the silver bulletlike tip of which thread continued to unspool, all too well. Prodded by the wizard John Dee, the captive fell to the floor.

"Jules!" Garet exclaimed with a concern that would have piqued Will's jealousy if he hadn't been more pre-occupied with glaring at Dee.

Dee was the cause of all Will's misfortunes, as Will saw it, having seduced him in 1602 with the promise of immortality so he could be with Marguerite as her peer, and having delivered it in the noxious form of turning him into a vampire. Were he not restrained by the chains, he would have been rushing to choke Dee, or do some-thing worse to him, he told himself. Meanwhile, Dee was shoving his new captive up against a wall slot and mak-ing him fast with the chains and padlocks hanging there, even as Marduk was similarly imprisoning Garet. Dee so far had not given Will a glance. But Will gazed relent-lessly at him like a leopard eyeing prey, not allowing him-self to be distracted by Garet's duress.

Marduk introduced Will to Dee.

"Sir Dee, you recall the Will Hughes creature," he said in a jovial voice, "that we vampired in 1602. He stands right here against the wall, poor thing, cowering."

Dee, who was busying himself affixing Jules's chains just right, did not turn his head in Will's direction but he did nod. Will didn't mind Marduk's reference to him as a creature—coming from that beast it was a compliment—but Dee's mere presence continued to infuriate him. He was searching his thoughts for the right cutting thing to say when Kepler spoke to Dee.

"See here, man, you can't just run all over the streets and through the tunnels of Paris absconding with young people like this. Your luck will run out and the authorities will bring you to justice."

Dee laughed. Marduk took a step toward Kepler and slapped his face. "Silence your wickedness, mathematician," he said.

Kepler fell silent.

Dee stepped back from Jules with the final clang of a padlock and clapped his hands together, as if in admiration of his jailer's handiwork. "Now, as to what to do with these whelps," he muttered. "It would seem a pity to ever let them go, so well chained as they are."

"Shouldn't their corpses just rot here?" Marduk asked. "This is, after all, the catacombs."

"Corpses? You are being a bit hasty, my good wolf. Have you lost track of their possible future uses, of our possible needs?"

Just then Lol fluttered upward out of her dank and murky corner, like a miniature dervish, to and through the broad opening Marduk and Dee had made before reentering. And just beyond a savage leap Marduk made at her. He howled with disappointment, seeing the impossibility of pursuing her in her speedy flight down the corridor.

"Never mind, my heathen," Dee consoled him. "We will deal with the fey soon enough. After all, even they need food to eat, and a collapse of the global commodities market may well leave them as impoverished and starving as all the other Parisians. As all the other

Frenchmen. And as all of humanity worldwide, for that matter." He laughed. The sound resembled a cackle.

"I say, out of breath, out of pulse, out of mind," Marduk grumbled. "Let's take care of them now and not give their fates a second thought during our meeting with Vice Chairman Renoir. I can feel eternity in this place, a black and cold one, licking its lips for them. So hungry to feed on such vermin, Kepler not included."

Will was trying to stay calm, but he couldn't help shuddering upon hearing these words. Nor could he bear to glance at Garet and observe what she might be feeling. They were now so desperate that they were reduced to relying on *Dee* as their savior!

"I say leave them!" Dee exclaimed with some anger, wheeling on Marduk. This seemed incongruous to Will, the frail wizard menacing the hulking manbeast, but Marduk took a timid step back, leaving little doubt as to who had a hold over whom. At least, for the moment.

"In any event, my good heathen"—Dee's tone softened slightly—"aren't you forgetting something pertinent?" He nodded at Will. "Isn't Renoir expecting to meet in secret with hedge fund manager Will Hughes, whose Green Hills Partners fund has earned him deserved preeminence? Hasn't that been our passport to meeting Renoir?"

In his overwrought state, one that made careful consideration of facts difficult, these words flowed like honey into Will's ears. The reprieve that Dee seemed to hint at for him, to attend a financial meeting with these two monsters, would be like visiting heaven compared to staying locked up in this hell. And it might afford, as a practical matter, opportunities to escape. He was startled that Dee thought he could arrange Will's attendance in a secure manner, given all Will had endured and learned. But such obliviousness was something for him to take pleasure in.

Mention of a financial meeting brought to mind his flirtations with finance before leaving London in 1602: Guy Liverpool's seductive talk of a new era in which alchemy occurred with stocks instead of lead. Will was a novice, really, and would have to be a silent observer for much of the upcoming meeting lest he reveal the gulf between himself and his four-hundred-year-old namesake. Who, Will realized, must have had quite the career with money to be a tool for engendering financial mayhem worldwide. He wondered—

Marduk was upon him then, fangs in his neck, inflicting a piercing pain. Will fainted with the shock and blood loss, and it was only when he woke back up to a rebricked cell empty of their captors a few minutes later that he groggily realized it was going to be Marduk who would be Will Hughes, hedge fund manager, at the meeting. Marduk had assumed Will's appearance by drinking his blood, pseudo-Kepler melting into pseudo-Will as the blood change suffused throughout his vile cells and organs. Pseudo-Kepler lay with the ashes of time now.

But the real Kepler survived, Will reassured himself with a sideways glance, as did his beloved, and the man who'd come with her, subsequent glances told him. So hope did too.

And then he heard a scraping sound he'd heard once before, from the other side of the bricked-over aperture.

Lol. She'd returned.

a Rose's Dream

I was astonished, then relieved, to see Lol in the dim candlclight, flitting from thc corridor into thc chamber. I recalled her well from New York City the previous winter—especially the time she had saved my life from a paralysis spell that her master Oberon had placed on me—and I shouted hello to her now. She seemed to nod at me in midflight with the hint of a smile, then flew to the slender, older man chained up next to Will.

The tiny file she pulled from her backpack did not inspire confidence, but as she set to work I could see that she started out on a link already partly cut. So she was perhaps returning to a job she or someone else had started. I was relieved by that thought, but not nearly as relieved as when I saw a kind of green and yellow mass fluttering in the vicinity of the aperture Lol had come through, as if a storm of butterflies had materialized from the subterranean clouds, a late-night thunderstorm of color. Dozens if not hundreds of Lol's close friends and relatives, all barely distinct from her in appearance, were fanning out now in the chamber to attack chain links with files. There was a high-pitched screeching noise the likes of which I'd never heard before for a minute or two, and then we all found ourselves free of our chains. Then the horde turned its attention to widening the aperture, so we'd be able to make our escape to freedom. That work proceeded swiftly as well.

The minute the opening was wide enough, Jules edged through it. I imagined he was going to check on the welfare of Annick, whom we'd left on guard at the entrance to the catacombs. He would have to break it to her that their colleague Jean-Luc was dead, his neck broken by the savage Marduk. Even though I'd only known Jules for a few hours I guessed that he would take full responsibility for Jean-Luc's fate, even though there had been nothing either of us could have done to save him. Jules hadn't seemed to want help searching for Annick, so I turned my attention to Will and the older man with him, who I assumed must be the man Will had referred to as Kepler.

I was so happy to see Will still robustly alive after being in Marduk's clutches that I could have hugged him with relief, but I retained a concern about not encouraging him romantically. So I turned instead to the older man. He bowed to me. Then Will said, "As horrified as I was to behold you imprisoned by those monsters, dear

Garet, it is with much greater solace that I behold you free before me now!"

This might have been quaint, affected speech to me, but for him it was (Elizabethan) reality. Certainly I could see relief shining in his eyes. I stepped forward and gave him a kiss on the cheek. Then he went on, "It gives me great pleasure to introduce to you, Garet James, none other than the esteemed mathematician and astronomer Johannes Kepler. Johannes Kepler, please greet the unutterably lovely Garet James."

The man with him bowed to me again with much grace, his gesture describing one of the parabolas or ellipses—I couldn't recall which—from my high school science class. Will's bow had been authentic, but this man's bow was elegant. Still, could it really be Kepler? I didn't want to embarrass either one of them by questioning it: after all, I currently lived in a world in which John Dee could be my contemporary, my enemy, and a historical figure all at the same time. But it was daunting to believe that Kepler—who, if my high school memory served me correctly, ranked with Galileo and Copernicus—stood in this dingy cavern with us. What was he doing in 2009, and how on earth had he gotten mixed up with the awful likes of Marduk? NASA had recently named a US space program after him, for goodness sake! And I had no idea what the real Kepler looked like, which put strict limits on my ability to identify him.

As if responding to my uncertainty, Will elaborated,

"Mr. Kepler, like myself, is a refugee in time, a colleague in wandering. Also like myself, he's the victim of a misunderstanding, or, in his case, something worse: of greed, of trusting the wrong person—"

"Of being naive," Kepler interjected. "I was always more sophisticated about the planets than about their inhabitants—Earth's, at least. Witness aspects of my marriages, or at least my first one, if I may so mention." He smiled in turn at both of us, and we both smiled back uneasily, startled by such a forward comment. I knew nothing about his marriages, that was for sure.

I did, however, know that Will was truly four hundred years out of his time. Hesitantly, I decided to go along with the premise that Will could have met Kepler, fellow time traveler, in contemporary Paris. The man certainly had old-fashioned mannerisms. He bowed to me again and said, in a soft voice, "If I might, my lady." And then he recited:

"My lady's face is like a rose's dream
"Of beauty greater than itself. The sun
"Itself cannot shine brighter than your eyes;
"Yes, Will has lauded you, but my surprise
"At your perfection is beyond all words.
"You turn this cell into a garden, filled with birds
"And flowers; nor could there be a grander theme
"Than you for any art. I worship at your throne"—

here he interrupted himself to bow slightly toward me, making me blush more than I cared to—

"And pray that you and this most earnest Will

"Will understand each other very soon."

Kepler shot a warm-eyed look at Will that I perceived as one of grandfatherly fondness for him, again to my embarrassment, as I wondered what "understand" could be a euphemism for. Kepler concluded with,

"Rejoice!—as we are cut loose from this hell."

I wondered if Will had put him up to this, a poem that had an Elizabethan ring to it as Will's poems did—though I suspected, without exactly recollecting, that Kepler was from the same era—but Will's features held no emotion but pleased surprise. He'd been anything but a convincing actor with me, so I adjusted to the idea that a scientific genius, whom I had studied in high school astronomy, was attempting to play Cupid in my personal life, centuries past his time. That was too much of a brainful for even the last forty-eight hours, but I decided it was not considerate of me to simply stand there in stupefied silence, so I thanked him. "I have never heard of you as a poet, just as an astronomer. Am I ignorant on this point?"

Kepler smiled. "I'm no poet. In my youth, as a student at the University of Tübingen, I did have a few years in which I frequently wrote sonnets, composing them while walking in the woods, on scraps of paper I then stuffed into my pockets. The sonnet was a popular form at the time. But I was not able to continue to write them, under the heavy but welcome burden of calculations required to verify my planetary theories. However, I listened to this brilliant young man recite a spontaneous poem of his own a little while ago, and it inspired me. Reawakened my poetic voice."

"You heard my poem?" Will asked him.

Kepler nodded. "I was too weak to respond, but I did hear it. It was one of the few things that helped me keep my sanity during those dark moments of imprisonment."

"This exchange of poems and pleasantries is all very well and good," Jules's prim voice came from the opening of the cell, "but are we going to stand here talking poetry while those madmen are loose? They have killed my colleague Jean-Luc, and now Annick has gone off in pursuit of them."

"Annick followed them?" I asked. "How do you know?"

"She texted me," Jules said, holding up his cell phone. "It was *most* irresponsible of her after I specifically ordered her to remain in hiding at the entrance of the catacombs."

"Ah, but most intrepid," remarked Kepler. "Perhaps the young lady will be able to tell us where Marduk and Dee have gone."

"*If* they don't kill her first," Jules snapped. Then he turned on his heel with military precision to march away from us—an effect ruined by his having to stoop and turn sideways to get through the hole in the brick wall. We followed him in silence, cowed by his anger and by the sight of Jean-Luc's body, his face covered by Jules's jacket, lying on the catacombs floor. Another corpse to add to the mounds of the subterranean dead, I thought, recalling the piles of bones and skeletons we'd passed on our way here. I shivered, imagining the corpses of Marduk's victims piling up in the same abundance on the streets of modern-day Paris.

11

Black Pools

Few would have suspected the true identities of John Dee and Marduk as they strolled, a few minutes before seven a.m., into the glossy glass lobby of Global Financial Fund headquarters on the Rue Cuvier near the Quai Saint-Bernard. Both wore Brooks Brothers suits and white dress shirts. Dee had on a well-knotted tie to indicate that he came from the traditionalist world of private banking; Marduk's open collar was actually a conformist gesture toward the freewheeling culture of hedge funds.

Though at one time the tie, or lacking one, represented a divide between California funds and East Coast or European funds, the financial consultant Dee had seen in advance of this meeting had told him that tielessness had now spread like a contagion, everywhere but into the Far East. The consultant, David Ferris, a dapper man in his thirties, had sniffed the air with disapproval while saying this, as if informality were a pestilence.

"We just need to look authentic," Dee had told him. "Will Hughes will be doing road shows to raise capital, and I need him to look like a manager—not that he isn't one."

Upstairs, in his expansive fourteenth-floor office, the man waiting to meet with them had an identity as public and transparent as Dee's was private and obscure. Vice Chairman for External Relations of the Global Financial Fund Jean Renoir was frequently quoted in the financial media, especially in the past year or two, when his comments had turned emphatically cautionary. None of the journalists whom he palled around with, and sometimes wined and dined, would have guessed that during this period Renoir increasingly seethed with resentment, bitter that his antileverage advice had not been taken by nations and individuals prior to the '08 crash.

His urbane demeanor remained the same. But, in his mid-fifties now, balding and with a paunch, Renoir had taken as a blow to his outsized self-esteem the fact that even though he had been so right and the world had been so wrong, he had been unable to do anything about it. He was neither the leader of a country nor the head of a national bank who could directly implement a tight credit policy, though his voice was heard in august financial circles. So when an opportunity for influence presented itself, in the form of an extraordinarily ambitious gold-buying scheme, a chance not only to punish nations and their currencies for overuse of credit but to profit massively in doing so, he had been all ears.

Renoir knew little about this mysterious John Dee who was riding up in the elevator to his office now, with the somewhat better-known hedge fund manager Will

Hughes. Dee's claim to be the head of an ultra-secret and high-asset private bank in Dublin, Ireland, one that specialized in providing financing to increasingly popular, off-market "black trading pools," could not be fully verified. But that was no surprise, nor even cautionary, given the secretive nature of that world. Of greater concern, perhaps, was his claim to be descended from the historical figure John Dee, an assertion improbable on its face. (One reason this meeting had been scheduled was to get a feel for whether or not Dee was some kind of crackpot.) People did have their vanities, however, and there was always the slight chance he was such a descendant.

Dee's colleague Will Hughes was better known and definitively legitimate—Renoir had seen him on any number of financial talk shows—and together Dee and Hughes had verified their access to billions of dollars, euros, and pounds, as well as to other currencies, to the satisfaction of Renoir's trusted chief of staff, Saturn Hicks.

His intercom buzzer made the familiar shrill sound.

"Mr. Dee and Mr. Hughes here to see you, sir," receptionist Carla Worth said in her best, perfectly accented English. They must have spoken to her in English. Renoir had expected it, but he would not have been surprised if they had used French.

"Send them in, please."

As they came through the door Renoir got up and swung around his desk to greet both men with a handshake. That was a gesture he did not make for all, or the majority, of his visitors. Many had to come over to his desk to meet him while he sat. Dee and Hughes then took plush chairs a few feet apart in front of the desk; both seemed distracted at first by the view out the wall window behind Renoir. The Seine glimmered with late dawn, and over Renoir's right shoulder rose the spires of Notre Dame. Sunlight at a low angle glowed in a patch on the rose-patterned carpet midway between the two men's chairs. Hughes seemed particularly interested in the angle at which it was traversing the window and soon had moved his chair a foot or two to his right, away from it.

"I see you fellows must be in love with Paris the way I am," Renoir broke the silence.

"Paris has been around a long time," Dee replied indifferently. Will Hughes seemed to be studying his well-polished shoes.

What cold fishes, Renoir thought. Ulan Bator had existed a long time too, and Marseille. Nobody loved them that he'd heard of. Maybe the natives. Maybe. Paris was a jewel. Despite his desire to be congenial, he didn't think he could reply to such a banal utterance.

Another silence.

"To me, it is the San Francisco of Europe," Hughes said ponderously. "All it lacks is an ocean."

A comment as silly as Dee's was frigid, Renoir reflected, but at least he had to give the man credit for trying. He studied Will Hughes briefly, before replying. Renoir recognized him from television and photos in the financial press, but he thought he could detect some tiny difference in his facial features, some obscure imperfection, right now. As if one of his eyebrows was a little longer than the other—maybe that was it—or was the peak of one of his ears too high? He couldn't tell, and then he warned himself against excessive nervousness at this meeting, not surprising given the monumental amounts of money involved.

"Yes, I like San Francisco too," he said.

Hughes nodded. Renoir observed Hughes's gaze to wander again, from the floor to the window to Renoir's own face now, not exactly meeting his eyes, and then to his neck. To the floor, and back to his neck. Was it his tie? Was it crooked? Renoir's hand found its way to the knot and found it straight. Will Hughes was starting to annoy him. He needed to bring the man down from his pedestal—but in a friendly way.

"Mr. Hughes, I have found my introductory discussion with your colleague Mr. Dee most interesting. I am of course familiar with your innovations in socially conscious investing, like the Green Hills Partners, which seeks to improve the lives of animals by selling short the stock of companies that engage in factory farming and other nonhuman practices. Audacious, and heartwarming, though you must tell me sometime how you manage the commodity risk with those trades."

"Commodity risk?" Hughes asked. He could feel Dee glancing at him anxiously.

"Livestock, of course, eats corn and grain, so the swings in the prices of foodstuffs must impact corporate profits."

"It's early in our friendship for me to be handing you trade secrets," Hughes replied.

Delicately, Dee said, "There are, of course, hedging

strategies to deal with any and all commodities, including gold and silver. Surely you, Mr. Renoir, of all people, should be familiar with that."

Renoir backed off. The pair was certainly high-strung . . . Nothing wrong with a little shop talk, was there? He shrugged and went on. "In any event, Mr. Dee tells me that you are, in the black pools, engaged in far more pioneering and unorthodox endeavors than with your admirable Green Hills fund."

Now Will Hughes smiled. And Renoir found something peculiar in the way he pressed his lips together. As if he was hiding something.

"You can give Mr. Renoir some of your thinking regarding the black pool possibilities, Will. Why don't you?"

"I've started off pretty old-fashioned when it comes to quantitative procedures," Hughes said. "Straight down the middle with risk metrics. Low exposure, high reward through repetitive trading gains. That's the mantra. But I am extremely progressive when it comes to investment themes. As you mention. Green Hills began as an environmentally concerned fund, expanded to advocating for humane practices on behalf of some of the most defenseless among us, animals being led to the slaughter."

Renoir was less than amused by this humane notion, which he had read about at some point a year or two before but not taken with any particular seriousness. The French economy depended heavily on agriculture. If the man's views became associated with his, Renoir's, name in public, it could be political poison for him. And his appointment at the GFF was, ultimately, a political one. However, he saw no immediate need to worry. They simply needed to keep their plot secret, at least until it was well under way and the results financial news. Renoir remained silent after Hughes's little speech.

Dee then steered the discussion in a more palatable direction. "What Mr. Hughes is trying to establish here, my esteemed Mr. Renoir, is that he is quite sensitive to the plight of the oppressed, whether they be two-legged, or four-, or a hundred-legged, for that matter." He laughed. "Bringing justice to credit-crazed capitalists whose predatory lending has caused so much suffering, by causing a collapse of the gold bubble, is an extension of progressive logic. And so we stand at the ready, sir, at your service!"

Renoir was reassured by these platitudes, at least as to Dee's sense of public relations, but he remained troubled by the tautness of Hughes's smile, which he observed from the corner of his eye. Then Hughes relaxed his lips, and Renoir found a little too much white gleaming at him, as if the man had spent excessively on some polishing treatment. Was there something wrong with his teeth? Finally Hughes returned to the neutral expression he had entered the room with, and Renoir's distraction subsided, but, still, this man was making him as uncomfortable as anyone with billions of dollars that Renoir wanted to speculate with could. It was time for him to truly take control of the meeting. He half stood from his chair, leaned on the mahogany desktop, and said tersely, "So the three of us stand agreed, then, that the corporate and banking greed unveiled to the general public in the fall 2008 crash goes unpunished a year later, in fact has been rewarded by a variety of bailouts and 'look the other way' investigations! And so therefore it's time that we, three individuals with unique capacities to carry out justice and punish the perpetrators, took matters into our own hands?"

Both men nodded. Renoir breathed a sigh of relief, then decided to go on to a more momentous concept.

"We will start out using three billion euros in the black pools with the utmost secrecy, as John Dee and I have already discussed, to raise the price of gold, first there, in the black pools, and then everywhere, as the consequences of the trades begin to affect the general market. And as we eventually—maybe in a week's time—leak reports of our success, consequently we will be able to raise almost infinitely more capital. Our assistants can meet during the next few days to work out the many logistical details of this plan.

"At gold's peak, we will of course short it and help bring it tumbling down, and then we will use our massive short *and* long profits to finance a global political party that will offer hope to billions of citizens—say, one citizen for every dollar or euro made—impoverished by this second, global, gold-centered crash, which will make 2008 look like a mere wrinkle in a riptide. We will offer a truly radical hope—no, not the tired clichés of communism"— his visitors joined him in shaking their heads—"but fair and equal treatment before the law for all, regardless of means, a first in the history of capitalism. The Fairness Party, we will call it."

Dee burst into applause. After a pause, Will Hughes joined him. Renoir beamed at them. "And if you imagine that I might consider becoming the head of the Fairness Party," Renoir concluded, "you imagine accurately!"

Dee got up out of his chair to grasp Renoir's right hand in both of his and congratulated him on his concept with enthusiasm. After yet another glance at Renoir's necktie, Hughes joined him.

12

Skin that Shines

The very same Will Hughes whom Garet James had met in New York City in the late autumn of 2008, whom she had gone to the Summer Country with in France the next summer and mistakenly left behind in Paris in 1602, sat at the Café du Pain only two blocks from the Sacré-Coeur in Montmartre. He enjoyed his splendid view of the city on the same morning and at the same time that Garet was trudging out of the catacombs with the other refugees from Dee and Marduk, far across the city from him and south of the Seine. A breakfast of café au lait and bread with cheese was before him on the red and white checkered tablecloth, drowning in a pool of sunlight the awning allowed, sunlight that was the greatest and most unexpected treat of all for him.

Late yesterday, in the furnished room near Gare de l'Est he'd rented upon his return to the city, he'd discovered, quite by accident, a tolerance for sunlight. A breeze had lifted the fringe of a carelessly closed curtain, allowing a patch of light to illumine his forearm. Even as he reflexively snatched his arm away, cringing at the sizzling pain he knew from experience was coming, hoping he hadn't burned himself too badly, he registered that he felt nothing.

Ever so cautiously, Will had moved his arm back into the light. The absence of pain was beyond a relief to him; it was soothing, as if the air were bathing his arm in medicinal bubbles. In a fit of daring, he reached out and flung the curtain aside and stepped into the crisp blaze of late-day light. Will tensed into a giant coil as he stood there, but, remarkably, he felt no different than he would have before he became a vampire—or was made one—on a terrible night in 1602. He waited, counting patiently from one to ten.

Nothing!

It was unscientific, of course, but Will had felt yesterday that he could have stayed in that room the rest of the day, watching the sun descend redly beyond the Seine, and not felt a scintilla of pain. Was he no longer, by some miracle, a vampire? He ran into the bathroom to try to check on the status of another "symptom."

No, he had seen with disappointment, he was still a vampire, if fangs were the test. Though they did seem to have diminished in size a little. But they were still there. On the other hand, he was able to see his reflection in the mirror, an experience he hadn't had since before he became a vampire. He was somewhere in between now. All in all, he'd need to be cautious with this newfound tolerance of sunlight. If he were brazen enough to go out in the sunlight tomorrow, he needed to assure himself of deep shadows or a shady interior nearby at all times.

Next, he had wondered if his appetite for humans as food had changed. This was hard to gauge, as he was at the time still hours away from the first meal of his nocturnal "day," but he had given it a try (even taking into account that he had been attempting to suppress his normal appetite lately for moral reasons, with encouraging though not always certain results). And yes, he did think a rich, juicy, rare, blood-veined steak, steer and not human in origin, was a more alluring and fulfilling prospect for him now than it had been on the previous day. Compared to his fondness for the more brutal food he had been consuming for centuries, this attraction to new forms of meat gave a sense of progress, which Will hoped was real. Eventually . . . he might progress enough even to eat more vegetables instead of meat!

Finally his thoughts had turned to how his alteration, modest or profound as it might be, could have happened. The quantitative streak in his thinking, the same quality that had led him to metrical poetry and stock trading, told him that, odds were, it had something to do with the young Will Hughes, whom he'd tracked down in a 1602 Paris alleyway and encouraged to have a rendezvous with Garet. That rendezvous, if it had happened, could have included young Will becoming a mortal by drinking Marduk's blood. He and young Will were two different people, of course, separated by four centuries of experience as identical twins might be separated by living in different countries, but that didn't mean young Will's departure from being a vampire couldn't have affected him in some way.

Apparently, it had. On the very first day on which, according to his calculations, Garet and his younger self would have traveled back to the present. His transformation must have something to do with his younger—and now mortal—self's reappearance in the present.

Obsessively, he had rechecked his fangs in the mirror.

No change: but only five minutes had passed.

He had then felt inspired to write a few lines of verse about the moment, about how an event happening to another could ripple so fortuitously along the rivers of time:

My Other Self

I don't know how, or why, or even if,
But Will, my youthful twin, you've lifted me
Halfway toward a restored humanity;
And for this I salute you, though the proof
Of such a transformation must await
Events, good fortune, further twists of time.
For now, my skin drinks light like a fine
*   wine,*
Affirming some benevolence in fate,
Though my harsh world sometimes succumbs
*   to hate.*
I welcome sun, as if my youth's restored

And sense my triumph—all these years, I've
   warred
Against my own foul nature—not too late,
Now a full day of freedom. Glory, light,
And skin that shines with sun. Farewell to night!

But the optimism of the poem had made Will nervous. He knew it took too much for granted: his new
tolerance for sunlight could easily depart. He didn't know
what had happened after he left young Will in Paris, and
even if his younger self had met up with Garet and been
transformed, he did not yet know for sure if he and Garet had made the journey in time to the present success-
fully. He and his younger self could be like twins, but
maybe time had reduced them to distant cousins instead. Still, he felt he could hope. But he had put the
folded piece of paper on which he'd written the poem
back in his pocket. Time alone would reveal what this
sunny moment was. He had told himself yesterday that
for now, he needed to try to enjoy it.

And then, as if out of nowhere, he had been startled
by a sudden resurgence of the old hunger, an ancient fire
that he'd doused with the worst of all blood-soaked
waters over the centuries, too many times. The pangs
had awakened him to the reality that he was still a vampire, even if possibly a hybrid one.

But even in that bad moment yesterday, he'd been
hopeful that, this morning, he might enjoy his first real
breakfast in four hundred years. And now, for the twenty
minutes he'd been sitting so near the sun at the Café du

Pain (not far from the shelter of the awning, of course), so far so good: he hadn't felt even a twinge of burning.

Will savored every morsel of his bread and cheese and sipped every drop of his café au lait, like a man without a care in the world. True, he needed to exercise discretion regarding a possible encounter with Garet and/or young Will, who would be in Paris now, assuming that their time transport had gone well. Such an encounter was . . . to be avoided. But Paris was a large city, and he had an excellent view of the entrance to the café.

Will lost himself momentarily in his surroundings, immersed his vision in the beautiful city sprawling out from Montmartre's hill, the white, gray, and pastel colors of its buildings, the spires of churches and occasional gold dome of a temple or mosque, the bustle of so many citizens even in the vacation time of late August. These were daylight scenes he could only have imagined for the past four hundred years, and he viewed every last detail of them passionately.

His fangs did not appear to have diminished any further in the mirror that morning, and he ran his tongue across them now, perhaps to prevent his mood from becoming too ebullient. His tongue did not detect any improvement. And then he returned to reveling in the view. Will swiveled in his chair and bent his head back, to take in the deepest of blue skies beyond the magnificent façade of the famed church behind him. The air itself seemed radiant. Will breathed deep to let the Paris sky fill his lungs, tickle his bloodstream, wash his flesh;

entertaining the fantasy that if he filled his lungs enough he'd be able to take off and soar like little Lol could.

He was a long way from religion, but then he entertained another fantasy: that sitting in such pure blond air was cleansing for his soul, a new kind of baptism for him.

antidote

When they left the building after meeting with Jean Renoir, John Dee, who had been on the whole quite satisfied with Marduk's performance during the meeting, observed his colleague to hesitate as they entered sunshine. Marduk quickly drew lavender felt gloves from his pocket and put them on. Then he doubled over as if with pain, shading first his eyes, then his entire face. He held his hands, fingers splayed wide, over his face so as to cover as much exposed skin as possible. He retreated back into the shadow of the building's awning and dropped his hands with a gesture of exasperation.

Dee was displeased, but not shocked. The vampire's antidote, an alchemist's potion that he had been working on for centuries, was being improved upon all the time, but it wasn't quite the finished product yet.

"What's wrong, my good man?" Dee asked Marduk, despite his being neither good nor a man. His colleague had resumed standing but still seemed to be gasping a little.

"Your remedy appears to be expiring, Dee. Not quite as it was advertised to me." Marduk turned a cold glare on the alchemist, one that made Dee shudder. Dee had seen plenty in his four centuries of dabbling with spirits, but there was no doubt that Marduk had a supreme sort of monstrous entity inside him. Babylonian (as in the evil described in the Book of Revelation), it had been long rumored. Dee was afraid of him.

Dee stood very still.

"I could use some water and another glass of the potion! What are you standing here like a grinning monkey for?"

Dee ushered Marduk back into the lobby, where a water fountain caught his eye. Dee pressed a pair of large square pills into Marduk's right hand and guided him toward the fountain. "It's best to take it in this form, in public as we are," Dee told him. "Dash them down with water. They will certainly take you to this evening's sunset, probably well beyond."

Marduk placed the pills eagerly into his mouth, gulped them down with long swallows of water. His expression brightened. "What a relief," he told Dee, apparently referring to the lessening of some burning sensation.

Dee nodded approval, though he hated to use these precious pills, the product of endless hours in his alchemist's lab back in Ireland. But if these circumstances didn't justify their use, what ever would? Marduk might have been a monster even to Dee, but he was also the key to a plot aiming at nothing short of world domination, his four-hundred-year-old dream.

They went back outside, Marduk showing no untoward reaction to sunlight, and made their way to the nearest Metro stop. Dee quieted any worries he was feeling over potion efficacy by reflecting that it was probably just a question of refining the dose. A sunlight suppressant was uncharted water even for an alchemical genius like himself, and perfection would not come easily. Vampires had been under the curse of sunlight peril for eons. That might stem naturally enough from their being creatures of the dark, but it created obstacles for the plot he had hatched, Marduk's very private impersonation of Will Hughes being its centerpiece. As to how the plot had gone this morning: so far, so good.

Then, before they got on the Metro, Marduk expressed to him in no uncertain terms his desire not to return to the catacombs as planned but to have a leisurely breakfast at a sidewalk café.

These liberated vampires, Dee sighed to himself—there might be no limit to their self-centeredness. But this wasn't the right fight to pick with Marduk; no doubt there would be other, more crucial ones. Aloud, he agreed to Marduk's plan.

So they veered away from the Metro entrance at Place Jussieu and lulled away the next couple of hours at Café du Dragon, a sidewalk café on the Rue Linné. On one hand, Dee did take pleasure in Marduk's ability to be out in the daytime, the culmination of so many years of research. It was an endeavor that had begun in the reign of Oliver Cromwell, when Puritan officials (whose values and religious fervor Dee despised) tended to be difficult targets for vampire assassination because they were out so much more in the daytime than at night. Marduk's wincing leaving the building had been a setback, as it indicated that the antidote's effects were disappointingly short, but the pills had so far worked like a wonder.

On the other hand, Dee was miffed at Marduk's lack of gratitude for the financial breakthrough with Renoir, irritated by his sullen personality—indeed, appalled by his lack of enthusiasm for the plan. Dee himself was most ebullient with the energy of his audacity. Enlisting a prestigious organization like the Global Financial Fund—or at least, one of its top executives—as an ally was a major achievement. He knew Marduk not to be the warmest of . . . creatures, but Dee wished that Marduk respected his accomplishment.

The bustle of crowds hustling past their table, the clamor of traffic, even the brilliance of sunlight glimmering in windows across the street all served as a chorus for his high spirits. Why then, he wondered as he finished up his bacon and cheese omelette and sipped the last few drops of *jus d'orange*, was he cursed to put up with the moroseness of a personality like Marduk's? Tell the truth, reluctant though he was to admit it, he wouldn't mind having breakfast instead with a spry young thing like that ingenue Garet James. She was on the wrong side of the battle, of course, but she had a twinkle in her eye and a bulge in her bodice that made Marduk look like the ghoul he was in comparison. (Even if Dee had in fact helped make him that.)

Eventually, Dee could ignore Marduk's truculent si-
lences no longer. He grasped the fellow's wrist in exasperation, moved it not so subtly into a shaft of sunlight
bisecting the table—to which Marduk evinced no
response—and exclaimed, "My dear man. Have you no
emotions? No sense of triumph, or even greed? We stand
on the precipice of an enormous victory. And you personally, thanks entirely to me, have the freedom to move
about twenty-four hours per day, more than doubling
your life in these long summer days. Do you not exult?"

Marduk took his hand away and put it back in shadow,
slowly. "What puts a damper on this for me is the need
to masquerade as that puny offal, Will Hughes. Because I
have fed on the young Will Hughes I haven't gained the
knowledge and experience of his older self. At least Kepler's form came with some interesting facts about the
stars. All I've gotten with this shape is an obsession with
the watchtower and a propensity to think in metrical
verse." He grimaced, showing more teeth than was wise
in a public venue. Dee hurried to reassure him.

"It's unfortunate indeed that you could not feed directly on the older Hughes, but unavoidable. How were
we to know he'd stay in 1602 and send his younger self to
the present? But do not worry, I have made an exhaus-
tive study of the world's financial markets. We should
have no problem as long as you do exactly as I say."

"Is that so?"

Marduk took Dee's wrist and moved it into the sunlight also, but squeezing so hard that Dee began to gasp.
The man's—creature's—strength was abominable.

"I follow no man's orders. I will try a fling at black pool stock trading tonight. It only takes place at night, right?"

Dee nodded, gasping, trying unsuccessfully to remove his wrist from the creature's grasp. He didn't want to beg or plead.

"Y-y-y-yes," he finally stammered. "I can get you an address. And a little money to work with." Anything to mollify the beast.

Marduk nodded. "Then I'll decide whose identity I use for the plot. But don't let anything untoward happen to Kepler in the meantime. Understand?"

Dee nodded that he did, and wouldn't. Marduk let go of his wrist with a triumphant grin. And Paris no longer seemed quite as electric with benign energy to Dee, as it had just a moment or two before. He rubbed his aching wrist, averting his eyes from Marduk's belittling gaze.

14

It Was Red

The apartment building on Rue E. Lumeau was the last place in Paris, or maybe in the world, that anyone would have suspected to house an activity as portentous as black pool stock trading. Dilapidated. That was the word that ran through Marduk's mind as he beheld, from across the street, the six-story grime-encrusted façade of the building, in one of the seedier sections of northern Paris. But when he carefully checked the address on the slip of paper Dee had given him against that on the torn awning protruding over a set of crumbling stone front steps, they matched. And as he continued to stand there, dumbfounded, a sleek black limo pulled up in front of the entrance and two young men in expensive-looking suits got out. They went up the steps, each carrying thin valises that could have been briefcases or computers, Marduk couldn't tell.

Curiosity overcoming him, he crossed the street after the men had entered the building, and he mounted the steps as well. The front door had a sturdy-looking lock,

but a mild push against the door with one shoulder revealed that it was actually broken, and Marduk slipped
inside. A narrow, rectangular lobby, which seemed to
run far back into the building, was dark and foul-smelling,
poorly lit by one Victorian-era lamp with a frayed shade
on a splintered table. Marduk looked around, feeling
further confusion. There was no directory, or elevator,
or even furniture to sit on. Again he wondered if he was
in the right place. He thought he detected a faint aroma
of stale urine.

Then he heard a distant clamor of voices, perhaps
from several flights above, muffled, as if from a crowd in
a tapestried room. He started up the stairs, which were
toward the back of the lobby. At the top of the second
flight, he took one stride onto the landing, where an am-
ateurish portrait of Napoleon hung in a cheap frame,
turned to go up the next flight, and found himself in a
different world.

A sheet of polished metal that could have been steel
but gleamed like silver blocked off the rest of the second
floor hallway; the polished wooden landing under its reflection was bright, almost incandescent. An oval-shaped
door, with a series of small red bulbs bordering it, was in
the center of the metal sheet. In front of the door, a
young man in a white, iridescent jumpsuit that resembled an astronaut's uniform sat a desk with a computer
in front of him. "Credentials, sir?" he asked Marduk.

"What?"

"Your credentials. No one is admitted to the trading
room without at least three forms of identification, one

of which must be a letter of certification, including bonding, from the CAC Quarante. The Paris Stock Exchange."

Marduk eyed the empty stairs below him. Short-tempered under the best of circumstances, he was of a mind to strangle this arrogant sentry, anxious as he was to start trading now that he'd come this far. At first he saw no potential witnesses below him, and the sheet of metal seemed to block any view from above. But then he heard voices, belonging to young persons judging by their laughing tone, floating toward him from the first flight of stairs. He strained his eyes downward and spied a few young men, dressed more casually than the others he'd seen, glancing up at him and sending looks of friendly recognition his way.

"Will! Where have you been?" the first up the stairs, a tall, gangling blond man asked.

"Haven't seen you in over a month!" a red-haired companion in an orange and white sweater exclaimed. The little group increased their pace up the stairs toward him, and soon three men, the third with dark hair and wearing a shirt with a photo of Elvis Presley on it, emerged onto the landing.

"Glad you fellows happened along," Marduk said. "I've forgotten my wallet and apparently this novice"—he indicated the man at the table with a nod—"has not heard of Will Hughes!"

The entry clerk, who mumbled apologies for being on only his third night on the job, was familiar with the new arrivals, for he opened the door for them without an ID request or further word. "We'll vouch for Will," the blond man told him, and Marduk joined them without further challenge.

The tunnel stretching out before them now seemed remarkably long given the external dimensions of the building. An optical illusion of some sort, Marduk speculated. It was oval-shaped like the door, made of luminescent white plastic with rows of twinkling red lights extending along it. The thick, rose-colored carpet they walked on, luxuriant as the Turkish carpets he had encountered during years spent adventuring in the Ottoman Empire, ran down the middle. Marduk tried to focus not on the modern and spacious design within such a rundown and cramped building but on parrying conversational forays from the others that he found disconcerting, given that they were based on aspects of Will Hughes's life he was not familiar with given that they concerned an older Will than the one he'd fed on. Forays concerning various "honeys," accompanied by laughter Marduk found shrill. Did these men go out drinking every night before they went to work here? he wondered. No wonder the economy was in the trouble it was in! He tried to confine his responses to grunts and monosyllables until one of the trio, the red-haired man, grew especially persistent.

"C'mon, Will. You recall. The one on your arm at the club last month." The man had the trace of a Scottish brogue. "Don't tell me you can't even remember her name!"

"They all have names," Marduk said, meaninglessly.

"I'll bet he remembers other things about her," the Elvis Presley fan piped up.

Raucous laughter. Marduk glanced behind him; the tunnel was empty. They were secluded enough for him to consider strangling all three, which he doubted would take him more than a minute. With a certain crushing pressure on the hollows in . . . but he backed off his dark idea, concerned there might be other checkpoints he'd need them for up ahead.

"Will's preoccupied with a trade," the Presley fan offered. "Any ideas you'd like to share with us, Will?"

"I'll share them after I'm done with them," Marduk rasped, angrily. "I'll share exactly how many millions I've made tonight." His voice sounded even to him like a growl, and he realized he'd forgotten to imitate Will Hughes for the moment.

The trio surrounding him fell uneasily silent, exchanging glances among themselves but keeping whatever thoughts they might be having about "Will Hughes" and his sullen selfishness to themselves. When they resumed their chatter, he was not, to his relief, included in it. They went on about stocks and women of various names and nationalities, as if they were interchangeable commodities, but without the good-humored undercurrent of earlier. Marduk was relieved when they arrived at the unmanned entrance to the trading room; he'd had to suppress the strong urge to throttle their superficial and inane selves every step of the way there.

As if making an ironic point, the black pool room had an intensely white decor. Marduk found the array of white objects greeting his eyes bewildering, and he wondered why all the traders weren't wearing white coats. White desks; white chairs on wheels; white computer consoles (though bits of color representing stock symbols flecked the screens); white walls, ceiling, and floor; white lamps above each console. But he wasn't there to critique the decor, he reminded himself—he was there to make money. If Will Hughes could do it, he could!

He looked around for the nearest empty trading post and spied one two-thirds of the way down the closest aisle. But just as he reached it and began pulling the chair out, he was accosted by a trading room attendant (who was in fact wearing a white coat)—a short-haired young person, revealed to be female only by the pitch of her voice, who asked, "Mr. Hughes? Why aren't you going to your post? We've been keeping it open for you."

Marduk, with great effort projecting some semblance of a personality, clapped his hand to his forehead and mumbled, "I confess to being distracted. Apologies. Can it be that age is creeping up on me?" He tried to smile.

He was acting lamely, he considered, but he didn't see an alternative. Certainly his first reaction—as always, to kill—was not practical with all these people around. Could he credibly say he'd forgotten where his post was when he was there to trade millions of euros in positions he had to keep by memory in his head?

When he didn't move right away, the attendant, after a quizzical look at him, took him by the elbow and led him to his post, two corridors farther away from the entrance. There, he found himself at a particularly grand-looking console and desk, set apart from the others and, alone among all the equipment in the huge room, not white. It was red.

Marduk was curious to know the thinking behind that color choice, which at the least showed Will Hughes to be a distinctive figure among stock traders. But this was not the time to be asking questions. The attendant left, and Marduk settled in before the screen. He was confident that he had mastered the necessary basics for this trading in the crash computer course Dee had given him during the afternoon, and Dee had assured him that his password, even though it wasn't Hughes's personal one, would work at this location this evening. And it did.

And it was remarkable how little time it took him to lose the entire ten million euro line of credit Dee had carved out for him for this one evening only.

He had been sitting at the screen only a few minutes when he started to get a visceral sense of how, whatever money might mean in the world generally, it meant something different during stock trading. Or, it meant nothing. The values of positions, especially the currency options and derivatives that Hughes—judging from the positions left over from his last session—traded, changed with shocking frequency, and seemingly in unpredictable directions. But Marduk had his mantra. A monster, which he reveled in being, could have a mantra. If Will Hughes could do it, he, Marduk, could do it even better.

Buy and sell. That was what Will Hughes did. Any idiot could do that, let alone an awesome being like he was. So he bought 100,000 options on the euro to rise in value against the US dollar from $1.3855 to $1.3875 during the six hours following the option purchase. The options cost about seven euros each, or about 700,000 euros all told, and "controlled," according to the screen—namely, gave a right to buy—hundreds of millions of euros in exchange. Granted, six hours wasn't so long a time, but it seemed a phenomenal amount of money to gain a gateway to for so little cost in return.

But in less than fifteen minutes, these options had a breathtaking plunge in value, from seven euros to under one, all of it because the euro had diminished from $1.3855 to $1.3819 in the blink of an eye. Marduk's position was nearly wiped out! Panicking, he sold it all for fear it would plunge to zero, so at least he'd have some money left from this mishap when the night was over. But he'd lost over six hundred thousand euros in less than fifteen minutes.

A half hour later, Marduk noted that his opening position, had he kept it, would now have more than doubled from its original price and would have increased many times over from the low point at which he'd sold it. For the euro, fluctuating extravagantly, was now at $1.3897, and the options had moved up to approximately sixteen euros each accordingly. Meanwhile he'd lost similar overall amounts in two other attempts at trades.

And the night got worse from there.

15

Consolation of the Traditional Kind

"Black pools" didn't even begin to describe the trading he had just attempted, Marduk was thinking as he shut down Will Hughes's computer and, penniless for the moment, left the room. "Black quicksand" was more like it. Or a black river running so treacherously that the world's most expert swimmer would drown in it.

He had been tempted more than once to smash the computer screen with his fist or stand on the flimsy rolling chair and kick the screen in with his boot. But he was mindful of the need to stay in Will Hughes's character and not upset Dee too outrageously, at least until he was ready to serve up justice to Dee as well, for all the slights Dee had inflicted on him during the time they'd known each other. Yes, he restrained himself. Perhaps he could find some other, more anonymous outlet for his fury. Dee's time would come, surely and soon enough.

Marduk hadn't failed, though. Anything Will Hughes could do, he could do better. And Will Hughes had made billions as a stock trader. At least, by reputation. (For all

Marduk knew, he'd stolen it, or lied about his results, given Marduk's inability to, at least immediately, duplicate them.) But assuming that Will Hughes was authentic, all Marduk had done here was gotten off to a poor start. He would catch up. Because he was more than Will Hughes's equal. Much more.

His exit was simpler than his entry—no long tunnel, no security checkpoint—and he wasn't sure how that was possible, but he simply went down two interior flights of shabby stairs and emerged on the same dilapidated front steps as earlier. When he had arrived, the sky had been pale violet; now it was pitch black.

As he descended the steps, Marduk detected, out of the corner of his eye, a flash of color down the otherwise deserted street. One moving slowly toward him. He smiled a smile of satisfaction. An entirely deserted street wouldn't have been good, but nearly deserted was excellent. With the stealth characteristic of even the most run-of-the-mill vampire, he turned away from the bottom of the stairs and pressed his back against the brick façade of the building, so that he became nearly invisible amidst coagulating shadows, especially to the casual passerby. Then he waited, each pulse pounding in his chest with greater and greater anticipation, as a blond young woman wearing a short silver dress and black high-heeled shoes came closer. Marduk wondered what she was doing dressed like that on a dangerous street like this, but hey, people had lives to live. Including her. He wasn't a judgmental sort or a prude. Maybe she was a black pool trader or had a party to go to. Either way, no problem. He had stationed himself so that he could grab her just before she reached the stairs. There was a convenient storage space underneath them, right now half occupied by black garbage bags that would be easily thrust aside. He licked his lips, and his pulse flared an extra pitch of intensity faster. The only remaining risk seemed to be that she might suddenly cross the street away from him—he wasn't sure he was willing to risk scrutiny from a car or person at a window in pursuing her—but that became less likely with each passing instant. Yes, life was good tonight.

Death would be even better.

A half hour later Marduk headed west down the completely deserted block, in the same direction from which the young woman, whose name was Jill Lautrec (though he wouldn't learn that until reading about her in *Le Cirque* the next morning), had approached him. He had a look of quiet satisfaction on his features, even as he wiped a filament of pale flesh off his too-red lips. As it happened, it was a remnant of the smooth underside of Jill Lautrec's breast. Marduk didn't generally care if his victims were male or female or follow gender-related procedures with them, but he'd been in an erotic mood tonight, perhaps brought on by the frustration of losing so much money.

He reached the corner of the Boulevard Raspail and Rue de Babylone, and turned in the direction of a Metro sign for the station at Serres Babylone, reflecting further.

He had no doubt he would soon, with a little practice, get the hang of stock trading and begin to exceed Will Hughes's achievements. Such a confident perspective was in fact enhanced by the revelation he'd had at the computer screen, that money did not mean the same thing in the stock market as it did everywhere else, and also by confidence that Dee would replace the missing funds. If Dee balked, or even hesitated, Marduk's hands around his pale and effete neck would encourage a better attitude. In the meantime, he'd satisfied the savage anger he felt over his "losses" with a consolation of the traditional kind. Now he could slip off anonymously into the black loveliness of the Paris night.

Marduk would be in no rush about another meal, either. Dee's antidote was thrumming potently in his veins; he could feel it. He would head back by Metro to the small apartment Dee had arranged for him in the Latin Quarter, near the Jardin des Plantes, where he could take refuge. Who could guess what fine repasts might await him now, even in the sharp sunlight of tomorrow?

16

We have Maps

We all emerged from the entrance to the catacombs blinking back robust morning sunshine, as sweet and light-rich as the air in the tomb had been fetid and cadaverous. This would have been one of the first opportunities for my lover Will and I to be together in the daytime had not the wrong Will accompanied me back to the present. I lamented the error again, even as I glanced over at young Will and saw that he seemed to be having trouble navigating. He had stumbled off the curb into the street and back at least three times, as if his vision were dazzled. And now he seemed to be searching for shadows to walk in, hugging the three- and four-story buildings lining the Avenue Denfert Rochereau, which intermittently blocked the low trajectory of morning rays. It was as if he had taken a step toward being a vampire. From what I understood, if he were a full-blooded vampire, even his brief experiences of sunlight as he crossed the narrow alleys between buildings would have broiled his skin to a crisp. But he was making his way through them unharmed, even if wincing.

Then it was my turn to wince, as I recalled Marduk's fangs biting the soft flesh of Will's neck in the tomb; and with that image I also recalled something Will had said to me in 1602 Paris, about Marduk's ability to create vampires with a bite. After all, wasn't that how Will had originally become one? Then why wasn't he a full-fledged one again now?

We were walking four abreast, with me on the outside and Will on the inside, Jules and Kepler between us, Jules obsessively checking his phone for a text from Annick. I hung back a step or two, sidled over to the right, and engaged Will in conversation from slightly behind him.

"Do you feel OK?"

He slowed and walked next to me. "I am uncomfortable, my lady, now that you mention it. Perhaps a mild fever. I seem to be more at ease when I'm away from the sun. Perhaps something's gotten to me from breathing foul air in the dungeon."

I couldn't tell if he was dissembling for my benefit, not wanting to be suspected of the taint—however involuntary—of vampirism, or if he genuinely did not realize he could be suffering a side effect from Marduk's bite. "How's your neck?" I asked. As far as I could see, all traces of the monster's fangs had vanished.

I observed Will's hand quivering as he felt his neck, but it didn't linger there. "Can't feel a thing, my lady."

"Perhaps a sound sleep back at the hotel might be

useful." I suspected he had been up all night in the cata-combs. Perhaps he did have a fever, from exhaustion.

"*Pardon,* Mademoiselle James," Jules said in an offi-cious voice, half turning his head toward me. I had been speaking almost at a whisper, but he'd still been able to listen. "I have told Annick to meet us at the institute and you must come too. There are reports to be filled out and plans to be made."

"Can't all of that wait . . ."

But Jules insisted that it couldn't.

I kept a careful eye on Will's demeanor all the way to the institute. He managed to stay with us, but he wasn't quite right. He gravitated toward shadows wherever he could find them. When he was forced by their absence into bright sunlight, he would sometimes cringe, or pant, or even moan audibly, which, however, no one but me seemed to notice. But he did manage to straggle along, and eventually we reached the block on which the alley leading to the institute was located.

I thought of taking Will by the arm and guiding him toward shadows he sometimes seemed to miss, but I didn't want to embarrass him. I did sympathize with his problem, no fault of his own but rather the apparent re-sult of imbalances in whatever supernatural realm vam-pires lived in. Or were dead in. I strongly suspected Dee's and Marduk's machinations had triggered this im-balance. So I observed him closely, this nearly identical twin of "my" Will, or, as I sometimes thought of my Will now, "real" Will. I sensed that on occasion, in addition to sympathy, a sliver of passion for real Will—not this one, I reminded myself—confused my perspective. Needless to say, I suppressed that sliver with the same shudder anyone might stifle an inappropriate impulse with. Or tried to.

As we approached the alley from the south we saw Annick hurrying down the rue Saint-Jacques from the north. I heard Jules let out a sigh of relief, immediately followed by an exasperated exclamation.

"There you are! Do you realize that you broke at least three rules of mission protocol? You abandoned your post, you conducted a reconnaissance mission without permission, and you failed to report directly back to the institute in the event of losing communication."

Annick stamped her foot. "Would you have had me stand by like an idiot while our enemies sauntered by me? How could I ask permission while you were out of cell phone range? And here I am, reporting back to the institute with more valuable information than you have found, I wager . . ." Her voice faltered as her eyes ranged over the group, counting heads.

"Where is Jean-Luc?" she asked, her anger replaced by fear.

"Jean-Luc was killed by those fiends. You see how dangerous they are? They could have killed you too!"

A flicker of anger passed over Annick's face, quickly quelled by sympathy. She placed her hand on Jules's arm. "No wonder you are so upset, *mon ami,* to lose another agent so soon after—"

Jules flinched away from Annick's touch. "I am concerned, Agent Durant, that we are losing valuable time while murderers roam free on the streets of Paris or in its catacombs! What is this intelligence that you risked your life for?"

"Dee and Marduk went to Global Financial Fund headquarters after leaving the catacombs," Annick explained. "I was able to observe from tracking their elevator's destination, and referring to the building directory, that they met with a Vice Chairman Renoir." Then Annick bristled and drew herself up to her full height—all of five feet in heels. "Furthermore, there was no need to yell at me, Jules Henri Maupassant!"

Maupassant?

"You know as well as I do that sometimes an agent in the field has to use initiative and," she added, her voice softening, "that we all know the risks. Poor Jean-Luc knew them too. I'm sure you did everything you could to protect him. No one will blame you for his death. Come, let us tell my grandfather what has happened. He and Claudine will know what to do . . ."

Once again Annick attempted to put a comforting hand on Jules's arm, but once again he shook her off and, squaring his slim shoulders, preceded us down the narrow alley, determined, I guessed, to be the first to report the casualty of our mission. Annick glanced at me over her shoulder.

"At least you recovered your Will," she said with a wistful look at him.

"He's not—" I began, but a gasp from Jules cut short my protest.

We hurried to the end of the alley where Jules was holding back the ivy that, only yesterday, had covered the door to the institute. Only now there was nothing but a brick wall.

"The Malefactors," Jules finally said. "They've removed the institute from the time stream. It is as if the institute never existed."

"Hellhounds," Annick said.

"What?" I asked.

"Who are the Malefactors?" Kepler asked. That worried me. He knew about the farthest reaches of the solar system, so if he didn't know, they must be pretty inaccessible. I should have followed up more thoroughly when I'd heard the term used once before.

"Malefactors are rebellious *chronologistes*," Annick explained. "As a practical matter, *chronologistes* gone bad."

"If you're familiar with thinking about time as a two-edged sword," Jules said, "good in what it gives us, bad in what it takes away—as the Bard phrased it in sonnet 19, "Devouring time" with its "lion's paws"—Malefactors are *chronologistes* who have come to view time darkly. They're a gang of outlaws who try to ambush eternity instead of working with the beauty and malleability of time as we do. Shakespeare, however well intentioned, could be called their spiritual godfather, while Einstein and his softness on time through relativity is ours."

Annick interjected, "Or to put it more simply, while

we Knights Temporal are sworn to maintain the time line, the Malefactors shape time to their own selfish ends. There are many rumors about how they came to so hate time—some theories quite sinister and horrible. They are our sworn enemies. They try to disrupt us. Still, in recent months they have been quiescent, as our current leader has adopted a vigilant stand against them. So what's worrisome here is the timing. It seems possible that Dee and Marduk may have made some arrangement with them. I just hope everyone got out alive when the institute was attacked."

"Possible," Jules said. "They're evil as a practical matter, but they don't hate living beings as much as time itself. And, somewhat contradictorily, the reason for that hatred is that they view time as a killer. They are big proponents of the ends justifying the means."

"Interesting concept of time," Kepler commented. "It is quite apparent that they must be atheists."

"They've got a fair share of company on that," Jules replied. "Especially in the past couple of centuries."

I shuffled my feet impatiently. We had a big new problem now, and I wasn't in a mood to listen to an academic or theological dialogue such as might occur at the nearby Sorbonne. "Weird," was all I could think of to say. And Will looked totally befuddled. At least the alleyway was shady for him.

My eyes swept the end of the alleyway, trying to imagine a force powerful enough to make a place as large as the institute simply vanish as if it had never existed.

Then I spied, at the foot of the wall, a crumpled sheet of paper. I opened it up as Kepler, Annick, and Jules rambled on about meaning in the universe, and I saw that it was a poem by a poet named Pui Ying Wong. At the top of the page, using a stamp such as a postal service might employ, the word *portal* had been printed in thick black letters.

Père Lachaise

Uphill, then downhill
deep in the cemetery
greenway crammed with graves

But we have maps, sold
in every flower shop, all
on Rue Gambetta

We veer tomb to tomb
reading names off grime-flecked stones
in plane tree shadow

Statues of weeping
Magdalene, angels with wings
too heavy to fly

Behind the temple
Jim Morrison's "a white ball
of fire," wrote a fan

Hear the music, hard
as it punctures and punctures
we keep migrating

Remember hunger
that burns like insomnia
may have led us here.

"Let me take a look at that." Jules interrupted my reading. He grabbed the paper out of my hand. Annick read over his shoulder, and Kepler joined her in doing so. Will stood aloof; I noted that light from the climbing sun was now starting to filter into the space where they were all standing.

"What could the PORTAL stamp possibly mean?" I asked.

"The poem may be a portal map," Annick suggested. "What else would the phrase 'we have maps' refer to? Remember that the institute itself has been a portal, perhaps the most reliable one in all the city of Paris except for a certain bookstore"—she nodded at Kepler, and he smiled slightly—"so perhaps there's a temporary replacement for the store at the cemetery, Père Lachaise. Or maybe it refers specifically to Jim Morrison's grave. Or maybe the Rue Gambetta is actually the significant reference."

"Or the statue of the weeping Magdalene," Kepler said. "Not everyone, you'll notice, is an atheist."

"The first riddle we need to solve," Jules proclaimed, "is whether this message was left for us by friend or foe.

There is no magical certainty in our world regarding the otherworld—some would say, not even on the question of whether it exists or not—so we must rely on our instincts. Père Lachaise could be a portal, or it could be a fatal trap."

"In that case," Will spoke up, "I urge that we seek shelter immediately back at the hotel. We can discuss our options there without being exposed like we are right now, so close to the scene of an attack."

I could tell from his trembling tone how much he feared the impending full daylight.

"The hotel sounds good to me," I chimed in.

Kepler agreed. "Even if we are going to explore the cemetery as a portal, we can't do it in the daytime. I have had occasion to visit the graves of the great poet Apollinaire and the astronomer Jérôme Lalande—who measured the distance between the earth and the moon—there. It gets very crowded."

"Jim Morrison's more than anyone's," Jules agreed.

"The hotel, then," Annick said. And we all nodded agreement, starting virtually as one back up the alley toward the rue Saint-Jacques. But I stopped suddenly, though the others kept on walking.

I stopped because I'd heard a violent clap of thunder from the sky behind me; some stormclouds must have crept up unnoticed while we lingered in the alley. And for a moment I thought I could smell the seashore, as though this were an Atlantic storm that had retained a trace of its origin while traveling over land. But then a quick glance told me that in fact the Paris sky remained an unbroken blue.

I heard a second peal of thunder, and the world around me seemed to go entirely black. I couldn't see the rest of the group in front of me, or the alley or the buildings adjacent to it, or anything. I felt physically fine—no dizziness, no unsteadiness, certainly I was quite conscious and alert—so I wasn't terrified. But I was unnerved. And then, suddenly, I found a compass by which to navigate this crisis.

Memory.

I'd experienced this particular sensation before.

It was when Will had transmigrated my—and his—atoms back in New York City, first to avoid hitting a tree in the limo and then to bypass traffic chaos so we could get to Van Cortlandt Park. As now, I had been immersed in a total, chilly blackness. And now, as then, I wasn't dizzy, but I could feel myself slowly spinning, as if I were standing on the nucleus of a gigantic atom at the edge of the universe, a nucleus slower than the whirling electrons around me, but rotating nonetheless. The closest galaxy was moving with my atom, as I could sense rather than see: a galaxy that was a magnificent whirl at the boundary of the universe.

Then all was suddenly still again, and I could open my eyes. I caught a quick glimpse of the group turning left at the entrance to the alley, toward the hotel, all of them oblivious to my delay. My chilliness had vanished. I could only wonder why my atoms had transmigrated again. Could this happen without an outside intervention? Why had I wound up this time exactly where I'd started out? I certainly hadn't willed it myself.

Then I saw the flash of tiny, whirring green wings. Lol. I recognized her right away. She flew back up over the wall of the alley to my right, retreating as if from checking up on me. She had been there at both transmigrations in New York City also, helping Will out in some way he had never explained to me.

Annick had nailed it. In this "other" world, I had nothing but my instincts to rely on. If Lol had brought us the poetic portal message—and a quivering sense of excitement told me she had—then she had just transmigrated me for emphasis. To make a point. She was tiny, but she had a phenomenal force in her. And I didn't use the word *phenomenal* lightly.

I blew a kiss in her vanished direction and hurried to catch up with the others.

a Swimmer Dives

Marduk slept late. He'd had no intention of staying in bed until eleven in the morning. But it was hard to say what was normal for him now, with Dee's antidote allowing daytime activity for the first time.

The studio apartment was sunny and bright. In his newfound trans-vampire confidence, he hadn't bothered to pull the curtains all the way closed before retiring. But his mood upon awakening was dark. He still found it impossible to believe that he had failed at something Will Hughes had succeeded at. And now he was even angrier about it than he had been the night before. But another meal, in daylight—and the possibilities for one were fiendishly infinite—was not going to satisfy this anger the way his meal outside the trading pools had. He could feel that new reality the moment he awoke.

Fact was, there was only one way Will Hughes could have outperformed him at something. And that was by cheating. Marduk needed to figure out a way to take that advantage away.

It seemed late for breakfast, so, after putting on a gray business suit with a black collared shirt and no tie, he decided to go down to the ground floor café, which shared the front of the building with a pair of small apartments, and have an early lunch there. He sat at a secluded table in the corner farthest from the street and ordered a cheese sandwich and a glass of red wine. Someone had left on his table a copy of the sensationalist tabloid *Le Cirque*, in which he read a news story about his meal of the night before while waiting for his order. He was grinning at his exploits, the reading about which was calming him down, when a shrill male voice said from behind him, "Mr. Hughes! What a pleasure! And what a surprise to see you in the middle of the day, you night owl!"

Marduk swiveled around in his chair and tried to smile, wondering how this particular insect could have made out his features from the rear. Perhaps the man had seen him in profile when Marduk first entered the café; a glance toward the front door told him that was possible. The insect was a middle-aged man, freckled and with crewcut blond hair, wearing an open-necked white shirt and a dark blue sports jacket. Marduk clasped the insect's hand and suppressed the strongest urge he'd felt since arriving in Paris to strangle or better yet decapitate someone. Almost simultaneously, a new idea struck him.

With one Will Hughes imprisoned by daylight, now that Marduk had bit him in the catacombs—and with Hughes's older self, even if he did turn up in Paris, still a vampire as well—what was to prevent Marduk from impersonating Hughes, albeit briefly and cautiously, in the daytime? Dee had mentioned Hughes's fund having a Paris office. Assuming it was open during the day—and it probably was—what was to stop him from going there and unlocking Hughes's trading secrets, the ones that made up his cheating advantage? No doubt the office staff wouldn't be used to seeing Hughes. But there was always a first time! His face was an unimpeachable ID. And something else was for certain: neither Hughes had access to Dee's antidote!

This insect had once worked, Marduk gleaned from their awkward conversation, for Hughes's fund as a trader and had left recently to start his own firm. Once this had been established, Marduk was adroit enough to send the insect on his way, mentioning an imminent meeting he had to attend. Fortunately the creature was not interested in, or comfortable enough to attempt, sitting down with him. There *was* going to be a meeting all right (by telephone). He'd call Dee right now and find out where Hughes's office was located.

Dee did not answer, and Marduk was not in a mood to leave a voice mail. But he searched "Will Hughes, hedge fund manager" on the smart phone Dee had provided for him (a useful contraption that made him wonder if all the vital energy of these insectlike creatures teeming through the streets had been sucked up by this time period's technological inventions) and found a Paris address for Green Hills Partners, along with ones for offices in London, New York City, and San Francisco. And off he went, his mood improved.

Sunlight lit up many alluring human delicacies as he

strolled through the crowded noontime streets toward 34 rue de Ballanchine. Strong cravings arose, far beyond the appetite he'd felt for the cheese sandwich. But the satisfaction of these fresh cravings, which he reserved for later on that day, would be nothing compared to that breaking into Will Hughes's computer promised. He was the great Marduk. Hughes was vermin.

Nonetheless, right outside the building, Marduk had a fit of nerves. Unwilling at first to open the door, he stepped away and felt a wild craving for the flesh of every passerby. He wondered if the stakes of Dee's financial plot were actually too high for him. They seemed to involve the destruction of the world's economy, followed by Marduk's rule over this rotting carcass of an Earth (technically both Dee's and Marduk's, but Marduk planned to murder Dee the moment the scheme was achieved). In theory it was an imposing, breathtaking ambition, but though Marduk hated the world, he did feed off it, and he feared going hungry if it no longer existed. But after a walk to the end of the block and back to calm himself, he shrugged his shoulders and was ready to move forward. His worries were premature. It was as if something alien had possessed him at the door. Something weakening and . . . human, if he had to find a sufficiently negative word for it. Something that reminded him of the gnat, Will Hughes.

Now that alien something was gone.

When he arived at the Green Hills office on the eleventh floor, he did not need to be buzzed in. The receptionist, a West African woman in her twenties wearing a rainbow-hued head scarf and matching dress, looked at her boss through the front office window, if with a puzzled expression, and buzzed him in.

"Mr. Hughes, you're back from lunch so soon," she said as Marduk passed by the front desk. "And with a suit on instead of your running clothes!" Behind her were impressionistic paintings of a variety of farm animals, in pastel colors, underneath a silk banner with the inscription: GREEN HILLS PARTNERS: BUILDING A HUMANE WORLD FOR ALL."

Marduk did his best not to let his shock show. Will Hughes come into work? Today, in daylight? Had the world gone mad? He mumbled something about having gone home to change.

"Lunch date a dud, sir?" the woman asked him solicitously.

"Something like that," he grinned, feeling like he might be sliding away from this particular problem. But of comparable concern was that Marduk was not certain which of the half dozen or so closed doors he was confronted with led to the absent Hughes's office. None had a sign on it. Marduk had imagined a very small setting: after all, the fund had three other offices spread across seven thousand miles—what did this one need lots of rooms for? But, being that he *was* Hughes at the moment, he needed to know which door led to his own office. He was befuddled briefly, as unprepared for this as he was for the shocking fact that Hughes had come to work . . . *in the daytime.* And, not surprisingly, wearing different clothes than he had on.

Marduk was quick to affix blame for the confusion. It must be the fault of some imbalance between Hughes and that youthful facsimile he had neglected to kill in the catacombs. Neglected because Dee had intervened against it. Turning the youth into a vampire with his bite must have somehow afforded temporary immunity to his older time-twin. Dee might have been a good alchemist, but he was a bumbler in the realm of vampires. So Marduk was now Dee's victim, standing here embarrassed in Hughes's office. Dee would pay for it, not far down the road.

"Is anything wrong, Mr. Hughes?" the receptionist's smooth, West African voice interrupted his revery. "You look puzzled. Did your lunch date not show up?"

Better to play along, keep it going, than flee in a panic. He had one more idea. "Yes, we had a no show. So I took advantage of the extra time to change—into something—more suited to my fairly sober mood. Ms.—Senghore," he read off the name plate on her desk, "I'm going to need some help now, moving something around my office. Could you come with me please?"

"Sure," she smiled. "But why so formal, Mr. Hughes? Am I no longer Margaret?"

With great effort, he smiled back. "I'm preoccupied with thinking about a trade, Margaret," he offered.

She came around the desk and, to his relief, walked down the corridor ahead of him. He heard another woman's voice chirping away behind one of the closed doors they passed. A loafer, too lazy to even go out to lunch like the other pathetic employees.

Marduk let Margaret get to Hughes's office a few strides ahead of him. It was the last door on the central aisle, though there was nothing on the door to set it aside from the others. It opened onto a large office likely more impressive than the others, one with three desks, a wall-size picture window, and a large video security screen mounted on another wall that showed the interior of all the other offices and the lobby simultaneously, in a number of smaller shots. On yet another wall were more farm animal posters, a slogan painted above—GREEN HILLS PARTNERS: A VOICE FOR THOSE WHO CANNOT SPEAK—and a hand-lettered quotation, attributed to Leonardo da Vinci, on a placard: *The time will come when men such as I will look upon the murder of animals as they now look upon the murder of men.*

"Oops, I just recalled that I've got to do something online before we move those . . . boxes," Marduk said. There was in fact nothing visible in the office that could have required help to move, but there was a closed closet door that might have concealed boxes. Marduk hoped his comment didn't sound like gibberish. Margaret, to his relief, began to back out of the doorway, though looking at him quizzically. "When would you like me back, Mr. Hughes?"

He glanced at his watch for show. "A half hour would be fine . . . Margaret." He grinned uncomfortably. She left.

Marduk breathed heavily with anticipation as Margaret closed the door. He locked it from the inside, then gave the video screens a close inspection. All the offices were empty at the moment except for one, where the woman he had probably heard in the corridor sat before a computer, pecking at the keyboard. She had no privacy from the ceiling camera. The system seemed to be meant to put pressure on the employees.

Each subdivided screen had an audio switch, activating a separate listening device. Marduk debated with himself, then turned on the switch for the lobby. If inane chatter interfered with his concentration, he could turn it off, but at least he would have some warning if Hughes suddenly turned up. From what Margaret had said, he might not be back for a while. She was working at her desk, and all that could be heard from there was a Brahms symphony she was listening to on the radio.

Marduk settled in with an air of anticipation at Hughes's own desk, which he assumed was the magnificent mahogany one in front of the picture window. From the correspondence, paperwork, and personal effects scattered about the blotter, he seemed correct in his assumption. The first item he looked at was a lettter on Will Hughes's letterhead, signed but not yet sealed in its envelope. Why he wasn't using e-mail for this, Marduk didn't know. But traders were famous for their eccentricities, and perhaps it was harder to spy on postal mail than electronic. The letter read:

Mr. Barnes,

Enjoyed our conversation. I will see you in exactly three days, at 6:30 p.m., in San Francisco, and we can conclude our trade of all trades. In person, off market. Down by the bay, as you suggest, maybe west of Marina Green, right before the Gulf of the Farallones Sanctuary, seems perfect. On a bench by the beach—why not? After all, when we're both trillionaires, the entire world will be our office, won't it?

Yours as ever,
Will

Marduk puzzled over this note. What could they possibly be trading that could make them both trillionaires and that could be traded outdoors, even given all these electronic devices people seemed to be using? Didn't one side always win and one side always lose in a financial trade? That's what Dee had emphasized during the crash course he'd given Marduk on trading and the computers connected to it, and what all the online textbooks he had crammed had said. This note had the scent of trickery to it.

Fraud!

That was his judgment on Hughes. He'd love to be the one to impose moral clarity on him, and Mr. Barnes, a few days away in San Francisco.

Then he turned his attention to the computer screen. It opened up with the same password he'd used at the black pools (the one Dee had stolen for him), and it quickly filled with currency option positions, all flickering and seeming to change every instant. He was starting to jot some down when he heard Margaret's voice from the screen, as audibly as if she sat in the room with him.

"You are quite the magician, Mr. Hughes. How did you get from your office to the elevator? I didn't know there were secret passages around here. And how did you manage to change your clothes yet another time?"

"What?" Hughes asked. "You're confused, Margaret. I'm just returning from lunch now. I haven't changed any clothes."

For Marduk, this was a moment when the urgency was so great that the body became the brain. Bluster and hatred aside, direct confrontation at this point was a disastrous idea. The only way out would be the window, not so daunting a prospect to one with his strength and agility.

He could see Will Hughes on the monitor striding down the corridor toward him, walking purposefully, Margaret a pace or two behind him.

Marduk had immunity to fatality or even injury except in a very few ways, none of which were threatening him right now. He was also a superb swimmer—as Hughes had once learned to his perpetual sadness at Pointe du Raz in Brittany—and had diving skills to match. He did a back flip through the picture window just as the office door was opening, his musculature enabling him to shatter the glass with ease. There was a millisecond of eye contact with a glaring Will Hughes—which Marduk would have preferred to have avoided—then he flipped himself over, head down, for a better view of his destination in the few seconds he had before impact.

While he knew the water wasn't going to help much, he guided himself toward a reflecting pool with a fountain, in a plaza adjacent to the building . . . and landed in it. Marduk raised his head sharply and poised his torso upward in the instant before hitting. His sinews were tested with excruciating pain, muscle and bone absorbed a terrific impact, a shock wave went through his body as though he'd dived into the center of an earthquake, but after an instant, vampire physiology ruled.

He rolled onto his back and watched a shower of shard and crystal, the window in a kaleidoscope of pieces, flutter sunlit toward the ground. Then he came spryly afoot, if still aching from head to toe, and walked briskly toward a Metro stop. The group of passersby who had observed his fall stood stunned, rubbing their eyes in doubt, wondering if they'd just seen a film stunt, a falling manikin, or a robot. Had anyone tried to approach him Marduk would have broken into a run, but no one did. He went down the Metro stairs, the crystal shower settling onto the concrete plaza behind him.

18

Viper

Will Hughes stood before the empty space where his window had been, beside himself with fury. He watched with exasperation Marduk's successful landing and flight, the shard spectacle coalescing on the ground, and tasted bitterness in his mouth, as if he had drunk something rancid. He itched to take up pursuit, but already his secretary was standing behind him, cell phone in hand, calling the police. He did not need to attract even more attention to himself than this unfortunate incident might.

The fiend! Marduk was trying to steal his identity from him. The temerity: the awfulness of it!

He'd have revenge, he soothed himself. But he'd have to plot it out with great care, given that he had the hybrid's disadvantage (as well as advantage). Daylight freedom was wonderful, but he was weaker physically both day and night.

Turning to Margaret to remind her to call building maintenance—the window, of course, needed to be replaced—he then returned to his desk . . . and noted a subtle shift in the position of his about-to-be-mailed letter to the San Francisco billionaire Horatio Barnes. Good. Perhaps Marduk had read it. If so, there was an idea for setting a trap. No doubt the trillion dollars mentioned could have whetted the appetite of the viper. If anything could.

He took a few steps toward the window, to let the afternoon sunlight strike him full blast. The tingle he felt was only the normal radiance of sunlight on human skin. He wouldn't be able to get into a wrestling match or other physical combat with Marduk anytime soon. But there was more than one way to cut off a viper's head. Animal rights fund manager or not!

He closed his eyes, tilted his head up to the sunlight as if to gather strength from its rays, stretched out his hands . . . and felt something alight in his palm. He opened his eyes. For a moment he thought the sunlight had coalesced in some form. A creature with wings the color of sunstruck grass and hair the fiery red of the sun's corona sat cross-legged in the palm of his hand. Then he recognized her, of course. Lol.

19

Earthquake in Eternity

"Black swan," someone was murmuring in the distance. Over and over. It brought into my groggy thoughts visions of a swan, gliding peaceably on a pond brimming with afternoon sunlight. The swan floated from the center of the pond toward a tangle of overhanging trees at the opposite shore from where I was standing. Kepler sat under the shade of a tree along with a man in ancient Greek garb whom I guessed in the dream was one of his heroes, maybe Pythagoras. They appeared to be observing the angle the swan's glide made in relation to a line drawn between their location and mine, glancing at me repeatedly, discussing the angle like a pair of high school math club members. Kepler jotted a few notes, and the Greek man moved beads along an abacus in his lap. But it was the swan that riveted my attention.

I strongly suspected that this was the same swan, a mortal, who was going to be assassinated in some inchoate future (from the time of the dream), killed for the crime of trying to be the lover of my ancestor Marguerite's sister. Marguerite, first love of Will Hughes. But right now, in dream time, the swan hadn't even met my ancestor yet . . .

I slowly woke up. I'd dozed off in an overstuffed chair in the sitting room off the lobby of the Hotel des Grandes Ecoles, which was filled with ornate antiques and their facsimiles. Despite the decor, there was a TV tuned to a cable financial channel on a stand that resembled a classic Greek column; someone had apparently turned it on while I napped. A panel of experts seemed to be discussing whether or not another "black swan event" like the one in the fall of 2008—in other words, an improbable disaster—was on the way, and perhaps the phrase had insinuated itself into my sleep. I tried to keep the dream alive even in my waking thoughts, as the gliding swan was of much more interest than the percentages being discussed on TV. But though I could recall the images and stare at them in my mind's eye, the dream had lost its vitality.

Then I sat bolt upright, eyes wide open, at the sound of a familiar voice I couldn't place at first.

"Garet James!"

She appeared in the doorway, wearing a less formal version of the attire she'd had on when I'd first gone to her apartment. A sea-green tunic embroidered with a white, multitentacled octopus design billowing over slim white capris, no doubt concealing her six other arms; I only saw two of them.

"Octavia La Pieuvre!" I exclaimed, getting up from my chair. "You survived! You're alive!" We embraced.

The last I'd seen Octavia she lay weak and gasping, drying toward death in the Val sans Retour. Seeing her so healthy-looking now was like a miracle. I couldn't wait to hear how she'd survived. But first I needed to introduce her to my friends, who were staring at her and me.

"Here is Johannes Kepler, the astronomer," I said, guiding Octavia by the elbow into the parlor. She was a sea fey. No point in hiding otherworldly facts from her. "I have recently met him in the catacombs." With all the gallantry I would have expected, Kepler stood and bowed, then approached and kneeled, and kissed Octavia's outstretched hand. She beamed at him.

"And of course you remember Will." I thought it impolite to Will to elaborate on the nature of this Will as opposed to the one she'd previously met. If she noticed any difference, she didn't show it. Will duplicated Kepler's aristocratic courtesy; he had been raised as a late-sixteenth-century noble, I reminded myself.

"Madame La Pieuvre is a woman of the sea," I proclaimed, though "woman" was not quite accurate. "Yet she courageously accompanied me on a land adventure once, at considerable risk."

Kepler nodded. "You exude courage as well as charm, madame. I too have been fascinated by the sea, although—or perhaps because—I grew up in landlocked terrain. Won't you join our little group?"

Octavia reached a slender, glistening third arm out from between the folds of her blouse and patted Kepler on his arm. If he noticed the extra nature of the arm, he didn't show it. Then she sat down in an overstuffed pink armchair with a lavender crescent moon design. Garish, but comfortable-looking.

"What brings you to the hotel?" I asked her.

"I'm here to visit Adele," she said. Adele Weiss, besides being the concierge of the Hotel des Grandes Ecoles, was her lover of long standing.

The subject under discussion by the TV panel lurched from black swans to new funds being proposed by various financial managers. One of the panel members characterized the funds as creative financial vehicles that arise in the wake of calamity. "Restoring order to ashes," she said. Whose payroll is she on? I wondered, as I rose from my chair to lower the volume.

"Wait," Will piped up, looking at the screen. "This interests me."

"Even with all your—shall I say, years—of financial experience by now, ey?" Octavia said. "So much of what is said about money on these sorts of shows strikes me as drivel. People who really know how to profit from things don't share their knowledge for free." Clearly, she didn't realize she was talking to a younger version of the Will she knew.

Will got up and came close to the set, better to hear the lowered volume. "Have you never seen a TV before?" Octavia asked him.

I suddenly observed another familiar face, that of Adele Weiss, in the sitting room doorway. Octavia had gone to find the Summer Country with me in order to have herself made mortal, so she would not live on in eternal pain without the mortal Adele. (I hoped to soon learn what the fate of that quest had been.) Adele, an elegant woman in her early eighties, was looking urgently at Octavia now. But Octavia's gaze was fixed on Will, and how he was staring at the TV set. Adele looked at Will, and from him to me.

"Oh my goodness! Look who's here!"

She rushed over to me and embraced me warmly.

Adele had been a friend and confidante of my mother, whom she knew in Paris. I don't know if she'd have greeted me so warmly otherwise, given my involvement with Will, of whom she disapproved. Right now she gave him a fleeting glance and said a cold hello. Will stood and extended his hand formally. "Have we met?" he asked, confused.

I stepped into the breach, introducing the two of them before Adele had a chance to elaborate. Better to have her confused than Will, who was my responsibility. I started to introduce her to Kepler but before I could proceed she said, "My dear man, you bear a striking resemblance to the famed astronomer." Adele had been educated at the Sorbonne.

Kepler looked pleased. "My dear woman, there's an explanation for that."

Adele peered more closely at him, then at Will and me, and sighed. "I have strange news for Octavia, but I suspect I'm about to hear stranger news than I bring." She sat in the last empty chair, a shaft of sunlight catching her profile and illumining her elegant wrinkles. Briefly, they made her look her age. I wondered again which option they had chosen: joint mortality, or going their separate ways. She took a few deep breaths, chin in upraised palm, and suddenly looked on the brink of tears.

"What's wrong, dear?" I asked her. Octavia was staring at her.

"I have been visited by two . . . by two . . . Malefactors," she blurted, her eyes wet. "Barely alive, they looked. Almost stick figures, dressed in black from head to toe, so emaciated it was like if you glanced at them from the wrong angle you couldn't see them.

"They came in last night about ten p.m., sat down at the bar where I'd been having a nightcap with Tony, the night manager. They asked Tony to go in the room behind the bar and then spoke to me. They said there'd been a cataclysm in 'mega-time'; I think that was their term for eternity. One of them called it 'deep time.' An earthquake. As a result, all of the time portals worldwide—which they depend on for survival much as whales rely on coming to the surface for air—were shut. They asked if I knew the location of any secret portals in Paris. They said they'd been told that there was one still open, known only to the fey. When I denied knowing of such a portal, which was the truth, they mentioned your name, Octavia, and said they knew I was the lover of a fey. They said they'd be keeping an eye on the hotel, and one out for you, though they didn't seem to know where you live. I apologize for my incompetence in not letting you know sooner, but now that you and the others are here I have to warn you. From here on out, avoid the hotel and me. At least for the time being. Please! They had a brutal attitude about getting the information they wanted.

And it seemed to me that if you don't have it, they might not believe you, and could take extreme measures with you. As it was, only my sobs seemed to stop them from hitting me. An old woman like me!" She shuddered.

I thought to distract her. "What could an 'earthquake in eternity' be?" I asked, trying to keep my voice calm, looking first to Kepler for an answer. I did not see anyone suspicious in the lobby outside the sitting room, at least that I could observe from my vantage point, but that didn't mean that no one lurked about.

Neither Kepler nor anyone else answered me right away, and I thought of the sense of transmigration I'd experienced in the alley a few hours earlier. Could that have been the outer wave, the ripple, of some seismic time event? Or the equivalent of an aftershock? No one else had seemed to feel it, but no one else had been as close as I to the vanished portal at the time, either. Another reflection was on the physical resemblance between the entities Adele described and the thieves who had robbed my father's gallery back in New York City in the fall of 2008. Was there a connection?

Kepler finally spoke. "Such an earthquake sounds reasonable or at least possible, when one considers that time is a physical dimension, like the other three we experience without any instrumentation. Not to mention the dozens more dimensions, or even the infinite number in parallel universes, that are speculated about nowadays."

"Annick and Jules might know something on this topic," Will observed.

They were still sleeping in one of the new rooms we'd

taken upon returning to the hotel. "Can we summon them?"

"Who are they?" Octavia asked.

"*Chronologistes* from the institute," I told her. "Yes, we should do that," I agreed with Will.

"Perhaps you should all come to my apartment instead of staying at the hotel," Octavia said. "By ones or pairs, so as not to attract too much attention. That includes you, Adele. After all, security has been compromised here in some way. But my apartment can be safely sealed off. We can await further developments there. From the little I've heard of them over the . . . years, Malefactors are not to be trifled with. Running around without their portals now, they must be crazed."

hieroglyphs of Shadows

I left Will and Kepler to the task of rousing Annick and Jules. I needed to take a stroll by myself, to think things through more. We decided to meet back in the lobby in forty-five minutes to carry out the move to Octavia's. When I left the hotel, I had an urge also to spend a little time in the Jardin des Plantes. The day had turned hot, and all the cement and stone around me seemed like it could burst into flames at any moment. A thin haze of vehicle exhaust smeared the air. I walked briskly and reached the Jardin entrance at the corner of Rue Cuvier and Rue Linné in a little under a quarter hour.

I walked into the park, taking the tree-shadowed cement path on the right, seeking a favorite bench I had sat on during my visits to the Jardin during the weeks while I had waited for Will to show up in Paris. In fact, I had come here to meet a certain Monsieur Lutin, who lived under the labyrinth. I passed the entrance to the labyrinth now and looked up the hill to the cast-iron gazebo that crowned the top. I wondered if Monsieur

Lutin was somewhere in the hedge maze that lined the paths up to the gazebo, but I kept walking, not feeling in the mood to talk to the gnomish little man. Fifty feet past that bench the path ended at a gardener's shed, and this deterred pedestrian traffic that could disrupt my reveries and diminish my ability to feel sorry for myself in the beautiful shade. The bench was empty and I sat down, losing my gaze in a grove of young oak trees beyond the stone wall across from the bench. Their leaves were especially luxuriant in the afternoon sun, branches gleaming as if they stored warmth for the desolate winter ahead. The life these trees appeared to lead seemed simple—growing, greening, and shedding—while the gnarled shadows they spilled onto the path seemed complex by comparison, like hieroglyphs. I longed for the pristine life of a tree, no Malefactors, or demented alchemists, or vampires to contend with. It might be dull, but right now it seemed a lavish pleasure to sprawl in the sun all day.

I saw, out of the corner of my eye, a man striding down the path toward me. Purposefully, as if he was coming to meet me. I recognized Will and wondered how he had known where to find me. I had told no one where I was going. But as I puzzled over this, a new mystery opened up. The expression on the man's face was not the look of puppylike devotion I had seen in young Will's eyes. These eyes had seen centuries worth of pain. This was not young Will, but the four-hundred-year-old man I loved.

"Garet, is it truly you?" he whispered, holding out his arms to me.

I longed to embrace him, but I held myself back.

"I could ask you the same question. After all, there's only one of me and at least two more of you roaming around Paris. And the last time I saw you, you weren't able to walk in the sunlight. How are you doing it now?"

"Perhaps you can tell me. My daylight freedom started only a couple of days ago, and I don't know why. I do stand as comfortably in sunlight right now as I once did only in utter darkness." He stepped from the shadows where he stood into a particularly bright patch of sunlight, without flinching. Seeing him in the full sunlight filled my heart with love, but I still held back from going to him.

"Interesting," I said a little coldly. "Your younger counterpart has been losing his tolerance for the sunlight since he was attacked by Marduk. Perhaps you are connected with him in some way."

He laughed. "We are the same person. That was why I sent him to you . . ."

"Not the same person," I snapped angrily. "How could you have thought I'd be satisfied with a facsimile? And how could you have left me if you really loved me?"

He gripped his hands together in front of him until his knuckles turned white. "It wasn't because I didn't love you. It was because I love you so much," he exclaimed. "I'd realized how hopelessly inadequate I was to be your beloved. The crimes I had committed over the centuries, the . . . all my sordid and reckless history. My hope was that my younger, and shall I say purer, self could become a more worthy love for you. And by staying behind in 1602 I would have four centuries to relive, to be better, making up for or even preventing my worst moments. The Will I sent to you was not a facsimile, but my younger, better self."

I snorted. "Younger, yes; better, hardly. He's a silly, vain boy. Why, in his first day here he got himself lost, then kidnapped by Marduk. How could you have thought I'd prefer him to *you*? And how could you have cared so little about being with me that you would choose to be without me for four hundred years . . ."

My voice faltered as this realization hit me. The man who stood before me was not the four-hundred-year-old vampire I had fallen in love with last year in New York. He was over eight hundred years old. He had lived his long life over again and come through that second set of four hundred years—if the look on his face told me anything—apparently still in love with me.

"It is because I love you so much that I forced myself to spend the last four hundred years without you. I had to prove to myself—and to you—that I was worthy of your love. I have tried to make amends for my many crimes and to live a life that you would be proud of so that I could come to you cleansed. I set about sparing the lives that I had taken in my first life, and then I tried to save even more lives, culminating in the moral crusade I have taken my hedge fund on with its humane focus, unique in the financial world. I haven't made things perfect, but I have improved them. The last four hundred years . . ."

"Have been a love letter," I finished for him, remember-
ing the phrase Horatio Durant had used. Then, unable to
resist any longer, I stepped forward into his embrace.
Instantly his arms were around me, the strong arms I
remembered so well, and his lips were on mine. I remembered their curve and fullness, but now instead of
being made of cold marble flesh they were warm. I gave
myself to the kiss and felt transported. Transmigration
of atoms was nothing next to the transmigration of love.

After a few minutes we returned to the bench and sat
there together, holding hands. I was aware that time was
passing, and that a deadline was approaching for the
rendezvous at the hotel, but I didn't care. There was a
rightness to being with Will that transcended anything
in this world, so I went with it. Still, as we sat there,
even the trees seeming to grow closer together, a tricky
question or two began to trouble me. "How did you know
I was here?" I asked, leaning my head into his shoulder,
taking his hand in mine and resting it in my lap.

"Here?"

"In the Jardin? On this bench. Just now."

He smiled. "Lol," he answered. "She came to me twice
today, the first time to tell me that she had rescued you
in the catacombs . . ."

"She saved us there."

"Thank God. The second time, she told me where you
were staying. I went to the hotel and watched from the
café across the street. When I saw you leave I followed
you. I thought I could watch you from afar . . . but I

found that there was a limit to how long I could see you and not approach you."

He squeezed my hand gently. The gesture was worth a thousand kisses. And after I squeezed his hand back, I kissed him. He returned the kiss so passionately he took my breath away, pressing his mouth against mine so hard I felt his teeth click against mine . . . He pulled away abruptly, his face white. My tongue had brushed against two sharp fangs.

"So you are still . . ."

"A monster," he replied, an expression of self-loathing crossing his face. "After all I have done, I am still a vampire longing for blood. You are still not safe with me."

"And am I safe without you? With Marduk and John Dee roaming the streets of Paris? With the Malefactors sabotaging the very fabric of time . . ."

"The Malefactors?" Will echoed. "What have they done?"

I explained what had happened to the Institut Chronologique. Will listened, his face turning pale. "Those bastards!" he swore.

"You know these creatures?"

"Over the centuries they have approached me a number of times to try to recruit me to their cause. At first I thought they were quite benign. They told me that what I was doing—living my lifetime over to try to rectify my past sins—was *exactly* the kind of time travel they espoused but were hampered in pursuing because of the unnecessarily strict regulations of the *chronologistes*. They tried to convince me that the *chronologistes* were

my enemies because they would prohibit what I was trying to do. Over time, though, I came to realize that there
was a reason for the *chronologistes*' strictures, and although I was still committed to my mission, I began to
see the danger in it. For instance, now that my younger
self inhabits the same time line as myself, I sense that
there is a danger to the both of us . . ."

"You think that's why Young Will is becoming sensitive to the sun and maybe growing weaker?" I asked.

"That may well be the reason," he answered. "I would
like to consult a *chronologiste* about the matter, but unfortunately, because of the strict regulations about traveling within one's own time line, the *chronologistes* have
very little experience with such matters and are prohib-
ited from even talking about the possibilities."

"Hm—, personality-wise, I can well believe that Jules
would refuse to discuss the problem, but Annick might
feel differently. You can come back to the hotel and ask
her . . ."

Will shook his head and looked away. "I can't go back to
the hotel with you, Garet, as much as I'd like to." He
looked at me and I saw that his gray eyes were filled with
pain. "I can't risk being near my younger self. I know from
the little I've learned from observing the Malefactors over
the years that being in close to proximity to one's self can
be extremely dangerous—for both selves. I shouldn't even
be here in the same city as my younger self."

"Then let me go somewhere else with you," I said,
squeezing his hand. "Back to New York City. Or anywhere."

Will furrowed his brow and gave me a puzzled look. "You'd abandon him to this strange world? Strange to him?"

I blushed at the censure in his voice. "I'd hardly call it abandoning him. He'll have Annick, Jules, and Kepler."

"But he doesn't love *them*, Garet, he loves *you*. If I know him at all"—a wry smile twisted his mouth—"and I think I can fairly say I know him like myself, his only reassurance in this strange world is you. And if he really is growing weak from my proximity—and perhaps becoming a vampire again from Marduk's bite—then he needs you even more. Don't you . . . like him?"

"He's not you," I snapped.

"But he is me, Garet. To tell you the truth, I'm a little surprised and disappointed you have so little patience and liking for my younger self."

I was stung by the coldness in Will's voice. "I'm sorry," I said, "perhaps I haven't given him a fair chance. I'll try to be more patient with him . . . but you can't expect me to love him the way I love you. It's you I want to be with."

"And I want to be with you," he said, warmth returning to his voice. "But I'm afraid that the only way that will be possible is if my younger self goes back to his original time. And now, with the Institut Chronologique gone, I'm not sure how we can accomplish that."

"We'll have to find a way. I'll talk to Annick about it. In the meantime, what are your plans?"

"I will endeavor to stop Dee and Marduk from whatever mayhem they may be bent on committing in

Paris—and elsewhere—and to finally destroy them. You and the *chronologistes* must try to find out what the Malefactors are up to. I promise that I will keep an eye on you . . . and I have a feeling that our goals will bring us together again. After all, it appears to be our fate to be together, no matter what distances in space and time we travel."

It was the first thing he'd said in several minutes that I agreed with wholeheartedly. I thought that was the best note to part on. But first I needed to give him a hug, and he responded so intensely that I could feel the full weight of his sorrow over me, over the centuries. And, at the same time, I experienced his joy at our reunion: he pressed into me so tightly that he might have been trying a sort of will power transmigration of atoms, a merging of our bodies that corresponded to what might have been going on with our hearts and spirits. It was so hard to let go . . .

But then, reluctantly, I moved away and said good-bye, left him on the bench and walked off. When I'd gone a few feet, though, I felt another unbearable wrench at being parted from him. I turned to see him one last time, but the bench where we'd sat together was empty save for the shadows cast by the trees—hieroglyphs that now seemed to spell out a message of rejuvenated time.

21

Insolence

Horatio Barnes, the man Will Hughes was going to meet in San Francisco, was a "niche nabob." This was the term Dow Jones columnist Ron Boyd had coined for him, in the first article Marduk Googled about him back at his apartment. Marduk had made himself comfortable in a large armchair, with his notebook on his lap, sipping a Belgian beer and munching on French crackers. He still felt soreness but the beer seemed to lubricate it, facilitating its passage out of his body. And he didn't have to worry about getting drunk. Something about his blood.

Boyd compared Barnes to the man who'd received hundreds of millions of dollars for inventing intermittent windshield wipers. Barnes had developed a lucrative fantasy football consulting business by introducing the baseball concept of "errors" into quarterback ratings regarding intercepted passes. Marduk had no idea what football was, let alone what interceptions were, but he read that Barnes's system attributed some interceptions to an "error" on the part of a receiver, others to an "error" on the part of a quarterback, and thus made better predictions regarding the future performance of both quarterbacks and receivers. If a quarterback was suffering in the ratings due to poor receivers, the fantasy football coach could improve his team sharply by matching him up with better ones. There was a gambling fever in America regarding football, and Barnes had profited immensely as both consultant and pioneer of his own set of fantasy football leagues. Shrewd investments in commodities like gold, silver, and copper had done the rest.

Good for him, Marduk thought sardonically. Let him enjoy his bizarre nabob wealth for a couple more days. Marduk wondered, almost idly, if his blood would taste sweeter because he was richer. Or luckier. Hughes's terminated future, and that of this lackey Barnes, clearly decided in his own mind (he would ambush them both and somehow acquire their assets), Marduk's attention returned to the oncoming evening. Hunting time. Maybe the physiological imperative for it had been reduced by Dee's antidote, but the primal history, in his veins, in the fibres of his being, was still around. He needed to hunt that night, first for the seven million euros he had lost and seven million new ones in profit to establish his supremacy. Anything Hughes could do, he could do better. And then he might treat himself to hunting down a flesh feast again, afterward. The first gal had been tasty. The next might be even tastier. He called Dee on his cell phone.

Admittedly, he had not been anxious to make the call.

Dee would be irritated by the lost euros, which he might not know about yet, and if he said the wrong thing Marduk could be motivated to kill him sooner than was prudent, harming the project and perhaps hurting his cover in San Francisco. Plus Marduk had no way to resupply himself with antidote. But homicidal impulses were a chance he would have to take, Marduk told himself, swiveling his chair for a better view out the window. It wasn't as if he didn't have such impulses toward Dee anyway.

He gazed fondly at the gargoyles under the eaves of the 1885 building opposite—winged demons with teeth like daggers, splashed in sunlight that seemed unnatural given their menace—and dialed. He felt less alone contemplating the gargoyles—not that he was a social sort of guy—and thought their prominence on such a typical Paris street gave the dark side of the universe a respect it deserved. Perhaps in San Francisco—though he knew nothing of the city—the "public demonic" might be harder to find.

"Hello."

"Dee?"

"Is this the Duke?"

Dee's nicknamed familiarity with him annoyed him. He acknowledged no nicknames; his tone immediately became belligerent. "I lost all the money you gave me last night. All seven million euros. I need a similar amount to play with tonight. Don't even think of saying no or I'm calling a press conference to denounce you and Renoir. What a pair of bastards you are, by the way." Marduk laughed.

Dee, perhaps stunned, didn't say anything.

"And I need real credentials this time, you sloppy worm. I barely got in last night. I'll bet you were hoping I didn't. Also, I need a week's supply of the antidote, so I can have more flexibility with my schedule." He laughed again. "I'm going to count to ten, and I'd better hear, 'Yes, sir, Lord Marduk, the money, credentials, and antidote are on the way to your apartment right now.' One, two, three . . ." Marduk chuckled; how Dee's jaw muscles must be clenching with tension. Could a dead soul like Dee still have a stroke? He wasn't sure, but he hoped so. But if Dee did, Marduk also hoped it was after his necessities were sent to him.

"I'll go along to keep you happy, my good fellow," Dee said on "six." "But at three thirty tomorrow afternoon—the stock market open in New York—we will be starting the full-scale gold-buying blitz. If Renoir knows what he's talking about, headlines will scream, markets will gyrate, and the black pools may well have to shut down for a few days. So tomorrow night there will be no opportunity for your amateur hour. Make what you can tonight, good wolf. The party is ending."

"I'll make my own decision on that. And meanwhile, you have screwed me royally in another way as well."

"What are you talking about?"

"We should have killed the Hughes boy in the catacombs. Because his elder twin has surfaced in Paris and is somehow able to walk around in bright sunshine. You haven't been popping him antidote pills behind my back, have you?"

"Of course not, you idiot . . ." Dee fell silent, as if realizing his poor choice of words and hoping he hadn't pushed the wrong Marduk button.

For a moment Marduk's urge to kill blinded him with a kind of red film before his eyes; then he suppressed it. Lucky for Dee they weren't having this conversation in person. Then again, he doubted Dee would have called him an "idiot" in person!

". . . How do you know he's about in the daytime? Have you seen him?"

"I ran into him at his office while I was there starting a trade on his computer. I thought I'd pick up a few of his tricks. But all I really learned is that it's going to be easy to kill him in a couple of days."

"Have you lost your mind? Do you realize how dangerous your behavior is? And no, I have no idea how he could go out in the daytime."

Silence ensued, during which Marduk could *hear* Dee thinking, so great was Dee's distress. No matter. Marduk was in charge now. He had no idea what the worm was making of this mess of circumstances, nor did he care. "Just send over my necessities. And watch your tongue, alchemist. Lord Marduk does not tolerate insolence forever." He hung up, exulting in the anxiety he was confident Dee was feeling. He'd so enjoy the end of him when it came. Soon.

a Change in Fortune

Marduk had trouble frittering away the six hours until the black pools opened. He thought of going out to devour someone or something just to idle away time. The Metro and the sewers had workers, for example, not hard to surprise down a dark corridor somewhere. Many other categories of food supply came to mind. But he restrained himself. He wanted to reserve every ounce of energy for the trading room and the promised feast afterward.

The gargoyles provided a repast for his eyes in the meantime. They grew more ominous as the shadows lengthened. He delighted in their malice.

His more detailed credentials from Dee came around six p.m., along with a wire copy showing he had access to seven million euros in an account at Crédit Lyonnais, and a dozen glass bottles of the antidote in a padded box. Just after eight p.m., he was crossing the street toward the decrepit-looking building, licking his lips with anticipation. But he suddenly stopped, blinking rapidly. He wondered if his new exposure to sunlight was affecting his vision, even now, in early twilight. As he gazed on, he was more certain of what he was seeing, and he beat a hasty retreat back across the street, down the block, around the corner, and into a smoke-filled dive called the Black Lily, where the recent health consciousness of Parisians had not penetrated even a sliver. Marduk sat at a tiny, splintery table in the back, ordered a drink, and listened to the sultry jazz singer on a round wooden stage accompanied by piano, illumined in a weak gold spotlight. He wrapped himself in tobacco smoke. Dee, he thought, shaking his head to himself. A worm. An imbecile!

Those strange, black pencil line drawings in the air in front of the black pools building—about seven feet off the ground—that had caused him to beat such a hasty retreat had been surfacing Malefactors. Two of them, standing sentinel on either side of the crumbling front steps. Initially they were both in and out of time at the same time, so that a fully fleshed being like himself could only see their edges. But he was sure of what he was seeing. It was possible that Dee had been trying to collaborate with them, despite Marduk's warnings on the subject. Either Dee had double-crossed him, perhaps with the vulgar goal of preventing him from losing any more money, or there had been some sort of security breach. But Marduk had no doubt they were there to block his entry or ambush him. Even as he'd stood there for those few shocked seconds, more than their edges began to show. And so he'd fled.

Marduk feared little, but he did fear them. Their

capacity to move in and out of time almost at will made them elusive and treacherous. They unpredictably performed acts of mass destruction in pursuit of their mysterious and irrational agenda: both the 1900 Galveston, Texas, hurricane and the 1906 San Francisco earthquake were examples of "natural disasters" rumored to have been instigated by them. Both catastrophes had supposedly been designed to open blocked time portals, regardless of loss of life. At other times they seemed to value life: they had twice intervened on behalf of one of Marduk's prospective victims (in 1309 and 1727), denying him a meal and the pleasure accompanying it.

Even if they hadn't intended to thwart his stock trading tonight, they would not have allowed him to partake of a meal in that same locale. Bastards. Even without knowing what they were doing there, he'd been right to flee. His hand-to-hand combat with one in 1309 had been like battling a whirling dervish, and when he'd started to get the best of that dung heap, the creature had traveled back to an hour earlier, ambushed him, and practically killed him. Something similar had happened in 1727. He had no desire for a repeat engagement; he'd wait out the entire evening if necessary in this den of smoke and song, checking up on them occasionally. If they didn't leave, there was always tomorrow. And if not then, San Francisco.

He took surveillance strolls at roughly thirty-minute intervals, careful to reserve his table in the crowded dive with the waiter each time he left. The Malefactors persisted as sentinels until around ten p.m. At ten-thirty, the coast was suddenly clear. He went back to the club, in an eruption of manners tipped the waiter handsomely, and then once again found himself climbing the steps to the black pools.

He followed the same entrance route as the night before. This time his credentials were perfectly in order, and there was no encounter with acquaintances of Will Hughes. The apparent discrepancy between the long, futuristic corridor and the narrow, shabby building startled him once again, even with his limited ability to distinguish futuristic design when he was already so far into the future. But he didn't reflect much on the contradiction. He was there not to be an architecture critic but to demonstrate that he was better at stock trading than Will Hughes.

As he returned, this time unescorted, to Hughes's trading screen and settled in, Marduk thought he detected a difference in the atmosphere in the room. Faces looked more worried, voices were quieter, and he found a recurring pattern in overheard words like *gold* and *short selling*. He began to be concerned that Renoir had started his trading plan sooner than Dee had told him, or at least that rumors of it were being circulated. What sort of double cross could *that* be? He couldn't imagine that Renoir, or Dee, could be up to any good. He briefly took pride in being personally part of a machination that was evidently of concern to all these spoiled, wealthy traders. Maybe, he told himself, this was a rumor leaking not from Renoir or Dee but from a lower-level sort of person, maybe one of Renoir's assistants. After having a drink or two, or more.

He sat down at the screen. In the upper right hand corner a red band was pulsing, the word *alert* in bold black letters superimposed on it. When he clicked on it, text appeared on the screen:

ATTENTION TRADERS: DUE TO BASELESS RUMORS AND RESULTANT PRESSURES AGAINST LIQUIDITY, THE SHORT SELLING OF GOLD FUTURES HAS BEEN TEMPORARILY SUSPENDED.

Hmm. Rumors were rumors, but "pressures against liquidity" did not sound trivial. Renoir. That bastard. If word of the pump-and-dump scheme had gotten out prematurely, or intentionally, short sellers would already be circling like vultures. According to what Marduk had learned in Dee's crash course, they would sell into the pump and buy the dump, profiting from the difference. Except Marduk had made a point of listening to the financial news before leaving his apartment and had even overheard a snatch of some financial conversation in the street just minutes earlier—there'd been nothing in either about any unusual activity concerning gold, which, in France as everywhere, had its price reported to the public virtually by the minute. Of course, black pools were a different world . . .

He could behead Dee, if it came to it: perhaps with one swipe of his Acheulean axe, a fearsome prehistoric weapon he had found in the woods near Rennes in the twelfth century and had carried ever since. (Acheulean tools demonstrated that the human species had always been violent, even in early incarnations like *Homo erectus*, a fact Marduk enjoyed.) Behead Dee and save even better mutilations for Renoir, now revealed to be a beast of deceit and hypocrisy. Still: better to get on with the trading, before revenge. He was there more for the currency futures than the gold, anyway. He shut down the alert message. Currency was alive and well. Let the trades begin.

From the beginning, they went better. Whether because he'd learned something from his first experience, or because random luck ruled the stock market, or because his biorhythms had a moon-sourced pattern on the upswing . . . the profitable trades started early, multiplied, and piggybacked on one another. Forty-five minutes into the evening, having started out with seven million euros, he'd made back the losses of the previous session for a total of fourteen million. Ninety minutes into it and he'd made eight million *new* euros, for a total of twenty-two million, with the caveat that money did not mean here what it meant in the world outside: here it had a slick, slippery, even quicksandish feel to it. After two full hours at the screen, Marduk's profit was past twenty-five million euros and he decided to quit. Not because of caution or to save profits for a rainy day, but because he was getting hungrier for the meal he'd promised himself after victory. If this wasn't victory, what was?

Marduk opened a new, secret online banking account for himself at Société Générale and transferred all his profits into it. Dee might have fronted him some seed money—and any losses would have been Dee's, of course—but Marduk never questioned the idea that the gains would be his alone. Then he left, ignoring a few attempted hellos to Will Hughes that traders made as he went down the corridors to the exit. His days of having to imitate Hughes were numbered in the low single digits now. He'd kill him in San Francisco, then return to Paris to rule the world.

23

Neanderthal

Octavia La Pieuvre's apartment at number 1 Avenue de l'Observatoire, a lovely beaux-arts building, was as beautiful as it had been the first night I had seen it. I saw Jules give the naked statue on the landing a scandalized look, but even he had to admire the elegant salon furnished in gilt and silk-upholstered Louis Quatorze furniture and thick Persian rugs, all in shades of blue and green that recalled the sea. Will seemed transfixed by the floor-to-ceiling windows, which opened to a terrace affording a view of the Luxembourg and, in the distance, the Eiffel Tower lit up like a Roman candle, while Kepler was excited to learn that there was a telescope in the tower room.

The apartment was remarkably spacious—I'd only seen a couple of rooms the first time I was there—allowing us each to have our own guestroom. I showered in my private bathroom with great relief, letting the spray tingle on my skin like an endless-fingered massage. I hadn't showered since the grime and stench of the catacombs, and I felt as cleansed as if I were bathing in radiance. My hands lingered on the places on my face and neck where Will's kisses had lingered and left a heat that had nothing to do with the heat of the water. Although I'd finally and reluctantly agreed with Will's reasons for not joining our group at Octavia's, I couldn't help imagining as I climbed out of the shower and wandered into the luxuriously appointed bedroom what it would feel like to bask with him in the lingering lilac light of the Parisian dusk that bathed the spacious, soft bed. I had left the doors to the balcony open before my shower and now I stood, wrapped in a thick towel, gazing at the view of the Luxembourg Gardens as dusk gathered in the pollarded plane trees, deepened the colors of the ornamental beds, and turned the stone walls of the Luxembourg Palace a deep honey gold. Was Will out there somewhere? He had said he would keep a close eye on me . . . What better location than the park . . . ?

The sound of wings startled me. A covey of pigeons roosting on the ledge below my balcony took sudden flight, as if alarmed by some predator. Something landed on the balcony beside me. I opened my mouth to scream but a hand covered it. I struggled in the grip of the dark-coated figure until I heard Will's voice in my ear.

"It's only me," he whispered, his lips nuzzling the flesh beneath my ear. "I saw you standing here and I couldn't stay away."

I turned in the circle of his arms, the towel sliding lower on my breasts, and gazed at him. The rich golden light of the Parisian dusk bathed his face, turning his skin a sun-kissed tan as if erasing the centuries he had spent in the dark, but the same light turned his silver eyes the yellow of a jungle cat, reminding me that he was still a predator. I traced the lines of his face with my hand. When I came to his lips my fingers slipped between them and touched the tips of his fangs. He shuddered.

"Garet . . ." he began, but his time I covered his mouth with my hand.

"I know," I said, "you're afraid that if we make love you'll need my blood again, but you won't. You've spent four hundred years showing me how much you love me . . ." I took his hand and stepped back, letting the towel fall to the floor. "Let me spend a few moments showing you how much I love you."

After, I fell asleep in Will's arms. When I awoke in a darkened room, he was gone. One of Octavia's brigade of servants was knocking on the door. After checking that Will was really gone, I opened the door. A young uniformed maid held out a green silk dress.

"For mademoiselle, with madame's compliments," she said in careful, rehearsed English.

I thanked her and took the dress, which I found fit perfectly. Octavia, who had spent days traveling with me, and whose multiple arms might give her some unusual insight into space as well, had judged my size to a T.

I joined the others in the dining room feeling some semblance of well-being for the first time in weeks. Will and I were together again, even if he couldn't be there at the moment, and there was a sense of safety in the group and in my Will looking out for me and us that was sorely needed after the catacombs. My mood might have been irrational—we could all still be in the midst of who knew what degree of trouble—but I enjoyed it. And I wore the dress like a second skin, even more lustrous than my well-washed, so recently caressed, real skin.

On the way into the dining room I noticed a framed print of a poem hung on the wall, and I stopped to read it.

Morning

It's always the same Frenchman in his beret,
shopkeeper with her one good dress,
child with bateau à voile at play.
It's always the same Frenchman in his beret,
baguette that hardens towards end of day,
white cup with café espress.
It's always the same Frenchman in his beret,
shopkeeper with her one good dress.
The French of my dreams a palimpsest,
language lost with each new day.
All that's left is the regret,
the French of my dreams a palimpsest.
Black-rimmed glasses, cigarettes,
fresh flowers on a grave;
the French of my dreams a palimpsest,
language lost with each new day.

I was charmed by the poem—by an American poet named Elizabeth Coleman—by its evocation of character and atmosphere; it reminded me of what it was like to experience Paris as an ordinary visitor. I made a note to myself that, if Will and I survived all this, we should come back here and do all these ordinary, but magical, things together. The margins of the poster were embroidered with miniature sketches of Paris street scenes: a kiosk on a tree-lined boulevard, deep green leaves rippling in the rain; a sidewalk café, sun-lathered on a summer day, with a pair of lovers eating pizzas and sipping wine; the Eiffel Tower, surrounded by lacy clouds at sunset. These sketches were also reproduced in larger forms and hung in polished wooden frames at intervals around the dining room.

There were eight of us: the five of our group, Octavia and Adele, and a guest whom I inferred, as the evening went along, was an old friend of Octavia's, Dr. Frank Lichtenstein from Philadelphia. He was an evolutionary biologist from the University of Pennsylvania who had spent the past year as a visiting scholar at the Sorbonne. Frank was a tall, gangly man of about fifty, clad in a brown and yellow checked sports jacket and button-down beige shirt that looked like they had last been in style in the early 1960s. But his conversation was the opposite of his look: very contemporary and well informed. I could not help but wonder, of course, how far back his friendship with Octavia went: decades, or centuries, or even longer. But I thought it rude to inquire, and he did

not volunteer any information. If he wasn't a human being, there was no overt way to tell.

The dinner had so many courses to it, served slowly,
that it was hard to tell what the entrée was. Perhaps it
should have been accompanied by a drum roll. But at a
certain point a serving person did come around to ask
our preference among salmon, chicken, and vegetable
ravioli, so that was a clue. The question, coming at last,
encouraged me because, much as I loved the sensuous
and delicate food, elegant surroundings, quiet but witty
conversation, and most of all the sense of stability and
civilization, I had no desire to dine all night long as if at
some Roman feast.

Most of us chose the salmon, arousing my curiosity
regarding Octavia: did octopi eat salmon in the wild? I
was again too timid to ask such an otherworldly question. Dr. Lichtenstein elected the vegetarian choice. I
noted him gazing at Will after the orders were taken.

"Beg your pardon, Mr. Hughes," he said.

"Yes?" Young Will had seemed out of sorts all evening,
participating only on occasion in conversation. I wondered if he had some way of sensing my reconciliation
with his older twin, but I doubted it. He was probably
uncomfortable with the contemporary—i.e. French
politics—nature of the talk.

"I believe I've seen you on television recently. Are you
not some sort of financial manager involved with animal
rights? I would have assumed you were a vegetarian!"

"Animal rights?" Will asked. "What sort of rights

might a beast possess, other than to be eaten quickly?" He laughed. The rest of us tried to smile. I keenly felt the awkwardness of the moment, since I didn't know how fully Dr. Lichtenstein could be taken into our confidence. But Kepler was astute enough to intervene.

"My good doctor, Mr. Hughes has had no sleep for the past couple of nights, due to a variety of crises. He barely knows his own name at this point. You must forgive him." He extended his arm across an empty place and patted Will affectionately on the shoulder. Will glanced at him, still baffled, but respecting him. He'd go along with whatever Kepler said. "Everyone in Paris, and hopefully soon the world, knows about the dedication of Will's Green Hills Partners to humane justice. Don't they, Will?"

Will nodded vaguely, and the doctor smiled politely but still gazed with puzzlement at him. Then our dishes arrived and we all dug in with relish, smoothing out the awkwardness for the moment.

"In any event, I think vegetarianism is silly," the doctor elaborated, "so no aspersions on the young man's carnivorous choice or anyone else's. I choose the ravioli only because it's a favorite, extraordinarily well done under your direction, Madame La Pieuvre." He smiled at her, and she beamed.

"Silly? How so?" Kepler asked. "It seems like an extension of Christianity to me, not that I have the discipline or stoicism for it. Moving on from 'love your neighbor' to 'love *all* life.' What's wrong with that?"

"I have studied the human species all the way back to

its predecessors *Homo erectus, Homo habilis, Australo-pithecus*, and so on," Frank told him—pompously, I thought. "Six million years and counting. Studied them as a man of science, not as a priest. We've never been anything other than a killer bunch from the beginning, partaking of bloody flesh like air. *Homo sapiens* killed off the Neanderthal, if you ask me, about thirty thousand years ago in Europe; the final remnant fled pathetically to the Iberian Peninsula before being massacred as well. And now that we've run out of alternate species to destroy, we're getting ready to do ourselves in. Give twenty nations nukes and we won't make it through another century."

An ominous statement, if there was any truth to it. I wondered if Frank was fey; if so, had he been around for the Neanderthal demise? (Had Octavia, for that matter?) He certainly seemed to speak with authority about it. If he had witnessed their massacre, that could explain why he was still upset about it.

"All of what you say may be so," Kepler replied. "It's not my field, but no doubt Mr. Darwin has brought fresh points of view to all of us. But don't you think we might strive to rise above our violent origins, if the history is as sad as you say? Isn't it Christian to suppress the evil thoughts and try to be filled with good ones?"

"Sounds great, but I don't see any sign of us rising above anything. The centrality of 'Thou shalt not kill' in Judaism and Christianity shows you how far back, and deep, the problem goes. Must have been a lot of killing going on for that commandment to be so important. I'd settle, as I say, for us not exterminating ourselves any-time soon. That'd be a fine outcome. Believe me, it's a long shot."

Kepler put his hands together on the table and made an arch with his fingers. "Well," was all he said.

"This is one of the misguided goals of the Malefactors," Jules said.

"What is?" I asked.

"To go back in time and correct the problem of vio-lence. To alter the genes that have historically contrib-uted to savagery. Or even to try to see to it that one of the less aggressive competing species—such as the Neanderthal—wins out instead of us."

"Would that really be so bad?" Annick countered. "Look at the violence we've encountered in just the last few days! We didn't have to be like this. Gorillas aren't the killers chimps are. Fate just threw the dice this way."

"How can you even suggest such a mad attempt at re-versal, Annick?" Jules asked, appalled. "We of the Knights Temporal are charged with preserving the time line—what you so blithely call a *roll of the dice*."

"Evolutionary selection *indeed* threw the dice if any-thing ever did," the doctor responded, attempting to diffuse the tension between Annick and Jules. "But that's beyond human control."

Just then we heard a commotion from the front of the apartment. "Sir, you can't go any further," a high-pitched male voice cried out, and then came a crash as of some object tumbling to the ground. It sounded like it could have been a vase shattering. Then there was a muffled sound, like a shot fired with a silencer, then another and a third.

Even as we got to our feet and the quicker ones among us—Jules, Annick, and Kepler—started toward the front of the room, a man I recognized as Cosimo Ruggieri burst in, waving a large-caliber handgun at all of us. We slipped, shocked, back into our seats. Maybe if we'd rushed him in unison we could have overcome him, but he looked crazed, and at least a couple of us could have been shot en route to subduing him. He was followed into the dining room by three of the slenderest beings I'd ever seen, clad in black, with black ski masks over their faces. They were so slender as to suggest they rode the boundary between existence and nonexistence. Male-factors, I guessed, sliding through some crack in time.

Fear chilled me, worse than what I'd felt in the cata-combs. Ruggieri didn't look half as under control as Dee and Marduk had, and now we were all suddenly being herded, under the threat of the handgun and silver rods the stick-men carried—no doubt weapons of some sort—into a corner of the room. For better crowd control. Hopefully.

Ruggieri continued to wave his gun, a glossy steel Luger with a walnut handle, at all of us. He rotated it a foot or so in front of his chest, sweeping us with the rota-tion's circumference, a motion the others imitated with their silver rods, except they held them at shoulder height. But though he threatened us all, he spoke only to me.

"Precious Garet," he said with a mocking smile. "How I've missed our moments together . . . the breakfast encounter in the garden of that fine hotel . . . our lovely midnight session in the tower . . . I've longed for them so."

He was crazy. I'd never spoken to him in the garden, though I had first seen him there (and worse, I had gone up a tower with him, and, far worse, I had briefly been attracted to him, fiend that I didn't yet know him to be). Horribly, his face seemed to be alternating in its features between the pleasant, ordinary one I'd first seen him with and the decaying death mask that went with the purgatory of immortality he'd been condemned to, that of living forever in the state of his deathbed. His features fluctuated back and forth, turning my stomach with their ghoulish disrepair but even more hateful in their ordinary sneer. I glanced from side to side, trying to glean what the others might be thinking, but couldn't tell anything. No doubt they were as nervous and filled with dread as I was. Revolting as the face in flux was, I was afraid to close my eyes against it, afraid he'd open fire. Then the anger finally burst out of me.

"I haven't longed for any moments with you," I spat out. "Not once I found out in Brittany who and what you were and are."

"Tsk tsk, precious Garet," he said, continuing to sneer but without the grin. "I'm so sorry to hear you disapprove of me." His gun seemed to be trained more on me, the center of the circle coinciding with my chest. "You have a lot to learn, dear. You, a whore traveling without a chaperone, taking up with vampires and who knows what other filth." He took a step toward me and slapped my cheek with his left hand, hard enough so it stung. I wouldn't give him the satisfaction of rubbing the bruise, and quivered back my tears.

"See here, Cosimo," Kepler said, as if they were acquainted. "Your lack of respect for women is appalling. The girl happens to be a paragon of virtue."

"Who are you to talk? Former partner of John Dee, of all paragons of virtue."

"I did not know Dee's character until recently. The Dee I partnered with was very different from the scoundrel he turned into after too much trifling with the other world."

Ruggieri took a menacing step toward Kepler, but once again including all of us in the sweep of his gun. "You're such a genius, you should have known right away."

Then the dining room window suddenly shattered, affording an even clearer view of the illumined Paris night. My Will Hughes stood in the middle of the vacant frame, outlined fiercely against multiple shadows, myriad twinkling lights, and the vast black sky beyond them.

a Perfect Pair

Out on the crumbling front steps, puffed up with his triumph like a balloon with helium, Marduk observed that the street at this hour was more crowded than it had been the night before, and the sky more turbulent. A storm seemed on its way, but the first change was of greater concern. He had in mind to replicate the previous night's feast, but with two rather than one. It was a delicious challenge. And Lord Marduk, descendent of the Babylonian deity who had once been revered in a diabolical amulet called the Babylonian Triangle, now a stock trader triumphant, had no peers among vampires, or any other entities. Two weren't much more difficult than one, and he leaned to the view that two females could be especially delicious. But he could not afford the witnesses such a crowded street provided. It could be Will Hughes who wound up being arrested for his crimes, and it would be harder to kill Hughes in jail here than along the open byways of San Francisco. Prudence dictated he move on.

He walked a few blocks southeast, looking for a location that was less crowded, but not so desolate as to be unlikely to offer up a meal. Creature of habit that he sometimes was, he preferred a building that resembled the black pools'. And he found one. The street it was on had reasonable prospects if he was patient and if the storm—which would empty the street—continued to hold off. The clouds were gathering but the wind had slowed, and he still hadn't seen lightning or heard thunder. He made sure there was a secluded place under the front steps to drag his victims and found that, even better, there was a decrepit small room there, a storage area with nothing but a few cans of motor oil and a pile of grease-streaked rags in it. He licked his lips. Plenty of room to indulge. He left the unlocked wooden door that concealed it from view in place, for now. It wouldn't be any obstacle when the time came.

He passed on several young women because they were alone, and then he began to see lightning over rooftops to the west and faintly hear thunder. He wanted a pair, but now he felt the claw of anxiety, too. A downpour could deprive him of any meal. By the time the storm ended, it could be too late for pedestrians. He'd already conceded that he'd have to settle for the next solo victim when a perfect pair finally strolled into view, at the end of the block. Marduk pressed himself back further into the shadows that concealed him, trembling with excitement.

They contrasted with one another in physique, and variety was the spice of death as well as life, he thought.

One was tall, blond, buxom, tightly dressed in blue blouse and blue jeans. He could make out rosy blooms in her cheeks when she passed under streetlamps—a nice detail, he reflected. Her companion was much shorter, with close-cropped black hair and thin, almost hawklike features, and she wore a Cambridge University sweatshirt and gray shorts. At first Marduk thought she might be a male, but closer approach revealed a reassuringly petite bulge. Given the weather, he could have compromised on the gender point if he had to. He began to hear snatches of their conversation, which (despite the sweatshirt) was in French.

Lightning crackled closer.

He carried a weapon, a small-caliber Beretta with a miniature silencer that Dee had provided him with, and had it in his right hand now. Because there were two, he was going to have to be more aggressive than on the previous night. Yes, there were risks. But, thanks to the darkening weather, the street was almost deserted now.

He didn't even have to speak. He stepped toward the blonde, showed her the gun that glinted in the light from the nearest lamp, and motioned both of them down the stairs. Both women's eyes went wide as they saw the gun, but they seemed too startled to scream, and they meekly walked down the stairs. The calm expression on Marduk's face might have helped lull them into submission. No doubt they hoped it was a robbery, not worth getting shot over. He kicked the wooden door aside and shoved them roughly into the storeroom. Then he pushed them both against the wall and ordered them in French to remove their clothing.

"Please," the blonde whimpered. Her friend began to whimper as well. Neither touched their clothing.

"Undress." Marduk pointed the gun at the scrawny one, then back at the blonde.

"We have money. We'll give it to you. Please," the blonde stammered.

"You try my patience. I'd rather enjoy you alive. But dead will be nearly as good." He fired a bullet into the wall behind them, just over the blonde's head. She remained defiant but her friend suddenly fell to her knees, weeping, and began reluctantly pulling at her sweatshirt, to remove it over her head.

Then he heard a slight sound behind him, a scratching. An alley cat? When he turned for just an instant—it wasn't safe to take his eyes off the women—he caught a glimpse of a single black line, irregular in the semi-dark. It was hardly there. But Marduk, with a disgusted sensation, realized that it was a glimpse of a Malefactor. He cursed under his breath. No doubt they had continued to observe the black pools building somehow even after the sentries appeared to leave, and one had followed him here. One or more. He'd have to give this terrible turn his undivided attention.

He took two steps forward and swiftly knocked both the women unconscious with blows that combined the gun's handle with his fist. As they slumped to the floor he turned and watched the Malefactor materialize. His, or her, or its, sluggishness in crossing into this time encouraged Marduk. In dealing with these creatures in the past, he knew time transit didn't always flow so swimmingly for them. It could give him an inside track in a battle.

Indeed, he'd never actually seen one fully in the flesh, though the two that had nearly killed him had materialized sufficiently to do real damage. This one was taking what seemed like forever to materialize. Marduk didn't mind the thunder starting to boom outside or thick raindrops splattering the stairs, but when the blonde groaned, he realized Malefactor slowness could cost him the pleasures of living flesh. He couldn't allow the women to be living threats behind him while he grappled with the Malefactor, who didn't have enough flesh on him for Marduk to attack yet. And he'd foolishly not brought spare ammo with him; bullets in the women's heads would reduce his store for the main target. Worries were endless in this vale of tears, Marduk reflected.

But then things seemed to move along with a welcome sense of momentum. The single line became a floating tube, then a thick cylinder, and the cylinder metamorphosed into a torso. Before he could have snapped his fingers a young man in his mid-twenties was standing before him, grinning meanly, dressed in evening clothes that seemed old-fashioned to Marduk's frail concept of 2009. He was good-looking, dark hair swept back from a noble forehead, eyes that were all silver: no irises or pupils. They glowed as if they were made entirely of silver, and Marduk had to admit to himself that he liked the look, the primal nonhumanity of it. The Malefactor glanced at the bodies and asked, "Am I interrupting something? Indeed, that is my hope."

"You are the scum of the universe, Malefactor. I only hope the metal in my bullets proves a match for your eyes. Afterward I look forward to cutting your eyes up for use as gems in rings, making a profit to add to my fortune." He couldn't control his rage after this short speech. He fired twice, hitting each eye in turn with deadly accuracy. But the bullets clanged harmlessly off their targets, and he had to duck out of the way of one of them as it ricocheted.

The Malefactor laughed. "You are wasting your bullets, lord of the ghouls. Unfortunately I have no authorization to slay you, or you'd already be dead. I am sorely tempted." He nodded at the bodies on the floor. "I pity these innocent ones."

Marduk tried a bullet in the vicinity of the creature's heart, assuming he had one. It didn't clang; it seemed to pass right through him as if he weren't there, drilling a hole in the grimy wall behind him. The Malefactor showed no ill effects, and Marduk couldn't block puzzlement from his features.

"You think I can pass through centuries in a millisecond but that it would be a problem for me to rearrange my molecules to expedite the passage of a bullet? You are delusional, dark lord who is not, I assure you, my lord. But they're your bullets. Waste away, if you please." He grinned.

Marduk held his fire. They stared at each other.

The blond woman groaned again.

"You trespass on my kingdom, Malefactor. Why?" Marduk finally asked. Crushing his windpipe with his hands was going to take a lot longer than a bullet would have. If it were even possible. It hadn't been the other times. That was why he was going to try reasoning with him. After a manner.

"It's leaking out into our world, what you and Dee are trying to do. We have our own big project going on at the moment, Marduk. So we thought it prudent to keep an eye on you, check in on you from time to time. So there'd be no interference. I got called away from your trading place but happened to subsequently be in the neighborhood and catch a glimpse of you accosting these poor souls. Why should these girls have to die a horrible death at the hands of a fiend? Unfortunately communication is slow with all the dislocations in time going on, and I haven't yet received authorization to deliver justice. Or we wouldn't be chatting.

"Malefactors are not heartless. We are misnomered enemies of the one true Malefactor, time, and kill when we have to in that war, but we'd rid the universe of evil like yours too, if we could. So take this visit as a warning. We are watching. You disgust us. I hope I get authorization before I have to leave Paris."

But even as he spoke these last words his shape began to waver back toward shimmering cylinders, then lines. Marduk had an unbidden glimpse of a dinner party in the 1930s, and then the creature suddenly vanished. Though relieved, Marduk reflected on what the Malefactor had

had to say. Maybe he should lay off his now stirring victims. Why add an enemy as treacherous as the Malefactors when already in the midst of such a vast scheme as the one he was involved with with Dee and Renoir? Why?

Because he was Lord Marduk, he told himself. Descendant of a Babylonian demonic deity. His anti-spirit had many historical achievements, from the crucifixion of Saint Peter to the Satanic possession of Germany in the same 1930s the Malefactor seemed to be returning to. The fifty million lives lost in World War II were a good start but well short of the annihilation of the species that was the goal. What were the two fleas on the floor compared to that goal?

He kicked them into semiconsciousness, disrobed them, and had his way with them, then feasted on their flesh, harder to find on the scrawnier one but still available. He had thought of enjoying them sequentially so one would pathetically know what had happened to the other, but wound up doing them in simultaneous stages. He thought maybe the Malefactor would appreciate this gesture; it was a more humanitarian procedure.

Walking away from the site of his grotesque mockery of benevolence, Marduk found that, though his corporeal needs seemed satisfied, he still felt a brewing anger that needed to lash out. It stirred in him so fierily that he paused at a pay phone on the way to the Metro. Fumbling in his pockets, he found the list of phone numbers Dee had provided him for emergency use regarding the financial project. Renoir had a co-conspirator in the

Autorité des Marchés Financiers, France's rough equivalent of the SEC, whom they could call on in case there
was any unexpected trouble with the authorities. He
wouldn't be there at this late hour, but why not leave a
voice mail? And if someone other than the "safe" individual happened to hear the voice mail first, Renoir would
be in a whole lot of trouble. Maybe Dee too. As for Marduk himself, he was leaving the country now anyway, in
pursuit of Hughes. And he could make whatever fortune
the conspiracy might have resulted in on his own, anyway. Because anything those imbeciles could do, he could
do better!

He didn't have to look far for an inspiration for his
voice mail, either. The way Dee had ripped off Kepler
long ago was an excellent model for it, especially on the
point of eliciting sympathy. "Hello, Mr. Haussmanns,"
Marduk began, when the voice mail picked up. "My name
is Jean LaSalle and I am the treasurer of a small orphanage in Audierne, Brittany. We have invested our savings
under the advice of a certain Jean Renoir, who is a very
famous man, and we have now discovered that all the
money has been stolen. Renoir is likely to have done it,
and if you investigate bank account number 72-71-TAA
at the Société Générale, you will find a paper trail that is
astounding and confounding indeed. And he has had
help from the infamous Irish banker, a Mr. John Dee, in
his criminal pillaging. Please help me and the little boys
and girls! Please!" He stifled a giggle as he hung up the
phone.

Zany as the complaint might be, he had the thought that it just might work. Renoir was famous for having made enemies with his belligerent criticisms of the free-spending ways of national politicians and national banks around Europe. Some of his enemies would have paid for information like that Marduk had just doled out. And if they got a warrant to go into this exceptionally secure bank account, no doubt they would find all sorts of mind-boggling transactions, given the preparation Renoir was supposedly making for the gold manipulation scheme. Marduk's anger immediately subsided.

Moving forward then with ruthless efficiency, he dropped the Metro idea, caught a cab to Charles de Gaulle Airport, and found a late-night flight to New York City. From there he'd go on to San Francisco. If this phone message worked, Paris—all of France would no longer be safe for him. If it didn't work, or not right away, Dee would be disappointed that he'd left so suddenly, but Paris seemed a little too thick with Malefactors for his taste, and anyway, to hell with Dee. Marduk would kill him soon enough.

And Will Hughes would soon die at his hands in San Francisco.

25

Nuclear Jigsaw Puzzle

Older Will's vampirism had been diluted by sharing the same time with young Will. Along with his new ability to tolerate sunlight had come some reduction in strength and reduced immunity to violence. Where he'd previously only had to fear the silver bullet, now a copper bullet would be fatal—any bullet, in fact, was cause for concern.

But the psychological resources afforded by having lived over four hundred years—twice—were immense. Will was drawing on them now to convince himself that he could still be a full vampire whenever he wanted to be, that he could use that level of strength to confront Ruggieri. That was how he'd been able to acrobatically scale the outside of Madame La Pieuvre's building, after being alerted by the watchguarding Lol to the emergency.

He'd enjoyed his climb, both for the beauty of his view of the city's lights and for the confidence the climb gave him in his resurgent powers. Coming to rest now on the terrace, alarmed by what he had seen inside the apartment, he took a deep breath and shattered the window with a jab from his clenched fist, as if smashing a brittle film of ice.

Will had time only to observe Garet among the hostages before Ruggieri fired at him, three bullets in quick succession in the chest. To his relief, they passed through him harmlessly and flew on out into the night. His immunity to copper bullets might have been gone, but his extraordinary skill in manipulating his own atoms was still present, and he'd been able to part his flesh around the bullets' trajectory, lining his atoms up with those of the bullets so empty spaces between nuclei and electrons in both passed by one another. Like intersecting pieces of a jigsaw puzzle.

Lol had instructed him in the nuclear arts quite recently, in both Paris and London. At her tiny size, she lived much closer to the atoms and had more of a mystic rapport with them than he did. He had learned the truth of her argument that the barriers among nerve cells, synapses, and the atoms that composed them could be artificial and illusory. Her practical training had been effective: Will could elongate and stretch his atomic spaces now the same way he could take deeper and slower breaths to relax.

Observing the failure of Ruggieri's gunshots, the Malefactors fired, gleaming yellow filaments from their silver rods that headed straight for Will's head like lightning bolts. They lit him up like a luminescent statue, to the horror of the hostages, but had no more impact than the bullets. Will diverted their electric charges into nervous-system atoms that could readily absorb them.

Then he took a giant stride toward Ruggieri and began throttling him with powerful hands, turning even the ghoulish sequence of his alternating features purple as Ruggieri lost all capacity to breathe. The Malefactors, observing Will's strength and immunity to weaponry, began a prudent retreat. Limbs shrank to branches, heads to fruit, torsos to slender trunks, and as Will strangled the last of the life out of Ruggieri, they vanished.

The transformation in Ruggieri's appearance as he became a corpse got the attention of everyone in the room. As he slumped onto the elegant marble floor he gradually became shorter, his legs thicker and stumpier, his brow and features more apelike. Lying with a stiff finality, he looked like a bloated chimpanzee, hairy face smeared with blood, hand clutching a sharpened rock that had appeared out of nowhere.

Everyone stared at this hominid corpse. Garet noticed Dr. Lichtenstein's transfixed gaze; she wondered again how old he was and if his presence had anything to do with Ruggieri's corpse's peculiar devolution. Then she observed that the older Will had vanished. He had apparently gone back out the window. If he had left any other way he would have had to cross her field of vision. Garet cast a longing glance at the open window and the night sky beyond it. When she turned her gaze back to the room, the younger Will was no longer to be seen either.

Everyone was startled to see Ruggieri undergo one more transformation. All that remained of him suddenly was a small pile of silver ash, a pyramid of silver dust on the gleaming floor.

❀   ❀   ❀

Despite the disruption and its apocalyptic finale, Octavia was bent on bringing the dinner party to a successful conclusion. She ushered the guests back to the table with a solicitousness more suitable to interruption by unpleasant argument than by paramilitary event. But no guest had been injured, and there seemed little point to calling the police when the chief perpetrator was a pile of ashes and his cohorts had vanished to a different dimension in time. So vaguely normal conversation ensued as the dessert of crème brûlée and a choice of cappucino or brandy was served, accompanied by candlelight and a violinist who had suddenly turned up.

The conversation turned more serious. Jules and Annick were strong on the point that the available portal clues all pointed to Père Lachaise and, according to Pui Ying Wong's poem, to Jim Morrison's grave in particular. It wasn't much, but it seemed to be all they had, and it was crucial to find a portal. That would enable Jules and Annick to reunite with their fellow *chronologistes*, including, hopefully, Annick's grandfather. Kepler might find his bookstore and at a minimum expel Dee from his part ownership of it. And young Will could return to 1602, enabling the older Will and Garet to move forward in a more complete manner. But Garet in particular seemed nervous about visiting Père Lachaise, especially in the middle of the night, as Jules and Annick were proposing. Kepler supported the idea.

"I don't quite see the logic of it," Garet said.

"We'll wander around," Kepler responded, "and maybe run into a further clue. It's not a math equation, or the diligent calculations by which I found the orbits of the planets. It's more a logic of the wind. But the world's a funny place, dear Garet. Sometimes we must let instinct, and the wind, rule."

The others nodded in assent, and it was agreed that Octavia would call a car to transport the group to the cemetery. Dr. Lichtenstein, though he had not participated in the discussion, appeared to be listening intently. Octavia's acquiescence in his presence during this conversation revived speculation, for Garet, about whether or not he belonged to some obscure, neolithic category of fey. Certainly his familiarity with evolution and his fascination with the way in which Ruggieri had deteriorated backward through time, were suggestive.

"Doctor, what did you make of the way Ruggieri decomposed?" she asked. "As if he went through the stages of the prehistory of man?"

He smiled, grimly. "It's as I say. Once a killer, always a killer. Even when still half ape, hanging from tree branches. That's how we got here, killing off the competing hominid species. That's why you still get news of killings, every day. Evolutionary heritage. Some might say, original sin."

It was an answer, a philosophical one, but not to Garet's underlying question. She didn't mean to be rude, but she had to find out more. "Did *you* being here, in this room tonight, have anything to do with his changes?"

He smiled again, more broadly. "I have my sphere of

influence, yes. But only because of the history I've observed."

"*Observed?*"

"Dear me," Adele said fussily, as Octavia darted a disapproving look at Dr. Lichtenstein. "You all really do need to go downstairs to meet the car, which will be here any second now. So late at night, you don't want to lose a moment."

As everyone else rose from their chair, Garet settled for the thought that perhaps *chronologistes* and Malefactors did not possess the exclusive license to travel through eons of time.

26

January 13, 1967

Following the guidelines of Pui Ying Wong's poem, we
went first to Jim Morrison's grave. But moonlight revealed it to be cordoned off by yellow rope. The guard
standing nearby told us the grave was closed until further notice because of recent disturbances by fans, though
I couldn't see any damage to the gravesite.

We had no real information that a portal had to be in
the vicinity of the grave, so for a few minutes we milled
about aimlessly, uncertain of where to go next. The silence in the cemetery was deep, almost startling, so
heavy it was like a presence of its own. Here and there
were small stands of trees. I became distracted by the
way darkness was pooling in one of them, a darkness
seemingly blacker than the night. For a moment I
thought I could see shadows flitting within the black
pool, then figures, gaunt faceless things with amorphous
boundaries between their limbs and the air. I guessed I
was imagining them—I could not believe they were
spirits, unlocked from graves by nightfall—but then

they grew more skeletal, more dervishlike in their motions, the longer I watched. Fear crept up my spine like chill fingertips. Finally I reached out and touched young Will, who had been somberly waiting to rejoin us at the cemetery entrance, on the arm.

"Look at that." I pointed at the grove. At almost the same instant, Jules grumbled, "Are we just going to stand around here all night?" And either because he broke the mood of my revery or because some tenuous connection between me and whatever world those figures moved in had been snapped, they vanished. I observed Will continuing to stare hard where I had pointed, but then he turned back to me with a quizzical expression. "They went away," I mumbled. He didn't answer me.

"Why don't we explore more?" Annick suggested. "The clue may not have been Jim's grave. I don't see anything. The clue may have just been the cemetery."

"Great," Jules complained. "We could be here for years if that's the case."

As he spoke I saw something else as odd as the shadow figures, about two hundred feet off to my right. A large reddish brown bird, something white in its talons, flew down from the branches of a tall tree, illumined by moonlight. It fluttered its wings to slow its descent to a glide and then fixed me in its gaze. The long bony head reminded me more of pterodactyls than of any modern bird. It moved so carefully that I could see exactly where it alighted: a plain white marker up on a hill, with a marble statue of a woman in front of it. It dropped the white object from its talons onto the marker; the object was something oblong like an egg. Or a stone. Whatever it was, it started to glow with a luminescence that took my breath away. Then the bird fluttered aloft again and vanished, suddenly, as if immersing itself in some other layer of reality that hovered above the cemetery. I felt an urge to examine the object more closely. "I think I may have seen a clue," I declared, "follow me."

The others looked at me, but no one asked what the clue was. No doubt they were relieved to turn our aimlessness purposeful, even if for only a few moments. I led the group about fifty yards to my right, to what turned out to be the composer Chopin's grave. He had a simple memorial with a stunning sculpture of the muse of music adjacent to it. Her marble skin glowed in the moonlight.

The object I had observed turned out to be an oblong crystal with hieroglyphs on it, holding a small gray envelope in place under it. I couldn't decipher the hieroglyphs, but I read aloud what was printed on the outside of the envelope: THE DOORS THEN, A DOORWAY NOW. SIX TICKETS.

"What doors?" Kepler asked.

"They were a late-1960s progressive rock group," Jules explained, as Annick took the crystal from me and scrutinized the inscriptions. "Named after a book by Aldous Huxley, *Doors of Perception*."

"That's right," I said, opening the envelope. "They're my friend Jay's favorite group. He's played me their music—oh my goodness," I interrupted myself. I held in my hand six tickets, looking brand new, with that gloss they have when first printed. But they were to a January

13, 1967, concert at the Fillmore West in San Francisco featuring the Doors, the Young Rascals, and Sopwith Camel.

I passed them around.

"Of course!" Annick exclaimed. "There is another institute of the Knights Temporal in San Francisco. This must be a sign that we should go there."

"So the institute is at the Fillmore?" I asked, confused.

"Probably not," Annick replied. "After the attack on the Paris institute, all the other institutes of the Knights Temporal would have gone into hiding to avoid detection from the Malefactors."

"That's the protocol," Jules agreed.

"How does an institute hide?" I asked.

"Within the time stream," Jules and Annick replied together. They exchanged a surprised glance at their unusual agreement, and then Annick, at a gesture from Jules, continued. "The institute is still in San Francisco, but it cannot be reached unless you travel through a series of time portals. In order to alert other *chronologistes* to the new location, clues are sent out. They're usually relics of the past, like these tickets. This concert hall will be the first step in the time trail that should hopefully lead us to the new location of the institute . . . and hopefully my grandfather and the other *chronologistes*. I guess we'd better get ourselves plane tickets," Annick said. "Unless anyone has any other more reliable, and I emphasize, *more reliable*, ideas." I thought her gaze lingered more on Kepler than the rest of us. He was shaking his head no, he had no ideas.

"At the moment, I can't even find my own bookstore," he said.

"And you all think this is authoritative?" I asked, though I was fine with the adventure of going and was already thinking about offering the sixth ticket to Jay. Back in high school, Jay, Becky and I would play a game we called If You Could Go Back in Time, in which we each had to choose the moment in time we'd most like to visit and then defend the choice to the others. Becky always picked political events of significance—the signing of the Declaration of Independence, Lee's surrender at Appomattox, the passage of the Women's Suffrage Amendment. I always chose an artist's studio at the moment of creation—Van Gogh painting *Starry Night*, or Leonardo da Vinci painting the *Mona Lisa*. But Jay always chose historic concerts—Woodstock or the Beatles' first US appearance or Simon and Garfunkel in Central Park. I thought that an early Doors concert might have been on his list. Just thinking about Jay and Becky gave me a sharp pang of homesickness. Perhaps I could have a quick layover in New York . . .

"What do you mean?" Annick startled me out of my thoughts.

"This envelope seems to come from some other world." I tried to explain myself as we strolled away from Chopin's grave, toward the cemetery exit. It seemed that we had our directions and wouldn't be receiving any further ones. But I remained a little tentative. "I saw the most distinctive of birds bring it to the grave, one that was dinosaur-like. Talk about time travel! But does that necessarily mean it comes to us from a good world? Could it be evil misdirection?"

Jules held up the oblong crystal that Annick had handed him. "Your concern is a thoughtful one. But the language etched on this crystal is an ancestor tongue of the *chronologistes'* language, comparable to Latin's relationship to French, and though neither Annick nor I seem able to totally translate it, it is in our tradition. And we happen to also have an office in San Francisco, which occasionally opens a portal there. Finally, the poet Pui Ying Wong's work is known in San Francisco. I can't explain why we have been communicated with this way. But the message seems genuine. As leader of this mission, I declare that it's imperative we now travel to San Francisco."

Annick immediately objected to Jules's high-handed approach. "You can't just keep ordering everyone around, Jules. We have to work together."

"Mission protocol demands strong leadership," he countered. The two of them had stopped and were bickering over a tombstone adorned with a weeping angel, whose posture of head buried in hands seemed an agonized response to the argument of the two *chronologistes*.

"Come," Will said to me, "those two would argue over the color of the sky."

"It's because they like each other but are both too stubborn to admit it," I said, turning to walk with Will.

"Really?" Will asked, intrigued. "You think Annick cares for Jules? She often acts as if she thinks he's an idiot."

"Well, that's because he *does act* like an idiot most of the time. But he's acting that way because he's insecure and wants to impress her—and she knows that, so even while she's exasperated with him, she still likes him."

Will furrowed his brow and looked confused, but then brightened. "Ah, so a lady might feign annoyance with a suitor but in truth be in love with him?"

Damn. Self-absorbed as he was, I should have known he'd apply my words to our case. Now I'd have to explain that my annoyance with him was not a covert proclamation of love. Before I could embark on this correction, though, we were interrupted by a strange sound. In another grove of trees like the one near Morrison's grave, I spied a second black pool, the outlines of gaunt skeletal figures dancing around each other within it. They sharpened slightly into more explicit skeletons as I gazed, and I observed with revulsion that some strands of decaying flesh still clung to a few moon-white bones. Somehow, they seemed to be moving closer to me. I heard the grim cackle of laughter floating toward me—the sound that had caught my attention.

A skeletal hand suddenly reached out of the black pool for my throat, materializing out of the night air as if the line between the living and the dead were much thinner here. The touch of bone-sharp fingertips was remarkably cold, and the pain was excruciating as soon as they began to squeeze. My vision blurred, then doubled. I saw two Wills through the murk. One fell to the ground, but the other drew a sword and swept it through my ghostly assailants.

I heard the sound of bones splintering, of joints cracking in the moon-latticed air. The hand at my throat slipped away, and the other hands vanished.

Even as I continued to gasp for air, and my body shook with convulsive sobs, Will was taking me in his arms and caressing me. I knew instantly it was my Will, newly armed. As my vision began to clear from my tears and I regained enough composure to glance beyond Will's powerful shoulders, I saw young Will stretched on the ground. I freed myself from Will's—*my* Will's—embrace and ran to his younger self. He lay still and pale in the moonlight, as lifeless as the marble statues that stood sentinel on the tombs around us.

"Will!" I cried, shaking him.

"I'm afraid my younger self has more courage than sense," I heard my Will say from behind me. "He threw himself into the fray without a weapon. I believe he loves you very much, Garet. Ah, look, he awakes . . . aroused by his lover's touch."

Indeed, young Will was beginning to stir. Reassured he was still alive, I turned toward the other Will. "Cut that out . . ." I began, but I spoke to shadows. My Will had vanished again. I turned back to his younger self and vented my anger at him and his newly absent twin. "You're both idiots!" I told him.

He only smiled. "Whatever you say, my lady. Your anger is balm to my ears . . ."

I didn't wait to hear the rest of his tribute. I stalked off, planning my escape from these romantic complications. I was beginning to think that battling shadows was an easier task.

27

Complications

Back at Madame La Pieuvre's, I was able to convince Annick, Jules, and Kepler to travel on to San Francisco without me while I made a stop in New York, but young Will insisted on accompanying me.

"Someone has to protect you," he informed me solemnly. "If I hadn't been with you at Père Lachaise, those ghouls might have devoured you."

I didn't have the heart to tell him that it had been his older self who had rescued me—or to send him away. He could barely tolerate sunlight anymore. Although he had not professed a desire for blood, he seemed uninterested in any other food. His weakening had seemed to increase after his encounters with his older self. I had consulted Annick about my concerns, and she admitted to noticing the same phenomenon.

"It is never advisable for two versions of the same person to inhabit the same time line," she told me. "It is strictly against the law of the Knights Temporal to travel back in time within one's own time span. No one knows exactly why, but those who have usually sicken and fade into nothingness. Indeed, some believe that the Malefactors were originally *chronologistes* who traveled back to change their own pasts, but who found they only created worse fates for themselves. They would travel back again— and again—trying to get it right, until they created so many versions of themselves that they went insane. *Chronopersonality disorder* is the technical term for it."

I shuddered. "How awful. How can we stop that from happening to Will?"

Annick shook her head. "There's no known cure. We can send him back to his time, but the other Will is there as well. Perhaps we could send him back to a more distant past . . . my grandfather would know what to do . . ." Her brows creased with worry as they did every time she mentioned her grandfather.

"If your grandfather and the other *chronologistes* had time to escape when the Malefactors attacked, they must have gone to another institute. They may well be in San Francisco waiting for us," I said soothingly.

Annick nodded, wiped away a tear, and firmed her mouth, trying to look hopeful. "And perhaps someone there will know how to help young Will." Then, with an impish smile, she added, "I see you're coming to care for him, eh? Has he replaced his older self in your affections?"

"No," I told her abruptly. "I still think he's a silly, vain boy—but that doesn't mean he deserves to vanish into the time stream."

✿　✿　✿

By the time we reached New York, though, I had revised my opinion. Young Will had spent the seven-hour flight pestering me with questions. How did the plane stay in the air without flapping its wings? Why was the food sealed in transparent wrappings? Why were the bottles of spirits so small? Why did the sunset last so long? When I explained time zones to him he'd become agitated, suspecting that I was tricking him into going back in time. As we approached our destination his questions had turned in a different—no less irksome—direction.

"Who are these friends Jay and Becky? Are they married to each other?"

"No. They're just friends . . . and band mates. They play in a band called London Dispersion Force."

I thought the name of the band would interest him, but he remained fixated on my friends—or rather, one of them. "So this Jay, he's unmarried? And you've known him since you were children?"

I sighed. "Yes, but we're just friends, not that it's any of your business." I didn't mention that I'd realized last winter when I'd acquired mind-reading abilities that Jay had more amorous feelings toward me. The last thing I needed was Will feeling jealous of someone else. Hopefully Jay had gotten over his feelings for me. Becky had mentioned something in an e-mail about a Dutch girl he'd met on tour . . .

Mistaking my preoccupation for mooning over Jay, Will subsided into a jealous sulk for the rest of the trip, giving me time to brood over what would await me in New York. Although I'd only left for Paris two months ago, it felt as though I'd been gone much longer. Of course I had traveled back in time four hundred years in the interim, making the time seem longer. But while I might be able to explain that to Jay and Becky, who knew about the supernatural nature of last winter's events, I had no such excuse to explain to my father why I hadn't sent him so much as a postcard all summer.

"What troubles you, my lady?" Will asked as the plane began its descent. "Is it this Jay fellow? Are you worried he will be jealous when he sees you with me?"

"No," I snapped, although now that he mentioned it, that *was* another possible complication. "I'm thinking about my father. I haven't talked to him all summer."

"And you're afraid he'll be angry with you? My own father had a terrible temper. Is your father . . . um . . . an able swordsman?"

I glimpsed in Will's worried eyes a scene from his past—an angry man in a jerkin and doublet wielding a sword . . . and then caught a wisp of a thought. *Will Garet's father challenge me to a duel?* I laughed out loud. "No, Roman is definitely more of a make-love-not-war kind of guy—although he does have his World War II service revolver, which he'd reported as lost in 1946 . . . but I'm not worried that he'll be angry with me. I'm afraid he'll be hurt I haven't been in touch with him all summer. I can't explain to him all that's happened."

"Don't worry, m'lady, I have an idea . . ."

I would have liked to know what that idea was, but a

sudden lurch in the plane as the landing gear descended wiped Will's face clean of everything but alarm. "It's okay," I told him, taking his sweating hand, "we'll face our fears together."

Although I'd e-mailed ahead to tell Becky what flight I was returning on, I'd assured her that because of the ungodly five a.m. arrival time we would take a taxi into the city. I was surprised, then, to find a welcoming party waiting for us beside the luggage carousel. Becky spotted me first and let out a whoop that woke up my fellow jet-lagged, bleary-eyed passengers. She tackled me, all four feet, eleven and a half inches of pent-up energy nearly knocking me to the floor.

"James! You're back! You look like shit! What happened to you over there? Did you—?" Her voice froze as she spotted Will. "You found him?"

Because of the complicated state of affairs, I hadn't written to tell her that I'd found young Will and would be bringing him with me.

She let me go, approached Will who was trying to assemble his best courtier's smile to greet Becky. "Ah, you must be the fair Rebecca—"

Becky socked him in the jaw. Will fell back into a pile of luggage.

"That's for abandoning my friend and leading her on a wild goose chase across Europe!" Becky said to the astonished, reeling Will.

"Beck, hon, I thought we agreed to no violence." Joe Kiernan inserted himself in front of Becky, his eyes warily on Will. For all he knew, this was the old Will— the vampire—who could snap Becky's neck in an instant.

"*You* agreed. I never agreed to anything," Becky sniffed, shaking her hand out. "Hey, James, your boy-friend crumpled like a piñata. What's the deal?"

"He's sick," I said, helping Will up. "And he's not my boyfriend."

"You mean you went all the way to Paris to find the schmo and he's *not* your boyfriend?"

Hearing my father's querulous voice, I turned and embraced him. He felt frail in my arms, and when I held him at arm's length he looked older than I remembered. And smaller. But somehow being in his arms made me feel safe for the first time this summer.

"It's complicated, Dad . . ."

"Only because your generation makes it so," Roman James said with an expressive roll of his eyes. "You loved this Will Hughes fellow enough to travel across the ocean to find him, right?"

"Yes," I admitted, "but—"

"No buts from you, young lady," he said, holding up an admonitory finger and turning to Will. "And you, young man, do you love my daughter?"

Will straightened himself up under my father's gaze, summoning all the dignity that a man who's just been decked by a 103-pound woman can, and bowed deeply. When he lifted his head he met my father's eyes. No mean feat when Roman James was taking you to task.

"Yes, sir, I do, and what is more I most humbly beg your permission to seek her hand in marriage."

"Harrumph," my father said, turning to me. "See, now what's so complicated about that?"

Jay met us outside the terminal with the van—an ancient sixties VW van painted in Day-Glo green and teal.

"Ohmygod," I said, hugging Jay. "You stole the Mystery Machine from the Scooby gang."

"We needed more room for Becky's enormous amp," he told me, looking over his shoulder at Will. "I see you found him. Good to see you, man." He curled his hand into a fist and jabbed it in Will's direction. He was only attempting a brotherly fist bump but after his experience with Becky, Will threw up his hands in self-defense.

"It's all right, Will, Jay's just being friendly." I demonstrated the fist bump, and gently probed Jay's mind. It *was* okay. Although Jay was happy to see me and still loved me like a friend, his thoughts were full of a blonde named Gisela. I didn't probe any further.

Will returned Jay's greeting and climbed into the back of the van with Roman, whom he'd taken an obvious liking to. Jay and Joe took the middle seats, as Becky insisted on driving and on me sitting up front with her. I had a feeling that all of this had been arranged. Jay and Joe's loud contentious discussion of the New York Jets' apparent decision to roll the quarterback dice on rookie Mark Sanchez formed a sound barrier between us and Will and Roman.

"Okay, James," Becky said as she navigated out of JFK. "Spill it. Something went wrong over there. That guy . . . he's not the Will Hughes you fell in love with."

"No," I admitted, glancing guiltily back at young Will chatting amiably with Roman. No doubt he thought he was charming my father in order to win his permission to marry me. While the idea that my father had any say in that decision rankled me, it was a natural perspective for Will, and it also softened me toward him. "He's a younger version. You see . . ."

I launched gamely into an explanation of everything that had happened to me in France—modern and Renaissance. Becky listened without interruptions—a rare feat for her—and without once taking her eyes off the road as she deftly negotiated the pre-dawn traffic. When I got to the part about young Will's increasing intolerance to sunlight, though, she glanced in her rearview mirror. We were on the Belt Parkway heading west. The sun had just appeared above the long low peninsula of Coney Island behind us.

"Hey, Roman," she called back to my father, "would you close the curtain on that back window? The glare is distracting me."

"Thanks," I told her after my father cheerfully complied. "So far the sun doesn't seem to actually burn him, but it bothers him and he's getting weaker, while his counterpart, *my* Will, is gaining a tolerance for sunlight and getting stronger."

"*My* Will? Are you sure that's the one you love?"

She had that smile on her face, the one she always got

when she thought she knew me better than I knew myself. It had always bugged the hell out of me. "Yes," I answered firmly.

The corner of Becky's mouth twitched.

"What?" I asked. "You recognized right away that that man back there is not the man I fell in love with."

"Yeah, but he's part of him, right? He's his past, and if you really love someone, you love his past too." Her eyes flicked to the rearview mirror where she could see Joe still animatedly discussing football with Jay, and she smiled again. "Even if that past included Catholic school, dating a girl named Mary Margaret McDonald, and voting for Bloomberg for mayor in 2001 and 2005."

"Or if it included sixteen parking tickets and an arrest for making a public nuisance of herself at a demonstration for Greenpeace," Joe remarked back without missing a beat in his conversation with Jay.

"And besides," Becky continued, "from what your friend Annick said, it sounds like they really *are* the same person. They share the same soul—that's why they can't exist in the same time frame."

"Oh man," Jay said, leaning forward and resting his arms on the back of my seat. "It's like that episode of *Star Trek*. The one where Kirk gets split in the transformer into Good Kirk and Bad Kirk and they fight—only they need each other to survive."

Leave it to Jay to find the appropriate sci-fi geek reference. "How'd they get them back into one body?" I asked.

"They sent them through the transformer," Jay supplied readily.

"Great. We don't have a transformer."

"Yeah, but you have this time portal thingy in San Francisco," Becky said.

"A time portal!" Jay said loudly enough to draw Will and Roman's attention from the back seat. "Cool!"

"We're not even sure it's still there," I hissed back at Jay, hoping he'd get the hint to lower his voice. "It could have been destroyed by Dee or Marduk or the Malefactors . . ."

"So let me get this straight," Becky said as she honked at a BMW trying to take the parking spot she'd spied right in front of our town house. "You have to stop Dee and Marduk from killing, and whatever other evil they're up to, stop these crazy time-thief bastards from destroying time itself, and you have to send young Will unwillingly back in time to save your present Will. Did I leave anything out?"

"That's about the size of it," I admitted, sighing at the hugeness and diversity of the tasks Becky had outlined.

"Uh huh. One minute." Becky twisted herself into a pretzel to get a good view over her right shoulder and then swung the VW van into the parking spot with barely an inch to spare. With that accomplished she turned to me and grinned. "Right, then—let's get cracking."

a Brownie Gries to help

First, though, we had to have bagels. Maia, who managed the gallery on the first floor of the town house, had bought two dozen assorted bagels. "I bet you didn't get these in France!" she told me, giving me a fierce hug.

"No, nor do I think I saw a single French woman to equal your sartorial splendor."

Maia laughed and brushed away my compliment, but it was true. Today she was wearing an elegant white pleated skirt with a sleeveless black turtleneck and black ballet flats. Will was goggling at her. I introduced them and left Maia to explain to Will what a bagel was while I greeted Zach Reese, my father's oldest friend and the gallery's most illustrious and profitable painter. I hugged him, gratefully inhaling the scent of turpentine on his clothes. For the last decade I'd far more often smelled liquor on his breath. After my mother (whom Zach had loved) had died, Zach had stopped painting and started drinking. But last winter, shortly after I'd found the mysterious silver box and encountered an assortment of supernatural beings in New York City, Zach had started painting again—to spectacular effect. He'd had a successful show in the spring just before I'd left for France. I knew, though, through experience with artists, that success could just as often lead to chaos or failure as it could to more success.

I held Zach at arm's length and looked at him. His eyes were clear, his skin glowed, and there were flecks of paint on his blue workshirt. "You're painting," I remarked.

"Am I ever!" he replied, laughing. "Like a man possessed! I'll show you later. Eat! I bought your favorite lox from Grimaldi's Deli."

Since we couldn't discuss supernatural events around Roman, Zach, and Maia, I settled down to a feast of New York bagels, lox, and cream cheese with my friends and family and heard about their lives over the last two months. The gallery was doing amazingly well, considering we had thought we were on the verge of bankruptcy last winter. Zach's show had pulled us out of our slump, and then there'd been the unexpected sale of the two Pissarros, which I still suspected had been purchased by Will Hughes. Since then, there'd been a steady stream of new customers flocking to the gallery.

"They must have heard of us through Zach's show," Roman said, "a most exotic bunch. A West African prince, a young Welsh woman whose father made a fortune in baked goods—"

"The biscuit heiress," Maia broke in, "very shy and she wears the most adorable homemade caps."

"—a diamond dealer who had a sudden yen to collect

art, a homeless man who found a winning lottery ticket . . ."

As my father and Maia listed off the new clientele, I began to get an uneasy feeling. These patrons sounded familiar.

"And the best thing is the effect they've been having on our painters," Roman crowed. "The biscuit heiress visited Zach's studio a few weeks ago and made a chance comment that started him on a whole new series."

"I think it was the scones she left," Zach said, patting his belly. "They brought back memories of my childhood."

I exchanged a glance with Becky. We had experience with some magic scones last fall, baked by a Manx brownie named Fenodoree. Was she the one visiting Zach? And the West African Prince . . . could that be Oberon, king of the fairies? All the fey I had met last fall had disappeared after I'd banished Dee from the city. Oberon had abandoned me in Van Cortlandt Park. I hadn't seen him since. I remembered, though, something he'd told me once: *The humans we touch bloom in our company. They do their best work while we drink of their dreams.* Were the fey visiting Zach and our other artists, playing muse to them? Were the fey back in New York?

"We've had the same kind of luck with our band," Jay said. "Remember that DJ Ariel Earhart on WROX? Well, she started an indie label and has offered us a great contract. After we met with her last month I haven't stopped writing songs."

Ariel Earhart was definitely a fey—although I'd never known exactly what kind. Some kind of wind spirit. She'd taught me to fly and how to listen to people's thoughts. I took a peek into Jay's head now and found it was full of song lyrics . . . and his new girlfriend, Gisela . . . and song lyrics *about* his new girlfriend Gisela. Maybe she was fey as well.

My friends did, indeed, seem to be blooming, but I wasn't sure I liked the idea that the fey had been lurking around my friends and family while I was gone. I gave Becky our long-established "we need to talk" look, and within minutes Roman had been deputized to show Will to his room in Roman's apartment on the second floor, Maia and Zach had been reminded that they had a client coming into the gallery in ten minutes who wanted to meet Zach, and Joe (a police detective), clearly used to Becky's efficient mode, said he had to report in to the station. Jay put on another pot of coffee.

"How long have the fey been hanging around?"

"It started a week or two after you left," Becky said. "We weren't sure at first, but then I caught that Welsh chick leaving a bag of rugelac for Roman one day . . ."

"You *caught* Fenodoree leaving baked goods?" From what I recalled of the Manx brownie, she was extremely shy and furtive. "You didn't thank her, did you?"

"Hell no! I threatened to get my policeman boyfriend to haul her in for questioning and get a cease and desist order."

I laughed. I knew brownies hated to be thanked, but I didn't know how they felt about cease and desist orders. "What did she say?"

"Nothing. She vanished. I mean literally. In a poof of

flour and glitter. It took me a week to get the stuff out of my hair." Becky rubbed her curly hair, which was as tightly wound as herself.

"Poor Fen," I said. "I don't think she's used to any humans being faster than herself."

"Poor Fen, my ass! A week later I came home from tour and found my apartment had been cleaned."

"You mean cleaned out? As in robbed?"

"No, I mean *cleaned,* as in straightened, dusted, and polished."

Becky lived in the one-bedroom East Village walk-up she'd inherited from her grandmother. She'd never had the heart to throw out anything her grandmother owned—including her two cats—and so had simply added her own stuff to the mix. So although Becky was an energetic cleaner of other people's homes, her own had layers of grime going back to the Eisenhower administration.

"Huh. Brownies usually clean up for people they like. Fen must have taken a shine to you."

"Ha, ha," Becky said humorlessly. "I bought new locks and put a security gate over the window. The next day I came home and found a pie cooling on my stovetop, and all my clothes had been washed and ironed."

"You should have seen her," Jay said, grinning. "She was fit to be tied."

"Finally I pretended to go out and hid in the dumbwaiter. I jumped her as she was sneaking in from the fire escape and handcuffed her to the radiator."

"You handcuffed a brownie? God, Becky, these are

dangerous supernatural creatures. You could have gotten hurt."

"Pshaw, I'd gotten a book out from the library and read up on fairies. I drew a circle of salt around her and threatened her with an iron poker until she told me what she was up to. She told me she was taking care of me because I was a loyal friend to 'The Watchtower' and you were going to need me."

"Need you for what?" I asked, suddenly sobered.

"She said she had heard from her French counterparts that you were in danger and would need our help when you came back to New York."

"Did she say how you were supposed to help me?"

"No, she honestly didn't seem to know," Becky admitted reluctantly. "But right after that we were contacted by Ariel Earhart and offered a deal from Prospero Records."

"Prospero Records?"

"Yeah, it's a major indie. They offered us a sweet deal. The only catch was they said they needed us to come up with new material by August. I thought it was too tight a turnaround for Jay . . ."

"But I thought I could write the songs by then," Jay said. "In fact, sitting there in Ariel Earhart's studio, I just knew I'd be able to do it. I felt this tremendous surge . . . like I was flying, and I started to hear stuff. Like voices and snatches of song on the air, like the whole city was singing to me."

Jay's face was lit up as if the lights of nighttime Manhattan were reflected in his face. I knew exactly what he was talking about. Ariel had taken me for a flight over the city and taught me to hear the myriad voices on the wind. It sounded as if she'd given Jay a taste of that magic.

"And since then I've been writing nonstop. It doesn't even feel like writing. It feels like I'm taking dictation from God."

I don't think I'd ever heard Jay utter a mystical view in his life, outside of his veneration for the Elder Gods of H. P. Lovecraft. I studied him, searching for signs of mania. The problem with the inspiration granted by the fey was that it became addictive. I'd seen what had happened to artists when that inspiration suddenly abandoned them.

"They're really good songs," Becky was saying. "The best Jay's ever written. We recorded them last month, and Ariel got us booked on a West Coast tour that starts in two days. We've got to be in San Francisco the day after tomorrow."

"San Francisco?" I asked, feeling a prickling at the back of my neck. Was it just a coincidence?

"Yeah." Becky beamed at me. "We're playing the Fillmore. How cool is that?"

"Pretty cool," I said, taking out three of the tickets we'd found at Pere Lachaise (Jules, Annick, and Kepler had kept the other three) and laying them on the table. Jay's eyes widened as he looked at them.

"The Doors in 1967! Man, I'd give my eyeteeth to have been at that show!"

"You may get your chance," I told him. "No tooth extraction necessary."

❖   ❖   ❖

By the time I'd explained to Becky and Jay the *chronologistes'* theory that the tickets were the key to a time
portal, I was ready to pass out from fatigue. Talking with
Jay about time travel wasn't helping.

"You mean these people travel back in time and
change things? Man, haven't they ever heard of the but-
terfly effect? What if we go back and change something
that keeps my parents from meeting? Would I vanish?
What if we come back to the present and everything is
different? What if the country's been taken over by Nazis
or people have three eyes . . ."

"You'll have to talk to Jules and Annick about all that,"
I said, yawning. "I'm going to get some sleep."

I left Becky and Jay in the kitchen positing alternate
universes and time lines, and I climbed the stairs to my
third-floor studio. Perhaps because of the jet lag, or the
length of time I'd been away, or all the talk about time
travel, when I got to my door I hesitated to open it. I had
the queasy sensation that when I opened it my studio
and bedroom would be gone. Who knew what changes I
might have caused by going back in time to 1602? What
if the life I'd left behind in New York was altered? I felt
as if my old self lay behind this door. What if I no longer
recognized that self?

I opened the door. Morning sunlight streamed through
the windows and skylight at the south end of the room,
reflecting off polished metal surfaces. In addition to my
jewelry business I made metal sculptures and mobiles
that hung from hooks in the ceiling. The most impres-

sive of these was a six-foot-long metal dragon welded (and rewelded after I'd removed the head last year) from chain links and spare automobile parts, with a hydraulic spreader—the so-called Jaws of Life—as its menacing long-nosed snout. I'd made it in my senior year at FIT after finding the jaws in a dump. They were a reminder of the horrible car accident that had taken my mother's life, which I'd later discovered had been caused by John Dee. I'd met a real dragon last year—Ddraik, who lived beneath the abandoned City Hall subway station—who had taken me back to that moment and made me relive it again and again, forced me to watch my mother die over and over again until finally I was able to get a message through to her—too late to save her, but in time to let her know that I would survive the accident and grow up. She had told me that was all she needed. And she had told me one other thing.

You can't change the past.

And yet I'd gone back into the past and brought a piece of it back with me.

"That looks like something out of my worst nightmare."

I turned around and found that "piece of the past" standing in my studio. His hair was tousled from sleep, making him look even younger than his nineteen years. But when he stepped closer to the dragon sculpture and narrowed his eyes at its rusty jaws, I saw a flicker of hard-won experience in his eyes. After all, in the last week he'd faced a monstrous vampire, an evil sorcerer, ghostly time wraiths, and his own future self. He wasn't quite the callow youth I'd met a week ago, and if he wasn't *my* Will yet, I could see the foundations of the man I would fall in love with.

"It *is* something out of my worst nightmare," I said, sitting down at my work stool in front of my drafting table and pulling over a stool for him. "Or, at least, I made it to confront my worst nightmare." I told him how my mother had died. Because he didn't know much about cars I had to explain what happened to metal at high-speed impact and how gasoline combusted.

When I was done he didn't say anything for a few minutes. Then he told me how his mother had died in a carriage accident when he was seven. "I was waiting for her arrival in the courtyard of Swan Hall. I saw the coach round the corner of the drive. My father was driving. I could tell by the way he was beating the horses that he was angry. He was often angry at my mother. She was much younger than he and she liked to laugh and sing . . ."

His voice, grown wistful, trailed off. When he began again, it was husky. "The carriage wheel struck the stone border of the drive and cracked. My father was thrown clear, but my mother . . . when I reached her, she was still alive. She'd been crushed beneath the iron wheel."

I winced and touched his arm. "I'm sorry, I didn't know . . ."

He snapped his head around. "You mean he—my older self—never told you?"

"No," I admitted, feeling somehow embarrassed.

"Well," he said, smiling faintly, "perhaps after four

hundred years I'll have forgotten it. That, at least, is something to look forward to."

I was about to tell him that he wouldn't have to live those four hundred years because we'd cured him of his vampirism, but then I noticed the way he'd positioned himself out of the direct sunlight and how pale and wan he'd become. He was turning into a vampire before my very eyes while *my* Will was becoming human. Even if we did find the portal and send him back to 1602, we might very well be sending him back as a vampire, doomed to live over another four hundred years battling his lust for blood.

You can't change the past, my mother had said.

I was beginning to think that she might have been right.

I was so exhausted that I must have slept through the entire day and well into the night, because when I woke up it was dark and the alarm by the side of my bed read 3:33 a.m. The sound that had awakened me was the rattle of chains. But I didn't think I was being visited by Marley's ghost. I'd made a few arrangements before going to bed, on a hunch.

I sprang out of bed, dressed in the sweatpants and T-shirt I'd gone to bed in, rushed into my studio and flipped the light switch. My hunch had been right. There on the studio floor, tangled in an iron chain and cursing a blue streak, sat Fenodoree. I grabbed the box of Morton salt I'd left on my drafting table and drew a circle around the irate brownie, even though I was pretty sure that the iron chain I'd rigged to ensnare her as she came through my skylight was enough to keep her in place. Every time she tried to pluck the chain off her ankles she drew her hand back as though burnt and uttered a string of Welsh expletives. When I had completed the salt circle I stood with my hands on my hips glaring at her. She looked much the same as when I first saw her working at Puck's Tea Shop in the West Village a year ago—a plump woman with sandy hair wearing a corduroy jumper, fingerless wool gloves, round gold-rimmed glasses, and a green corduroy tam-o'-shanter. It looked like I had snared Betty Crocker.

"If you stay still and promise not to try to escape, I'll take the chain off your feet."

She glared at me with a distinctly un–Betty Crocker-ish look, but then crossed her arms over her chest and nodded. I reached into the circle and unwound the chains from her striped stocking and purple Croc–clad feet. I drew the chain out of the circle and dropped it close by my side so I could throw it over her if she tried to escape.

"Hello, Fen," I said, sitting back down outside the circle. "Sorry about the trap. I had to make sure you'd stay long enough to talk to me."

"How did you know I'd be here?" she asked, pouting as she rubbed her ankles.

I waved my hand at the studio. "I've been gone two months and there's not a speck of dust anywhere. Everything's been polished except for the box of iron chain links. And Becky told me you'd been visiting the town house and cleaning her apartment."

Fen sniffed. "Your friend has the personality of a boggart—but a loyal one."

"Yeah, that about sums Becky up," I replied, grinning. "She said you told her that I was going to need her."

"And you do, don't you? You and your time-hopping friends are heading off to San Francisco without the slightest notion of how to open the portal and what to do if Dee or Marduk or the Malefactors attack you."

"How can Becky and Jay help us against Dee and Marduk or the Malefactors?"

"With their music of course!" Fen replied.

"Music can defeat the Malefactors?"

"Not just any music—it needs to have the right frequency. The right music can disrupt the wavelengths on which the Malefactors travel. Wavelength travel is just one method in their arsenal, but they've been using it more and more recently. That's why we sent you to a concert."

"You left those tickets at Père Lachaise?"

"Well, not me, per se," she replied with a sniff. "I have not set foot in Paris since before the Terror, when an impertinent French baker insulted my scones." She muttered a string of Welsh invectives under her breath. "But one of O—" She clamped her hand to her mouth suddenly.

"One of Oberon's crew? I should have known he was behind this." The last time I'd seen Oberon had been last winter when we'd escaped from our final encounter with John Dee in the High Bridge Tower. Oberon had left me unconscious and burnt in Van Cortlandt Park.

When I'd gone to look for him, I had found that the SRO hotel where he had lived had been turned into a boutique hotel, and he'd vanished. "Has he been following me?"

"We've kept abreast of your activities through our French friends—Monsieur Lutin in the Jardin des Plantes, the lumignon, and Madame La Pieuvre. A professor you may or may not be familiar with, Dr. Lichtenstein. And of course, Lol has kept watch over you."

"Yes, I saw Lol but I didn't realize she was working for Oberon." I didn't mention that she had been giving Will news of my welfare as well, or that I had indeed met Dr. Lichtenstein and observed what had happened to Cosimo Ruggieri's corpse in his presence. "The last time I saw them together, Oberon swatted her."

Lol had been trying to save me from Oberon at the time. The memory reminded me that Oberon had put a paralysis spell on me and left me. I would have died if Will hadn't saved me. Oberon had claimed later that he'd known Will would reach me in time, but still . . . "Why is Oberon watching me? And don't tell me it's because he's concerned about me. He tried to me kill me once."

Fen fidgeted. I knew that the fey couldn't tell an outright lie, but they could dissemble. I picked up the iron chain and rattled it at her.

Fen cringed. "Because if you don't open the San Francisco portal and defeat the Malefactors, all of mega-time will be destroyed, and without mega-time . . ." A single tear appeared at the corner of Fen's eye, magnified by her glasses. ". . . without mega-time, the fey will vanish from the human world entirely. We use mega-time to travel between the Summer Country and the human world. That's why there's always a shift in time whenever we travel between the worlds."

"That's why I went back to 1602 when I traveled through the Summer Country in the Val sans Retour?"

"Yes, and it's why human visitors to the Summer Country come back years after they left."

"Like Rip Van Winkle."

Fen giggled. "I told that one to Washington Irving over a pint of ale one day, but yes, that's why Rip came back twenty years after he'd left, and Oisín came back to Ireland hundreds of years after his visit to Tír Na nÓg, or King Herla left his Briton kingdom only to return two hundred years later to a land taken over by the Saxons. Time is a river and we fey know how to navigate it. But if the Malefactors have their way, they'll dam the river and flood both worlds. We have to stop them, and Oberon knows you are the only one who can."

"So why didn't Oberon just come to me and explain this?"

"Well, he didn't exactly part with you on the best terms," Fen said, blushing. "He was afraid you might be angry with him."

I laughed. "Yeah, well, he did paralyze me and almost kill me. But afraid of me? He's the frickin' king of the fairies!"

"And you're the Watchtower, Garet," Fen replied soberly. "Have you forgotten that?"

I stared at Fen, thinking over the last few days of fleeing from Dee and Marduk and the Malefactors. I *had*
forgotten it. It was time to stop running and face my
fears. "Thank you for reminding me," I said. I stood up
and broke the circle of salt with one foot. "Now, as Watchtower, I order you to take me to your king."

29

The Grange

We crept out of the town house and walked to the subway station at Fourteenth Street and Seventh Avenue, where we caught the uptown 1 train. Ordinarily I would have worried about taking the subway at four in the morning, but considering all the supernatural perils I was facing, such concerns seemed fairly pedestrian. Besides, I was sitting next to a brownie. A pissed-off brownie. When a crowd of obnoxious teenagers got on at Twenty-Third Street, Fen glared them into orderly silence. She herself maintained a huffy quiet until the drunk boys got off at Penn Station. Then, somewhere between Thirty-Fourth and Forty-Second Streets, she remarked, "I see you found Will."

"That's not my Will," I snapped automatically. "But the real Will is around. He's tracking down Dee and Marduk to stop their killing."

"Oh," Fen said. "I wondered about that."

I glanced at Fen and noticed that her round cheeks were pink and her glasses had fogged over. I recalled that she was Will's friend—Marguerite had asked her to look after him—but perhaps she had more than just friendly feelings toward him.

"The Will who showed up with you at the town house yesterday did smell right," she went on.

"Smell?"

Fen crinkled her nose, making her look like a rabbit. "I can always tell a friend by his or her smell. This Will smelled like my friend."

"He's young Will Hughes from 1602," I explained. "Will—*my* Will—sent him back to the future in his place out of some harebrained notion that I would prefer his younger innocent self."

"That's just like Will," Fen said with a wistful sigh. "So noble."

"Stupid, if you ask me. And now, having both of them in the same time line is causing all sorts of problems. He—young Will—is weakening. Annick, one of the *chronologistes*, thinks he'll vanish into the time stream if we don't do something."

"How horrible! We must think of something to save him."

"Maybe Oberon will have an idea."

Fen shook her head. "Oh no! Oberon hates Will Hughes. Better not to ask him. Can't one of the *chronologistes* save him?"

"Maybe. If we can find the San Francisco institute."

"That's what we'll do, then," Fen said with a decisive nod, as the train pulled into Seventy-Second Street.

"Don't worry." She squeezed my hand, all animosity over my recent treatment of her forgotten. "We'll find a way to save both our Wills."

We rode the 1 on up to the City College station at 137th Street and Broadway. I had been wondering where Oberon had settled since leaving the Jane Street hotel. The fey seemed to pick eccentric locations to inhabit— abandoned subway stations, tea shops that vanished overnight, the water tunnels beneath the city . . . perhaps Oberon was somewhere on the City College campus, living in some bell tower like Quasimodo.

But we didn't walk into the campus. We did walk east to Convent Avenue but then turned north to 141st Street. Even with a brownie at my side, I felt uneasy in this neighborhood. It was a section of Manhattan I hadn't spent much time in—Hamilton Heights, I recalled. The old brownstones we passed were lovely, but some showed signs of disrepair and neglect. Others were being renovated. Did Oberon live in one of those?

Near 141st Street we entered Saint Nicholas Park. We passed a man sleeping on a bench. Fen removed a scone from her pocket and tucked it into the man's pocket. We continued on the path toward a faded yellow house perched atop a hill: a lovely Federal-style house with bay windows and a colonnaded front porch. It looked out of place in the city park. In fact, from the torn-up ground around the house, it was clear that the house had been moved to its current location not too long ago. Something pricked at my memory about a landmark being moved in this part of the city.

"Is this—?" I began, but Fen hushed me with a finger to her mouth.

"Better let me go ahead and tell Oberon you're—"

"There is no need for sneaking about, Fenodoree." The deep male voice came from the front porch of the house where a lantern now glowed. "I've been expecting the Watchtower."

I squinted into the light of the lantern and made out the outline of a tall man with long dreadlocks. I blinked and realized that the light came not from a lantern but from the man himself. His eyes glowed green, and he was surrounded by a nimbus of sparkling gold lights that took the shape of enormous semitransparent green and gold wings. Oberon, king of the fairies, bowed to me. "Welcome, Watchtower, to the Grange."

He swept his arm toward the front door, the lights from his wings reflecting in the windows. I walked up the steps, studying the house. "The Grange? Do you mean Alexander Hamilton's Grange?"

I now recalled reading that the home of Alexander Hamilton had been moved to a park and was being restored. As I walked through the door I saw that the house was empty of furniture and was still in the process of restoration. You could see, though, that the bones of the house were lovely. The proportions of the entrance hall and the octagonal room beyond it were perfect. There was a restful feeling in the lines of the rooms, though also a hint of sadness in the air.

"Yes," Oberon said, following me into the octagonal room. "My esteemed friend, Mr. Hamilton, called it 'my sweet project.' We talked over its planning many times."

I glanced at Oberon. His face was wistful as he glanced around the empty room. "You were friends with Alexander Hamilton?" I asked. I don't know why I should have been surprised. Oberon had been friends with William Shakespeare. When I'd visited him at his apartment on Jane Street, I'd seen his likeness in paintings by artists from Leonardo to David Hockney. He had inspired countless poets, musicians, and artists. Why not one of our founding fathers?

"Yes, we met on his home island of Nevis. I proudly watched his progress here in New York when he joined the New York Manumission Society and defended runaway slaves for free, and when he founded the *New York Evening Post*. I like to think I inspired some of his writing in the Federalist Papers. He was a fine man, but one in whom the forces of passion and reason forever warred. Unfortunately, his passion was his downfall. He only lived here two years before he died in that tragic duel."

"Why didn't you save him?" I asked.

Oberon flexed his wings, his green eyes flashing angrily. "If we fey could always save the ones we loved, the world would be a different place. Alas, there are evil forces at work, often foiling our good intentions. You should know that by now, Watchtower."

"Yes," I admitted. "I do. That's why I'm here. I need your help." Oberon bowed his head and indicated that I should precede him into another room, which I found had been rudimentarily furnished with two chairs and a table in a small windowed alcove. "Come sit," Oberon said. "Mr. Hamilton and I often sat here and discussed our visions for the new republic. In fact, it has been a long-held dream among many in the fey community, including myself, to see one of our own installed in the White House. Secretary Hamilton shared that dream because he believed that, loosed from the strictures of mortality and the sort of ambition that leads to a desire to have eternal life through reputation, a fey president might provide more balanced, impartial, higher-quality leadership. And the secretary, who had an African grandparent, also identified with the fey as a fellow minority group member.

"For the longest time the US presidency has been restricted, given political realities, to white Protestant males. But in the last century barriers have fallen: disability with FDR, Catholicism with JFK, and now, most dramatically, race with Barack Obama. National ticket and serious primary candidates have included Mormons, women, Italian Americans, and Jews. So ambitious murmurs have arisen among the fey again recently, though if we get a groundbreaking candidate he or she may have to employ the same sort of discretion FDR did, concealing certain things from the public. After all, many ordinary citizens do not even believe in the existence of our group, let alone display any willingness to vote for a member of it. But our day will come!"

Oberon's eyes started to glisten. "And when it does, we will locate Mr. Hamilton wherever he is now, and I hope we—the new president, that is—can regularly receive advice from him. He was a crucial adviser to George Washington and can be to the first fey president as well!" He rubbed his eyes dry with the back of one powerful hand.

I waited for him to regain his composure—I understood how he could be so moved, having felt similar emotions myself regarding Obama although I was not a minority—then asked, "Why are you here now?" I sat down in the heart-backed chair, which I was pretty sure was an original Hepplewhite.

"I wanted to spend a little time in my old and hopefully future friend's home before it became a museum. Tell me why you are here, Garet James."

"As I said, I need your help. You've been watching me, so you know that Dee and Marduk are out and about in this time, killing again, and no doubt up to even deeper evil we haven't learned the details of yet."

"Yes, Lol told me of your little mishap in the catacombs. But meanwhile, I believe your friend Mr. Hughes intends to pursue the fiends. I have every confidence that Hughes will put an end to their machinations. Your vampire-lover is quite . . . ruthless in his way."

"I hope you're right. But that's not our only problem. The Malefactors are trying to destroy time."

"Yes, that *is* a problem. But one I think I can help you with."

He got up and walked over to a patch of wall that had been stripped of its plaster and reached into a dark hole, pulling out a burlap sack. He laid the sack on the table between the two chairs and sat back down.

"Open it," he commanded in a voice so compelling I would have obeyed even if the sack had contained live snakes, which, for all I knew, it might have. I reached my hands into the sack and felt something square, hard, and very cold. Like a block of ice. When I drew the object out, it glowed with an arctic blue light.

"The silver box!" I gasped, staring at the object. A nest of snakes would have surprised me less. This was the object that had started everything. I had found the box at John Dee's antiques shop last winter. It had been sealed then—it wasn't now—and John Dee had offered to pay me to open it, supposedly because of my welding skills, but really because it could only be opened by the Watchtower. After I had opened it, John Dee had sent thieves to the town house to steal it. He had then used it to summon the demons of Despair and Discord to New York City, just as he had once used the box to summon the demon Marduk to turn Will Hughes into a vampire. Will and I had tracked him down to the High Bridge Tower and closed the box. Then Will had taken the box and used it to gain access to the Summer Country . . .

"I don't understand," I said, tearing my eyes away from the glowing box. "How do you have this? Will brought it back with him into the past, where it vanished.

Morgane said it was a constant, that there could only be one box in any time line. And the box that young Will brought to Dee that Dee used to summon Marduk was still in Dee's possession in 1602. It must have eventually been sealed, or how else would I have found it in 2008 . . ." The blue spirals etched into the silver began to spin in circles—an endless Escheresque loop that my eyes followed unwillingly. I smelled the brackish tide of the ocean and was suddenly seized by an overwhelming sensation of vertigo.

"Quick, close your eyes and put your head between your knees."

Again, Oberon's voice was so compelling I instantly obeyed—although I'd never understood what good this maneuver did. After a minute, though, I felt a little better. I lifted my head gingerly and cautiously peeked at the box. The blue lines had ceased their endless loop.

"It's a time-loop enigma," Oberon said with uncharacteristic gentleness. "If you contemplate it, you'll go insane. Let's just say that Will Hughes took the box to the Val sans Retour and used it to travel back to 1602, but the box didn't go with him. I found it in the Val sans Retour and brought it here."

"You went to the Val sans Retour?" I asked. "But . . . ?"

"But only faithful lovers can travel safely through the Valley of No Return? That's true. You are wondering, perhaps, whom I love. I would have thought you would have guessed that by now."

I looked up from the box into Oberon's eyes. For a moment I felt, staring into their unearthly green depths, the same vertigo I had felt looking at the box. They were just as old and had seen as much. I saw what they had seen now in flashes that sped before me from the misty beginnings of time when the fey first roamed the earth freely with humans—and even before that, with hominids. Oberon had loved the humans more than any of his kind. I saw him sitting cross-legged in front of a fire in a cave, handing a shell filled with red ochre paint to a caveman, and saw him watch as the man painted animals and a creature who was half man, half antlered beast—and resembled Oberon—on the wall. I saw him standing on an African plain as tribesmen stitched his visage on leather and bone masks. I saw him standing on a Greek mountaintop as a sculptor chipped away at a marble block to sculpt his portrait.

But he wasn't alone. A woman stood beside him, a woman who looked like me. Marguerite. Together they walked among mankind, sometimes in human shapes, sometimes as animals—the great cave bears, saber-toothed tigers, lions, . . . and swans.

Then one day Marguerite fell in love with a human man, and she left Oberon for him. When the man saw her change into a swan, though, he shot her down with an arrow to keep her from leaving him. I saw Oberon standing at the edge of the pond, watching her die, but then he saved her by making her a guardian of the humans she loved. Still an immortal, but no longer able to come and go between the worlds.

"You loved her," I said aloud, breaking out of the stream of memory. "You loved Marguerite."

"Yes, I loved her, even when she chose to live among humans and become the Watchtower. I didn't mind her infatuations . . ."

I saw Oberon dressed as a Moroccan prince in a Tudor house, watching a bearded man writing wildly with a quill pen, Marguerite laughing as she looked over the playwright's shoulder.

". . . but when she chose to become mortal for one . . ."

I saw young Will at a party, eyes fixed on Marguerite, and then Will at the door later on, begging admittance and Oberon pushing him down the steps.

"That's why you hate Will so much." Another memory scrolled before my eyes. A street in Paris at dawn. Will Hughes set upon by a gang of rough-looking men, Oberon watching from the shadows.

"You tried to kill him."

"Yes, but she would not let me."

A woman came rushing down the street. She wore a yellow silk dress, elaborately styled wig, and dainty high-heeled shoes. I recognized her as Madame DuFay: one of my ancestors and a Watchtower. I'd watched her memories once, through an enchanted Lover's Eye brooch, but now I was seeing the events through Oberon's eyes as she rushed to save her beloved Will Hughes and was struck down instead by one of the assassins Oberon had hired.

"You tried to kill Will because you loved Marguerite," I said.

"Yes, many times, but the Watchtower always stopped me, even at the cost of her own life."

"How do I know you're not planning to kill him now?" I asked.

"Watch," he replied.

I looked into his eyes and saw him watching me from the shadows in Paris: in the Luxembourg Gardens, outside the Arènes de Lutèce, on the platform at the train station in Poitiers . . .

"You! You were the man in the black coat and hat I saw in Paris!"

"Yes. I knew you would lead me to Will and to the box."

I saw him, outfitted in olive green cargo pants, anorak, wide-brimmed hat, and wraparound gogglelike sunglasses, following Octavia and me into the Val sans Retour, and then following me into the reeds after I had left Octavia by the rock . . . but then he lost his way. The reeds were whispering to him. *How can your love be true when she loves another?* Then the reeds sang. *Only when you destroy what she loves will she be yours.*

"That's a lie," I said, tearing myself out of the vision. I recalled the seductive power of the reeds. They had tried to convince me that Will didn't love me. They were a trap set by Morgane to lead lovers into betraying their beloveds.

"Of course it was a lie. If I had listened to them I'd still be there. Instead, I heard another voice."

He compelled me back into the vision, and I saw a crazed and frantic Oberon wandering through the reeds until he came to a clearing where nine stones stood. I remembered the place. It was the tomb of the Watch-towers. I'd found my way there, too, and had discovered Will in the cave, half dead and raving. But Oberon had seen someone else standing in the entrance to the cave— Marguerite. The original Marguerite. She held her arms out to him, her eyes filled with tears.

"My dear Oberon," she said, "if you truly love me, why do you kill what I love?" And then she had shown him all the pain he had caused her over the centuries as he had tried to destroy Will, and she showed him how, in his spite, he had hurt humans by inspiring them to greatness and then abandoning them so that they always longed for that lost spark. He fell to his knees at her feet and wept. When he swore he would never hurt Will or another human again, she lifted him to his feet and handed him the silver box.

"Then take this back to Garet and let her use it so that she can finally be with Will. When you have done that, I will know you love me and you can return here and we will always be together."

Then she kissed him.

I felt the tingle of her lips on mine, and for a moment I was both people in the vision: Oberon, whose memories I was living, and Marguerite, my ancestor. When I opened my eyes I saw Oberon's face in front of me, his face wet with tears, his green eyes burning into mine.

"So you see," he said, "I have no reason to lie to you or wish you or Will harm. Take the box to San Francisco and use it to open the portal. You will defeat Dee, Marduk, and the Malefactors, save humanity, *and* save Will Hughes. Spend the rest of your lives together. I will return to the Val sans Retour and spend eternity with my Marguerite."

"But how . . ."

"You'll know how, Garet James. This is what you were always fated to do."

I nodded and took the box, which he'd wrapped back in its burlap sack, from him. He rose and saw me to the door. When I stepped onto the porch I saw that the sun was rising over all of New York City to the east and south. I turned to ask another question, but Oberon was gone. I tucked the box under my arm and headed to the subway station thinking of the question I hadn't gotten to ask. He had said I would save Will Hughes and spend the rest of my life with him. But which Will Hughes would I save?

30

Romance at the Edgemont

Marduk had been delighted to learn, on a Fox TV News monitor at JFK Airport in New York City while waiting for his connecting flight to San Francisco, of the arrest in France of Jean Renoir on suspicion of fraud and financial manipulation. French police had uncovered evidence of a "massive plot to undermine the world's gold trading" and were searching for another suspect in the case, the Irish banker John Dee, and also for the vanished source of information, an unnamed proprietor of an orphanage in Brittany. Yes, Marduk thought with great satisfaction, Renoir had his assortment of enemies, and it hadn't taken much. He suppressed laughter as an image flashed of Renoir being walked up the steps of a courthouse with a gendarme to either side of him. This reminded him of another French official's recent arrest in some sex scandal. Ah, the French. They had believed the likes of him, Marduk. Too bad they hadn't found Dee yet. But that might make it considerably easier for Marduk to kill him.

And now, several hours later, Marduk was really liking the San Francisco hotel John Dee had recommended to him, the Edgemont. One of the city's most legendary and finest, the Edgemont had famously been scheduled to open on the eve of the great earthquake in 1906. Hundreds of dignitaries had gathered back then in the grand ballroom for an opening gala, and supposedly some who had lingered until the wee hours of the morning had felt an early, cautionary tremor not experienced anywhere else. Crystal chandeliers had swung about wildly, and a huge wall-height mirror at the ballroom entrance had cracked in half. The damaged but not destroyed hotel had finally opened about two years later. Reading about this history on the hotel Web site on the flight from Paris to New York—what a creature of the Internet he was becoming—Marduk had felt his blood-rich saliva surge in his throat and mouth. He looked up the earthquake on Wikipedia; the details of the carnage were a feast for his thoughts.

He sat on the ninth-floor open-air terrace of the hotel, which was located at the intersection of Mason and California Streets. The terrace was part of a cocktail lounge called the Evening Room. Marduk luxuriated in the view, sitting with his cell phone at the ready on the white linen–covered table before him. He sipped a Bloody Mary—he liked the name and the color of the drink—and had the phone out because John Dee, who had managed to flee France, was supposed to call upon his arrival at the San Francisco airport. Dee's first flight had been delayed by weather in Paris, and then he had missed his connecting flight in New York.

Yes, Dee was furious at Marduk for tipping off the French authorities regarding the Renoir plot but, apparently insatiable in his greed and Machiavellian lust for power, Dee seemed compelled to rejoin him in San Francisco and try to jumpstart a US version of the plot in the midst of the small but growing financial industry there. Marduk chuckled to himself at Dee's ambition, taking another sip of his drink and pretending it was blood.

He took in the sparkling city view, sunlight gleaming on the Bay and off the windows of the skyscrapers in the Financial District to the south. A small white cruise ship moved at an elegant pace toward the Bay Bridge, bisecting the water perfectly as if it carried a convention of geometers. The ship's image of hospitality reminded Marduk of his own obligations in that arena. He would have to make a dinner appointment for Dee and himself in the Edgemont's fine restaurant, the Century (named after the approximate age of the hotel) as soon as he learned what time Dee was arriving. If it was booked, he'd consult with the front desk to find a comparable locale nearby. As to what might come afterward, why reflect on that now? For the moment, he thought he should prepare himself to be an excellent host. He spit on the floor sarcastically at this thought.

Just as a small red private plane, flying low, suddenly appeared in the sky to his left, the phone rang. He answered on the fourth ring. The great Marduk should never appear too eager.

"What an ordeal," Dee said, coming on without a greeting. "Remind me to use Air Fairy next time. If only such an airline existed. Mere mortals can't do anything right."

"Why didn't you just rent your own plane?" Marduk asked, inspired by the sight of the plane overhead, and feeling it might be useful to feign sympathy.

"I had to purchase a package deal from the official I paid off to avoid the fate of Mr. Renoir," Dee explained. "Specific tickets were part of it. I guess they wanted to keep an eye on me for as long as they could. All futile for them, of course: yet all due to the unfortunate act of betrayal that has occurred. Something you wouldn't know anything about, now, would you, my dear Marduk?"

"Of course not!"

Dee's tone turned impatient, which was fine with Marduk, since his tolerance for talking to this fool was not unlimited (he couldn't imagine how he was going to get through dinner with him).

"Well, whatever the truth may be, and however unreliable you may have turned out to be, monster," Dee told him tersely, "I am determined to take one more opportunity to talk sense into you. The greatest opportunity in the history of capitalism remains open. Where and when shall we meet to discuss it?"

"Come here to the Edgemont. Meet me in the lobby, seven p.m." Marduk hung up without another word, just to irritate Dee. The phone rang again immediately, probably Dee calling him back, thinking they had been accidentally cut off. Marduk grinned at the phone; he was too important to answer it. The caller tried several more times, eventually gave up.

Marduk lingered over his drink, savoring a few bloodred drops nestled at the bottom of the glass as if they were the last juice from a deceased victim. Then he took in the panoramic view from the terrace with a final sweep of his gaze, Dee's antidote still fortifying him as the sun-lathered breeze with a hint of Pacific salt caressed his features. He inhaled deeply: the sea tang, the sight of glimmering towers, and the red plane disappearing beyond the hills of Berkeley to the east all seemed to stimulate him. Then he stood up, leaving a dollar tip under his glass, and headed back to his room. He'd try calling in the dinner reservation. Then maybe some pay-per-view-porn to while away the time—he wondered if a tonily pretentious hotel like this one would offer it. The bloody, axe-slayer kind?

The moment he got off the elevator on the fifth floor, Marduk knew something was wrong. Traveling in other worlds as he did, it was not so difficult to sense the presence of a new and different one. A recent visitor to 2009, he was no expert in its furnishings, or lighting, or architecture, or music, so he could not put his finger exactly on how he knew he might be in a different year. He was not even sophisticated enough to know that these were gas lanterns lining the hallway, not electric ones. The air was no doubt dimmer, but he did not specifically recall that, where he now walked along a thick rose-patterned carpet, an hour earlier he'd strolled along a thin, pale blue one when he'd left his room to go to the cocktail lounge. He heard music coming from one of the rooms—from a violin, as if someone were practicing—and the bouncy, Irish jig–influenced rhythm of the song bore no resemblance to the music he'd been hearing in the airports in Paris and New York, in the streets of San Francisco.

Marduk had an indefinable sense that the change in time was substantial. Maybe it was that he doubted small shifts in time could be perceived so readily. But he saw no immediate alternative to returning to his room. Perhaps his sense was wrong, and he was just experiencing a hallucination, a delusional intuition. He shrugged and began to stride down the hall toward room 508. Then he stopped himself short, shuddering.

Faintly, like the hint of convoluted twigs in the shadowy air, he thought he caught a view of a Malefactor, a fading one, just outside his door. The creature had one clump of twigs—a forest hand—on the doorknob as he closed it, and now his remnants were drifting toward a nearby exit sign. The twigs drifted as though blown in a breeze, but there was no sign of air movement in the hallway. Was the Malefactor just now exiting Marduk's room? Could its malign presence in 508, even a brief one, have transported the entire hall, or even the entire hotel, to a different time? Marduk didn't know. He didn't want to know. He felt violated, infuriated by the Malefactor's seeming presence in his room, but not enough to pursue the beast—always a treacherous challenge, given the possibilities for time ambush. No, he needed to act with prudence, to go into 508 himself now and make sure nothing had been stolen or vandalized.

Marduk took long strides along the hallway, beside himself with fury, and flung open the door, which was unlocked. Horror that he was himself, he nonetheless recoiled from what he saw inside the room.

The bodies of a man and a woman clad in old-fashioned evening attire—still elegant despite the bloodstains—lay sprawled across the bed at odd angles to each other. The man appeared to have shot himself or been shot in the head, a small crimson hole behind one ear, an antique-looking revolver dropped from one outstretched hand to the carpet. Maybe it was Marduk's imagination, but the gun still seemed to be smoking, a thin trail of gray wafting up toward the ceiling. The woman was shot too, right in the center of her forehead, and further, savage mayhem had been wreaked upon her. Her throat was slit ear to ear, and there was an impossibly deep X in her chest right over her heart, which could be seen in all its bloody stillness. Her left breast was virtually amputated. The surprisingly modest steak knife that appeared to have done all this lay on the bed next to her torso, a knife broken in half from, apparently, the man's exertions. Marduk had done worse than this many times, but he nonetheless felt revulsion over what he beheld. Hard to say why.

In any event, he didn't think the Malefactor had killed these people. No, that creature had dialed the time back in his room many years ago to this event, but for what purpose? To pin it on him? To terrify him, not that such a thing was possible? The Malefactor knew of this probable lovers' quarrel–murder–suicide and had sprung it on him, Marduk. For what purpose?

As if to answer his question, footsteps and the clamor of voices were suddenly coming down the hallway toward 508. Of course . . . the gunshots would have been heard, back in time whenever this had happened. Instinct took Marduk swiftly out of the room, his face averted from the newcomers—who appeared not to notice him, as if he were a ghost—into the same stairs the Malefactor had entered. He went down half a flight, then stopped. He listened, more calmly than a moment earlier, to the shrieks, the yells, the horrified exclamations now coming from room 508. There were no indications anyone was pursuing him.

There in the stairs, he suddenly faced perhaps the most humiliating experience of his entire life. *He didn't know what to do.*

Marduk didn't know how to get back to 2009. And as tempting as it might have been to stay in this new time period and find a new slew of delicious victims to feast on, it was much more important that he get back to deal with Dee and Hughes. So, from the stairs, Marduk called John Dee on his cell phone. This served to emphasize his humiliation.

He didn't know what to do.

31

Bird Dust

"You're trapped where?" Dee asked Marduk.

Marduk didn't know why the fool hadn't heard him. There was a crackle of static in the connection, as if it were weakened by the time gulf. But he could still hear.

"I'm trapped a long time ago, like I just said. I don't know exactly when. Maybe in the early years after the hotel opened. A Malefactor was lurking about my room, and he twisted the time frame somehow." No need to tell Dee about the scene in his room. It was beside the point.

Dee started to laugh.

"Keep doing that and I'll kill you the next time I see you," Marduk told him coldly. Of course, he intended to do that anyway, but no need to be definitive about it at this stage. It would put Dee off.

Indeed, something in Marduk's tone might have cautioned Dee, for his laughter suddenly stopped. "All right. I have an idea. Go to the restaurant off the lobby, Fiorello's, which I think has always been a dining room of some sort, and sit in the southeast corner of the room. It won't be crowded at this hour. I'll get there as quickly as I can."

"But—"

Dee hung up. Marduk knew better than to try him again. Seething with anger, he made his way down to the lobby and found the entrance to a restaurant with a painted sign above its doors, "The Gold Mine," apparently a dimly lit predecessor of Fiorello's. Marduk noticed a lot of candles and lanterns around, but none of the bright electric illumination present when he'd checked in in 2009.

A waiter standing nearby took him with indifference to a southeast table in the largely deserted dining room, seeming to scarcely notice Marduk's no doubt eccentric-looking 2009 attire. Marduk ordered a glass of red wine and prepared himself to wait. But almost immediately the air around the table began to waver, then to develop little silvery ridges, and John Dee's limbs, then torso, then head fleshed out the ridges, a Malefactor-like process except there was no suggestion of a tree. And except that it left the nattily attired Dee with a fine coating of white dust over him, even his eyelashes and lips, one that Dee seemed oblivious to. He put a small silver wand on the table between them, one he'd apparently used to effect his transit, sat down, and gazed at Marduk.

"You look good," Marduk told him.

"Thanks, my good creature," Dee replied.

Marduk laughed. "You're covered in filth, you ignorant dunghill. It looks like you're shrouded in some sort of bird waste in powder form. You look disgusting." He turned away in his chair, as if he couldn't stand the sight of him.

Dee put a finger to his forehead, removed it, and gazed at his fingertip. He frowned, then wiped the tip clean on the tablecloth, repeated the process with his chin, his cheek, his lips. Marduk turned back to him.

"The dust of the centuries," Dee said grandiosely, as if acquiring it had been an achievement. "Time travel is so unpredictable. You must excuse me. I will find a wash-room."

"The dung of the centuries, you mean," Marduk told him, laughing again. With his finger, he helped himself to a daub of dust from Dee's forehead, placed it under his nose and made a revolted expression, though he smelled nothing. "You must have encountered a flock of time-traveling birds in your journey," he taunted. "What an unfortunate accident."

Dee got up, patting Marduk on the head as though he were a pitiable simpleton, and left. When he returned, much cleaner now in his gold suit, yellow shirt, and black tie, he had dropped the pretense of gentility. His eyes held only the cold glare of an inquisitor. "Yes, I did acquire some dust effect from the travel," Dee said. "Odd. These things never go perfectly. If Kepler had worked harder on the technology as promised, instead of wasting cen-turies pursuing me for nonexistent moneys owed, per-haps perfection would have been attained. Ah, well. Someday he'll see reason, and I can release his book-store back to him instead of having to conceal it as col-lateral against his wild financial fantasies. Anyway, speaking of imperfect beings . . . if you didn't tip off the police, any ideas as to who?"

"I know nothing about it. Nothing at all. But since you're starting to ask questions, I've got one for you."

"Yes?"

"Can a corpse be transported through time? Or does the passenger have to be alive for your tricks to work?"

Dee looked at Marduk suspiciously. "And your reason for wanting to know is?"

"Your deathly pale appearance in all that dung dust brought it to mind."

Dee frowned, but then appeared to ponder Marduk's question. "I've never tried it, but I'd have to guess the answer is no," he eventually said. "Living cells, and the living molecules that make them up, have a sort of elasticity to them, a vibrancy, a bounciness, that dead cells lack, and that's probably necessary to cling to the irregular passages, the freakish angles, that are necessary for a passage through time. Elasticity, flexibility: no, my good ghoul. I don't think the dead can be transported through time."

Marduk slapped his knee with enthusiasm, leaving Dee with a baffled expression. "Oh, thanks, Sir Dee. You're a well-informed fellow."

Dee, clearly puzzled by the compliment, went on. "Ah, then. Let's not dwell on the past. I'll assume you had your reasons for the double cross, whatever they were. You have your moods, and Renoir can be a pompous, irritating sort. And after all, he's merely been incarcerated. It's not like he's been hung—"

"Is there a point to this, Dee? I'll repeat, I admit to nothing!"

"Yes. The point is, we can still go on together, you and I. Plotting."

Marduk looked at Dee with an expression of amazement. Dee wanted another conspiracy, even after Marduk's treachery? Unbelievable, even for an idiot like Dee. There had to be some sort of trickery here. Treachery. But he stayed silent. Let the fool be a fool.

"In retrospect, perhaps it was an error to mimic Hughes in our machinations. Not that I think he was the source of the betrayal: he couldn't have known about the plot yet—I suspect you, denials or no—"

Marduk nodded, as if he had been complimented.

"—but once the plot got its inevitable public exposure, that could have led to complications with Hughes, given the hellhound's tendency to be disruptive, even vengeful. No, I've devised a more efficient strategy now, with an intermediary we can dispose of." Dee reached in his pocket and handed Marduk a newspaper photo of a man in his late twenties, long blond hair, handsome features, powerful build, making a gesture as to wave a photographer away. Marduk glanced at it.

"Mack Ames," Dee explained, "the so called 'meat billionaire,' savant of speculation in meat stocks and grain commodities. He's a Wharton whiz kid whose Page 6 reputation for late-night drinking and upscale fisticuffs is exceeded only by his wealth. You'll find him a juicy, sloshed target in New York City neighborhoods like

SoHo and Chelsea one night very soon. Dee glanced at his watch. "Probably too late now for tonight, though. After your meal of him he'll be gone for good, no time-trapped doubles to worry about, and he makes a nice counterpoint to Hughes on the pathetic vegetarian thing. No phony sensitivities for 'Meat Muscle Mack.'"

Marduk licked his lips with passion, even though he realized Mack was a meal he was unlikely to have in the immediate future. But best to play along with Dee here. The main thing was to be swift and precise when the moment came. He couldn't afford to make errors, or let his concentration slip, when the stakes were so high and the opportunity so fleeting. Marduk trembled with the imminent temptation, the orgasmic salvation of it. Play along, he told himself. Another question or two. "Who will be Renoir's equivalent?" he asked Dee. "Don't we need an inside man here, as we did in France?"

Enthusiasm seemed to show on Dee's features now, as if he thought he was, truly, getting through to his pet beast. He reached out and tapped Marduk on the shoulder. "It's America, remember. The grand old US of A. All we've got to do is wave a wad of campaign cash in the air, and we'll have our pick of the government. Everyone's available. Can't get reelected without c for cash, can you?"

"Hmm." Marduk pretended to be reflecting. "You know what, sounds interesting. But shouldn't we both move back to the present, by which I refer to 2009, right about now? So we can get down to some truly serious talking, put all the cards on the table? I mean, nothing to be done in 1912 or whenever we are, huh? No hedge funds or billions to run for office in 1912, right?"

Dee looked reluctantly at his wand on the table, as if he was enjoying the conversation now and didn't want to disrupt it. But then he muttered that Marduk had a point. He picked up the wand gently and went through a sequence of complex, circular motions with it, several inches above the table in a flat plane. The air immediately around them began to shimmer again, waver, as if it were trembling. Tiny, silvery ridges began to appear, and Marduk felt a sense of relief. He saw how he could start to grab onto the ridges and most likely ride them back to 2009, if Dee had calculated it all correctly. And Dee had gotten here from 2009, hadn't he? But there was no time for dawdling, Marduk reprimanded himself. Work to be done. He glanced at Dee, who seemed oblivious to him, carefully observing the strengthening fissures in the air around them. Now!

Marduk picked up the knife from the silverware laid out on the table, masking his right-handed motion with a left hand raised to obscure it, then reached out with the left to grab the back of Dee's head. His massively strong hand took a grip like a man palming a miniature basketball. He jerked the startled Dee's head farther back and slit his throat from ear to ear.

There might have been a hint of terror, and even of regret alongside terror, in those rolling eyes before the man lost consciousness. Dee's body slumped onto the floor, and Marduk took an easy stride over to where the air seemed to be opening the most, between two cracks illumined like slow bolts of silver lightning. He jumped between the cracks, felt a strong electric charge surge through him—no deft touch from that dolt, Dee—and then all went black.

When his vision cleared and he felt alert enough to focus on his surroundings, he found himself sitting once again at exactly the same table. But the song playing in the background in the restaurant—one with the phrase "Roman cavalry choirs are singing" running through it— was one he had heard in both Paris and New York in 2009. In a far corner, a staff person tidying up wore attire he also recognized from 2009.

He was back! And no sign of the recently deceased Dee. He touched his forehead, then glanced at his fingertip. Nothing. No trace of the dust that had smeared Dee. Marduk smiled a self-satisfied grin. He was better at stock trading than Will Hughes, better at time travel than John Dee. It was all in the nature of his genius.

He was the best!

Still, on further reflection, he recognized that it would be prudent to quickly find a new hotel in a different part of town. His short killing list of two was half completed, but a most significant target—Will Hughes—remained. The Malefactors seemed to be onto him here at the Edgemont, there could be a remnant of the time portal they'd opened floating around somehow, and who knew what hotel housekeeping and the police had made of the mayhem in his room, a century ago *or* now.

Or both.

Better safe than sorry.

He got up from the table and walked out of the hotel, leaving his bags behind in Room 508.

32

Mother and Child Reunion

Marduk's new residence was the Palace Motor Inn, a motel he'd found online after leaving the Edgemont. It was on Lombard Street near Steiner, named after the nearby Palace of Fine Arts, an elegant temple to creativity built for the 1915 Panama-Pacific International Exposition, which the motel resembled not in the least. But right now Marduk didn't care much what motel or hotel or even what city he was in: he was hungry.

It was two a.m., Marduk's normal hunting hour. Earlier that night he'd paid a visit to the San Francisco black pools location Dee had grudgingly given him the address of while they were both still in Paris. Though at the time he'd screamed at Dee and threatened him in order to get the address, once he was actually walking over to them, the black pools seemed a matter of little importance. He'd already proved his trading superiority to Hughes.

He had then found himself standing in front of a pastel-colored three-story apartment building on Beach

Street between Divisadero and Broderick, a setting that contrasted dramatically with the rundown one in Paris. The stucco exterior was beautifully painted, polished windows glimmering in the moonlight. Lights had been on on all three floors, and he had heard a clamor coming from all of them, especially the top floor. Yet when he walked up the front steps he found a note on yellow lined paper, attached to the glass door: NO ACTIVITY TONIGHT DUE TO CRISIS IN GOLD.

Marduk didn't like lies, and he had been tempted to kick the door to shards and shrapnel—he could *hear* activity, damn it!—but he had calmed himself down and strolled away. Instead, he had walked on along the shoreline west of Marina Green, a scouting expedition that was necessary for the upcoming ambush.

And now it was several hours later, and he was hungry. He hadn't eaten since a luncheon of salmon and roasted potatoes a little past four o'clock in the afternoon, in the excellent Italian restaurant Pepe's on Chestnut Street near the Moscone Center. Any satisfying effect of subhuman flesh like a fish's never lasted long: such fare wasn't quite nutritious enough for him, physically or psychologically, though he had still enjoyed the novelty of dining in sunlight.

The occasional headlights of a passing car threw bright reflections across the dark ceiling and walls of Marduk's third-floor room. Marduk surveyed the ordinary-looking bed, lackluster lamps, and stained beige carpet and wondered if he could stand being in the place any longer. It wasn't fit for royalty like him. Not at all. But it was the first place he'd found online with at least three stars, and he had been in a hurry to get away from the Edgemont to a different neighborhood. It wasn't worth moving again now.

Marduk went to his "city view" window to distract himself and gazed out at the long streets, Steiner and Pierce, Fillmore and Webster, that rose gently to the south for several blocks, then suddenly became steep hills. Lights in the apartment buildings that lined them were mostly out; the silence he listened to on raising the window for air seemed oppressive. And the misty, salty tang of the air was effete. He needed real nourishment. He made a final effort to distract himself, flicking a light switch and reading the poem on a poster that was hanging near the door, next to an impressionist still life of five golden apples in a silver bowl:

S. F. Bref
by Katherine Hastings

Sea fog, come through my gates of cabled gold
where nets once hung to catch any man who
flew. (They formed a club called Halfway to Hell!)
Cover me coldly with your blue-born breast.

My thousand eyes will greet you as fairies
do—many-colored and feathered. The bell
on the Bay will sway over shadowed waves,
announce your entrance with crystalline breath.

I am your queen waiting with skyward curves.
My body arcs up for you over old
treasure chests buried under black paved bones.
I have been loved before, sometimes to death.

Are my hills too high? My valleys too bold?
Climb me, fill me sea fog, where others fail.

Marduk liked the reference to flying. He had considered the use of a plane in tomorrow's operation, but he had decided on another mode of transportation instead. It would do just fine. As for poetry, he could appreciate the quality of this particular poem, but in general he didn't care for it. He knew the Hughes creep wrote poetry, and that was enough reason to condemn it. Once, centuries ago, another creepy poet was publishing such a book—sonnets, if he recollected—and a short man in a black cloak had hired him, Marduk, to destroy copies being sold in a shop near the tower. Said they were filled with paganism and too-manly love. Marduk had gotten fifty pounds for under an hour's work, and the copies, which he'd seized at swordpoint, had wound up in the Thames. That had been his most memorable moment with poetry.

He went out the door, down the stairs, and out onto Lombard Street. The air was damper and mistier than at the window, rippled by a sea breeze, but Marduk found it more refreshing to breathe than he had upstairs. Maybe he was just exhilarated to be outside, energized after the artificial stillness of the room. He could enjoy the outdoor air while he killed. At this solitary hour, assuming he could find a meal, he probably wasn't going to need an enclosure, a boarded-up shack or dilapidated storeroom, to drag his victim into. He could enjoy her (or him, if necessary) under the rolling black sky and whatever moonlight and starlight twinkled through fast-moving clouds.

He began with a slow, meandering route back to the black pools building, first going west on Lombard to Pierce, then back east on Alhambra down to Cervantes Boulevard, then onto Beach. He hoped to catch some late-night reveler returning drunk from a party, on foot or in the few paces between departing cab and front door, or maybe a sleepless dog walker. The pastel town houses and their spotless pavements were beautiful, but they failed to yield up a pedestrian. The black pools building had gone silent and dark, apparently deserted, the taped front-door sign removed. Marduk moved relentlessly on, along Casa Way to Marina Green. Somewhere in the city of San Francisco, he told himself, a lone pedestrian walked. He went in a new direction now, east toward the low silhouette of Fort Mason that jutted out into the Bay.

The vista was striking, with the Golden Gate Bridge and Alcatraz both shrouded in fog, and the breeze rippled black water that glowed silver where and when moonlight broke through the clouds, but Marduk was not there for the sights, and the bay walk looked as deserted as the streets of the Marina had been. He reluctantly pondered the possibility that he, lord of the

Babylonian underworld, might actually have to go hungry. All night. He considered returning to a city neighborhood, breaking down a door, and feasting on whoever he found inside, but that level of aggressiveness had considerable risks and drawbacks. Then, in the distance, just past where the path swung south around a rectangular inlet near Fort Mason, he spied a figure sitting on a bench, too far off for Marduk to discern the gender. His pulse quickened with excitement.

There was a problem, however. He could not stealthily approach in such open terrain. He should have thought of this problem before leaving the city streets, he reprimanded himself, but he'd hoped he might encounter someone so drunk as to not require any stealth. Which could still be the case. So he strolled tenaciously along, grassy field on his right, lapping waves on his left, breeze everywhere. The person could have glanced his way at any time but did not.

Marduk didn't walk with the enormous speed he was capable of: a few cars still rolled up and down Marina Boulevard, and he didn't need to attract the attention of the police or anyone else. He might have been erring on the side of paranoia, and he wouldn't normally have been this cautious, but with Hughes in his sights soon, and this fresh target almost within reach . . .

The person on the bench got up suddenly, stretched arms as if with relief toward the sky, and began to stroll slowly away from him, still without glancing back. The first street lamp revealed the person to be a young woman with red hair halfway down her back. Agitated with desire, Marduk couldn't help himself; he heightened his pace so that each of his strides gained more ground than three of hers. If a witness wondered what manner of being could cover five yards in a single stride, so be it. It was going to be much easier to surprise her this way, both of them in motion. The only thing missing from this perfect scenario was a cautionary glimpse of her face—no accounting for ugly—but young flesh was the spice of passion, and he'd take his chances.

Closer and closer. She never looked back. As Marduk got within a couple of strides, he could perceive the fullness of her figure and the lithe athleticism in her motion. Luscious. She was reaching the southern bar of the rectangle, and there was a dense grove of trees just off the path, which he could carry her into. To be fastidious about privacy. He—

With no warning, his prey stopped and turned to face him.

Though Marduk had no feelings in the human sense, he felt something now. Shock, and dread. A creepy coldness that made his bones shudder. He paused in his tracks as completely as she had. His world splintered.

The body may have been youthful, but the face wasn't. It looked thousands of years old. Though a monster himself, he found it monstrous. The one eye in the center of the forehead was the color of dung, the mouth was an open sore with a leech crawling on it, the skin was grayish yellow under the lamplight and oozing a foul odor. Worst of all, her hair was a menagerie of snakes, red-eyed and hissing.

Sure as he was standing there, this was Tiamat, she-devil of Babylon. Thousands of miles from home and thousands of years past her extinction at the hands of monotheism. Tiamat.

His one, his only, his primordial, mother.

She leapt at him, her vulture talons dripping with blood, not to hurt him but what he dreaded more: to kiss him. The resulting filth and disease would inflict on him a demise more excruciating than that from a slit throat. He jumped a full ten yards away from her.

Then he heard a stirring, a rippling in the black water to his left, and felt as much as heard a cascade climbing the air, as if a forty-foot waterfall had suddenly formed out of fog and mist. He looked up fearfully, he who had previously felt no fear. Shrouded in the tumult, the spontaneous waterfall, this same creature, Tiamat, appeared in a newly enlarged form, rising from the Bay. The smaller monster on the pavement in front of him vanished.

Behind the cascade, a half mile out in the Bay, fog and mist parted from Alcatraz, as if the rock and its edifice were liberated by Tiamat's manifestation. The dread overwhelming Marduk was unbearable. The vipers on the risen monster's head were a serious threat to him, many feet long and as thick as he was, slithering downward toward him.

He turned away and raced back toward the city, along the Marina path, at his maximum speed. Fortunately Tiamat made no effort to pursue him, but he could hear her cracked, demonic laughter reverberating after him.

"Son. I love you. Son."

He kept running. The Palace Motor Inn was a port of refuge compared to this hell. Maybe he wasn't so hungry after all. Maybe his next meal could wait.

33

City on the Edge of Time

We left for San Francisco the next day, lucky enough to get tickets on the same flight as Jay and Becky,

Or perhaps it wasn't luck.

Oberon had said I was fated to defeat Dee, Marduk, and the Malefactors and to be with Will. I was beginning to feel that events were rushing forward, carrying me toward my fate just as the moving walkways at JFK carried us toward our departure gate.

Will was much less garrulous on this flight. While he had taken a liking to Roman, his time spent with my father had made him realize that winning my hand in marriage was not so simple an affair as asking for it. He seemed sobered, as well, by the mechanics of the twenty-first century. Instead of marveling at the technology that kept the airplane aloft, he seemed daunted by the crowds in the airport, the security procedures, and the jostling of the passengers vying for available overhead compartment space. The twenty-first century was beginning to lose its interest for him—or maybe he was just still growing weaker. He slept for most of the flight, only waking when we began our descent toward San Francisco.

He perked up a bit on the drive into the city. While the skyscrapers of New York had overawed him, his first sight of the Financial District skyline swathed in layers of fog seemed to enchant him. The lathering fog *was* an enchanting sight. I hadn't been in San Francisco for years—not since a childhood trip with my parents—and I'd forgotten how spectacular the city was. The gaily painted Victorian houses perched on steep hills rising up from the deep blue bay, the dramatic banks of fog swathed over the city like cotton batting, the great ochre sweep of the Golden Gate Bridge . . . it all looked like a magic kingdom in a fairy tale.

"There's sure to be a portal here," I told Will as our taxi climbed Fillmore Street into Pacific Heights. "I can practically smell it."

He gave me a wan smile. "Yes, my lady, I believe you are right. This city looks as though it were perched on the edge of time itself. Do not worry. I will be, as your friend Becky so colorfully says, out of your hair before long."

I started to assure him I hadn't meant to say I was impatient for him to go, but we pulled up then in front of the three-story lilac and lime green Victorian house where we were staying. Jay and Becky's bandmate Fiona, whose new boyfriend Jared owned the house, were standing on the sidewalk waving. Then there were greetings and introductions and rooms to be sorted out. Assuming we were a couple, Jared had put Will and me in a room on the third floor. I was going to object, but Will had already sunk into a deep armchair in that room, in front of a window with a view of the bay. There were two beds and a sitting area, so there was ample room to spread out—and I'd be able to keep an eye on Will.

While Jay and Becky went with Fiona to do a sound check at the Fillmore, I called Annick on her cell. She told me that they were staying at a motor inn in the Marina district only a short trolley ride away; they'd be over in half an hour.

I made a pot of tea in the kitchen and asked Jared to let them in, and went back upstairs with the tea to tell Will that our friends were on their way, thinking he'd be pleased to see Kepler again. I found him still seated in the same chair, seemingly frozen to the spot. The view from the window *was* mesmerizing. A low bank of fog had moved across the bay, obscuring the water and the hills in Marin County except for their peaks, which seemed to float like islands in the fog.

"I've never seen a fog like this before," he said when I sat down in the chair beside him.

"I read in the guide book that it's caused by the warm air from the Pacific blowing across colder currents and then being pushed through the Golden Gate when the land temperature rises . . . or something like that."

Will smiled and shook his head. "That may be how your scientists explain it, but I can *feel* this fog in my bones. It is time itself, broken free of its moorings. I can feel it calling to me."

"Calling to you?" I asked, distressed at the melancholy tone of his voice.

"Yes. It knows I'm in the wrong time. It wants me to go back."

"How can time *want* anything—" I began, but a voice interrupted me.

"He's right."

I turned and saw Kepler standing in the doorway, his eyes fixed on the view. Annick and Jules stood behind him. "I've felt it too since we came to this city. The pull of time. This city rests on a seam in time—a gateway. I imagine that's why the terrain was called the Golden Gate. And no doubt that's why the Knights Templar built an institute here—and why the Malefactors want to destroy it."

"Have you been able to find the institute?" I asked, rising to greet Jules and Annick. Annick kissed me on both cheeks and then, much to my surprise, Jules did too.

"No," Annick replied, smiling at my surprise over Jules's warm greeting. "It is too carefully hidden, and the city is swarming with Malefactors. One followed us when we went to the Fillmore. Jules distracted him . . ." Her upper lip quirked into a smile. ". . . while I went to the ticket window."

"I pretended to be a lost tourist," Jules said proudly, "who could not speak English. Imagine! I, who attended Oxford for three years!"

"Jules has developed quite the gift for subterfuge," Annick said fondly.

I was glad to see that Jules and Annick were getting on better but was impatient to find out more about their progress in finding the institute. "What did they tell you at the ticket window?"

"The clerk was quite excited to see the tickets. 'You must be coming to our Doors retrospective,' she said. 'Only you're here on the wrong date.' Then she gave me this."

Annick took out a bright purple flier on which was printed, in pink psychedelic script, the words: "Travel back in time to the sixties with London Dispersion Force! Vintage Doors tickets will gain you free admission." The concert date was tomorrow.

"That's Jay and Becky's concert," I said. Then I explained how they had booked the tour after recording their new album with Prospero Records.

"And you say that this recording company is run by a . . . um . . ." Jules wrinkled his nose. ". . . what did you say she was?"

"I'm not exactly sure what Ariel Earhart is. One of the fey, certainly—some kind of wind spirit."

"An air elemental, no doubt," Annick said. "My grandfather taught me about them. They ride the airwaves and can hear frequencies we can't."

"Yes," I replied. "They can read minds too."

"My grandfather said that they could also sense time frequencies and were natural time travelers."

Jules snorted. "That's never been definitively demonstrated—" he began, but Kepler rushed to Annick's defense.

"Ah, but it coincides with my theories of time," Kepler

remarked, roused from his contemplation of the fog-shrouded view by the mention of his favorite subject. "A related point is that people with an aptitude for geometry may also have a capacity in the area of time travel, as they are more likely to detect polygonal patterns in the shapes around them. Where cracks in time are more likely to be hidden . . ."

I could see that Kepler was gearing up to deliver one of his long-winded lectures, which, while fascinating, would take up much valuable time. I had noticed that Will's eyes were heavy, and I wanted to get rid of everybody so he could rest.

"So, is it likely that the songs Ariel inspired Jay to write and that the band will perform tomorrow will have the right frequency to open the time portal?" I asked.

Annick, Jules, and Kepler exchanged glances and nodded.

"Good, then we'll go to the concert tomorrow. If the frequencies don't work, I have this." I removed the silver box from the laptop case I'd carried it in. When I took it out, Jules and Annick gasped. Even Will stirred himself and stared at the box apprehensively.

"That's Marguerite's box, the one I st— borrowed from her in 1602. Dee used it to summon Marduk."

"Oberon told me it can also be used to open doors in time."

"Of course it can," Kepler said, leaning closer to the box and peering at the spirals etched into the lid. "Those lines on it are time disrupters." He touched the lid, and the lines glowed blue and began to spin.

"Careful!" Jules cautioned. "I've heard about the device. It's extremely volatile. It can tear the fabric of time. We must be very cautious with it. If the Malefactors ever got hold of it . . ."

Jules didn't have to finish his sentence. We could all well imagine what the Malefactors might do with a time disruptor.

I shooed everyone out of our room soon after that, saying that I was jet-lagged and wanted to rest up for tomorrow. Really, I wanted Will to get some rest. He'd become agitated while looking at the silver box. As soon as everyone was gone I put it back in the laptop case, but his eyes remained fixed on it.

"That's when everything started to go wrong," he said. "When I took the box from Marguerite. What did Kepler call it? A time disruptor?" He laughed dryly, the laugh turning into a cough. "It certainly disrupted *my* life."

"Yeah, mine too," I said, helping him up from the chair and steering him over to one of the beds. "It was after I found the box in Dee's shop that everything went nuts: the town house was robbed, fairies started popping up all over, I met you . . ."

He turned his head to me and looked up from the bed. "Me? You mean my older self?"

"Yes, of course," I replied quickly, busying myself unfolding a blanket so he wouldn't see the embarrassed expression on my face. "That's what I meant."

When I drew the blanket up over his chest I saw he was smiling at me. "That's the first time you mixed us up."

"Yeah, well, I'm a bit jet-lagged. We all are. You should get some rest now. Tomorrow's going to be a big day."

"The biggest," he agreed, the smile fading from his face. "Garet?"

"Yes?"

"Would you . . . I mean . . . er . . . if it's no trouble . . ."

"What, Will?"

"Would you stay with me for a bit? Until I fall asleep? It's just that I don't want to be alone right now. I have the strangest feeling every time I close my eyes that I'm fading and that without something to hold onto I'll simply vanish."

I looked into his gray eyes and saw with alarm the reflection of the blue spirals from the box spinning into the void. He *was* fading. I lay down on the bed beside him. He looked startled for a moment, but when I put my arms around him and guided his head to my shoulder I felt his muscles relax and heard him sigh.

"Just hold on tight," I told him. "I'm not going anywhere and neither are you."

I dreamed I was standing on the edge of a pool, my bare feet gripping the mud bank. I stepped into the water and the cold rippled up from my feet, raising goosebumps all over my body. I looked down at my arms and saw that feathers were sprouting from my skin. I stretched out my arms and felt the wind rustle my newly fledged wings. I glided into the pool, my feathered breast cleaving the water, its chill now a delicious balm. I felt the release of shedding my human skin . . . but then I heard a twig break on the shore behind me, and I swerved my long neck to look back . . . and saw *him*. The human I'd come to love. I'd told him again and again not to follow me to the pool, but I might as well have sent him an invitation writ in gold on a silken banner, so drawn were these humans to the hidden and forbidden.

But wasn't that one of the things we loved about them?

It was the rule, though, that when they saw us in our natural—or *supernatural*—state, we had to leave. I had never questioned why—until now, when I saw the look of pain in his eyes. But already I was lifting off the water, beating my wings into flight, obeying the injunction, regretting the hurt I was causing even as he lifted his bow to his shoulder and aimed . . . and I saw in his eyes that he no more wanted to do what he was doing than I did, but we were both caught in this age-old dance, hunter and prey, lover and beloved, the wolf as compelled to chase as the deer to flee . . .

Then the arrow struck me.

I cried out in a human voice that was echoed by a voice on the shore, the ripples my body made as it hit the water spreading out in circles that would reach into the centuries . . .

He was striding through the water, reaching for me, his arms wrapping around me. "I'm sorry," he was saying, murmuring the words into my neck. "I'm so sorry, I never meant to hurt you."

"I know, I know, I never should have fled."

He wrapped his arms tighter around me to keep me from sinking into the water, found my lips and pressed his mouth to mine. I kissed him back, hungry for his warmth, pressing my self against his warm solid flesh to keep myself from sinking into that bottomless cold.

He lifted his mouth from mine and drew back, his silver eyes locked on mine.

"Garet?"

We were no longer in the water but on a bed in San Francisco. The man above me was not the archer, but Will Hughes, young Will Hughes . . . and yet he looked at me with the same love that his ancestor had felt for my ancestor Marguerite, and with the same pain.

"Do you know me, Garet? It's Will . . . young Will, not—"

I laid my finger on his lips to silence him, feeling my hand moving through water, parting the ripples of time to reach him.

"Yes, I know you," I said. "I've always known you." And then I drew his head back down to mine.

Still on New York time—or perhaps Paris time or, for all I knew, 1602 time—I awoke before dawn, alone in the bed. Will was standing at the window, staring out at the dark city. I wrapped a blanket around my shoulders and joined him, leaning against him. He put his arm around me and adjusted the blanket to keep me warm.

"What are you looking at?" I asked, peering into the

deep blue beyond the window. The fog obscured even the scattered lights of the city. We might have been floating through a midnight blue ocean.

"Eternity," he replied. "Can't you feel it? All of time is pouring through the city. We'll find our portal today and I'll go back . . ."

"Will—" I began.

He touched a finger to my lips, much as I had to his last night—was it already *last* night?—when he asked if I knew him. "It's all right, my darling, beautiful Garet, I'm not afraid any longer. Don't you see? All of time is happening *all the time* and so"—he smoothed a lock of hair back from my face and smiled, his eyes gleaming silver against the indigo sky—"the moments we spent together last night will always be there. As long as I have that, there's nothing in this world—or any other—to fear."

34

Piece of Driftwood

Horatio Barnes was a short, slender man of about forty, clad in an orange turtleneck sweater and white cotton pants against the stiff westerly breeze off the bay. He had on Converse All Star dark blue sneakers with thick white sweat socks. Like many tycoons of the Internet era, his unassuming features—mild blue eyes, soft cheeks and chin, thinning brown hair swept back from a high forehead—would not stand out in a crowd. Barnes was as physically removed from the Cornelius Vanderbilts and J. P. Morgans of a bygone era as today's movie usher was from Brad Pitt. But as he eagerly brought up two new ideas to Will Hughes, from whom he hoped to obtain a two-billion-dollar investment that could generate profits of at least two billion more, he showed a greed comparable to that which moved Vanderbilt or Morgan, or the even more rapacious Jay Gould and "Diamond Jim" Fisk (even if the "trillions" of which he'd written in his first query to Hughes were revealed at this meeting to have been a rhetorical flourish).

"Mr. Hughes, I feel so honored that you are willing to meet with me in my most favorite setting in all the world," Barnes said, as soon as they'd found a bench. They were on the Golden Gate Promenade, Crissy Field behind them, the beach and Bay in front of them, the Gulf of the Farallones Marine Sanctuary to their left. At six-thirty in the evening, the beach was mostly deserted except for the occasional dog walker, but the promenade had its share of strollers. Several varieties of shore bird soared, coasted, and tiptoed about. It was an eccentric locale for a business conference, but Will was happy to indulge. He liked it there, and he liked Barnes. So far.

"Anyone strolling along is going to think we're just a pair of friends chatting," Will commented. "We're more secure here than in a conference room, because someone's always going to be tempted to spy on a conference room."

Barnes responded by holding out his hand so they could shake firmly on the point of confidentiality, which they did.

On a rocky ledge at the western edge of Alcatraz Island, so densely shrouded in fog at this hour that no one along the shore saw him or his boat, Marduk laid aside the binoculars with which he was scrutinizing the Hughes-Barnes meeting and nodded approvingly to his lone deckhand. The conferees looked like they were settling in for a talk of some length, and six or seven minutes was all Marduk was going to need. Especially since there was no sign now of his mother, the monster Tiamat. They both clambered down a rope ladder to the boat, deckhand first (Marduk was always one to keep his own back secure). The boat was tied up along the rocks forty feet below, awash in the salt surge and foam of the incoming tide.

It was a gleaming, jet-powered hydrofoil, twenty feet long, equipped with miniature missiles that had been fitted with both wooden- and silver-stake warheads for this occasion. Dee had made the arrangements; Marduk had simply had to pick up the keys at a kiosk selling souvenirs on Fishermen's Wharf and rent a skiff to take him out to the island. As they got in the gently rocking boat and the deckhand made things ready for him—Marduk didn't have much experience with boats, but he knew he could steer one—he looked approvingly at the short distance to the Presidio shore. Three or four minutes at most, to bring the boat to high speed and . . . he licked his lips with anticipation. The appointed minute was at hand.

"I'll give you two examples of ideas that have been brought to me," Barnes was telling Will Hughes, "that, if not for the lack of ready capital, would be sweeping the nation."

Will nodded amiably, absorbed for the moment in the view, thirty feet of white sand down to the shore, against which gentle waves lapped rhythmically. Past it the western bay, dark water with an occasional white stutter of foam spoken by the wind, and then the red-orange towers of the bridge, rising out of grayish white fog like inscrutable copper shrines reaching for the clouds. Here and there, red rays of the setting sun broke through.

Barnes paused for a moment before going into more detail. The hesitancy was fine with Will. He might be disappointed when Will told him he wasn't doing any new investing now unless it involved compassion for animals.

"The first idea," Barnes finally said, excitement coming into his voice, "is similar to my fantasy football breakthrough of assigning errors with forward passes. It's to list all players' forty-yard-dash speeds alongside their heights and weights. It's a similarly intentioned strategy: the more available information, the better the gambling decisions. A modest-sounding plan, perhaps, but when you sit down and look at all the details, the capital needs can be quite intense. The teams would have to be paid handsomely for their proprietary information, and there's already the beginnings of competition in this space from players like Bloomberg and Reuters. So extensive advertising is a necessity. And we'd need expert consultants . . ." His voice trailed off, as if Hughes's lack of immediate enthusiasm had dampened his.

"Not much of a sports fan, my man," Hughes told him, "and the little I follow is cricket or European soccer. Can't you just turn on your telly, watch a game, and see how fast a player runs?"

Barnes gave him a friendly pat on the shoulder. "Just the point. By then, it's too late! You might have already lost your bet."

After another pause, Barnes went doggedly on. "In a different field, I recently sat in on a focus group of cardiac rehab patients. The modern theory is an aggressive one—challenge patients to work up to new exercise levels so they can rebuild heart muscle—and though it's statistically valid, such rehab can be frightening. The patients have a strong temptation to cheat when reporting the levels they're working at, due to fear, or fatigue, or even laziness. In most places a technician monitors their heart rates but not the actual program of exercise. So I propose new software and connections that will allow the technician to monitor the exercise, diminishing cheating. Better outcomes will attract more patients to the programs that do it this way!"

Cardiac rehab cheaters, Will summarized Barnes's second idea to himself. How large a group of people could that be, even in a country as big as the United States? It didn't seem that there could be a fortune in profits, and no animal protection angle came to mind. Still, he didn't want to be too critical or hurt this entrepreneur's feelings. He looked away for a moment, toward the fog-encased bulk of Alcatraz, looming out of the dusk to the east.

It happened so quickly that, even when he had the luxury of armchair reflection afterward, Will couldn't quite reconstruct the exact details of how it went. With Marduk at the throttle, the deckhand cowering near the stern, a hydrofoil was coming fast across the water at them, riding a foot above the waves and sending a cascade of foam and spray in all directions. Marduk looked like he might be intent on crashing the boat onto the beach, a plan that evidently was a surprise to the deckhand, who was kneeling and praying. Will noted a sharply pointed piece of driftwood at his feet an instant before the metallic arrow of the boat's prow struck the sand and began lurching up toward them at a still enormous rate of speed. From the prow of the boat some sort of missile came at them, a moving bolt of flame like a firework. Will noted the silver stake protruding from it. He swept up the driftwood with his right hand, then grasped Barnes around the torso with his left arm and launched them both away from the missile's trajectory at astonishing speed, so they skidded along the sand fifteen feet away from the path of the oncoming missile and boat. Then, while prone on the sand, Will hurled the impromptu stake with a violent flick of his wrist and unerring accuracy, directly at Marduk, who had a leering, self-satisfied grin on his face.

The stake struck Marduk in the chest. It combined the force with which it had been thrown with the momentum of the boat traveling at eighty miles an hour, shattering Marduk's chest, flying clear out his back, and clattering onto the aluminum deck drenched in the blackest, foulest-looking blood Will had ever seen. Marduk grimaced in great pain, and the furious gaze he directed at Will blazed orange-red, like the fire of the Babylonian hell he was descending toward.

The beach had been deserted at the moment of impact,

but shrieks and shouts of "Look out!" and "Get out of the way!" could be heard from the nearby promenade as the hydrofoil lost its elevation and with a loud scraping noise struck a cement embankment. The impact broke the boat in half, wrenched its fuel tank loose, and sent the deckhand somersaulting through the air onto the sand. Remarkably, the man was able to stagger to his feet and start running. Will hustled the dazed Horatio Barnes to his feet as well and began fleeing with him to the east, toward Fort Mason. Whether from the force of impact or a stray spark from the hell Marduk descended to, the boat blew up in a tremendous explosion. Charred fragments from the fireball fell no more than a few feet from the fleeing Hughes and Barnes, but they were unscathed.

Once they were able to stop and look behind them, Will dusted the sand and ashes off his clothes and took a few tentative steps back toward the twisted, smoldering wreckage. Initially, he saw no trace of Marduk's corpse nor, fortunately, of any other victim on the beach or promenade. Hopefully he'd have a chance to scrutinize the scene more closely later. Alone.

"What the hell was that?" the dazed Horatio Barnes asked him. "What kind of a fool drives a boat onto the shore?"

"You had the right key word in your first question," Will replied.

"What?"

But Will preferred not to elaborate.

Then Barnes put a grateful hand on his shoulder. "You saved my life, man. I'm forever in your debt."

Will patted him on his back in acknowledgment.

The first approaching siren could be heard, not far off.

35

Amulet

"Let's find a restaurant and grab a bite to eat," Will told his prospective partner as they walked away from the crash. "Finish our discussion. I don't think we'll be in the way of any seaborne mishaps on Chestnut Street."

Barnes gave a subdued laugh, and they strolled calmly back in the direction of the city streets. Neither one of them had any desire to remain at the marina as a witness and wind up with his name in the paper, especially in association with the other. But the facts would look reasonably clear to the authorities, Will reflected. Let the wreckage be examined for whatever mechanical failure had caused the pilot to lose control. He doubted that the murderous impulses of a supernatural being would be suspected.

From the man's lack of comment, Will also doubted Barnes had observed Will's fortuitous javelin throw, let alone the hellfire issuing from Marduk's eyes or the corrupt blood pouring from his chest. Good. Will would return later, maybe in the middle of that night, when the wreckage was attended to only by a line of yellow police tape affixed to metal rods in the sand. Then he could satisfy his curiosity as to whether any remnant of Marduk's existence persisted. If it did, he'd dispose of it properly. The world wouldn't be safe otherwise.

They went to Santiago's New York Coffee Shop on Chestnut near Fillmore and lingered over vegetarian omelettes and coffee. Will was reassured to see Barnes had researched him enough to follow the point of vegetarian etiquette. After about two hours they reached a partnership agreement, one that Will scaled back considerably from Barnes's hopes. He liked the man's passion and personality but was underwhelmed by his ideas, though he did appreciate the willingness Barnes finally expressed to consider investments that promoted the humane treatment of animals. (It was important to bring as much of the financial world as possible on board with the concept of cruelty-free investing, because nothing other than an economic force was going to change farm animals' world of suffering.) A second factor in his conservatism was Garet. She made him financially cautious. The future, and all that.

They would start with one hundred million each and see how it went. They sealed their agreement with a handshake.

Afterward Will returned to his five-bedroom San Francisco apartment. (He used it mostly to store the US financial records of Green Hills Partners, as the San Francisco office was too small for that.) It comprised the entire third floor of the white brick 1920s walkup at 891

Post Street, where *Maltese Falcon* author Dashiell Hammett had once lived on the fourth floor. There he slept a few hours. Nocturnal sleep was still a novelty, though he was getting more accustomed to it. He awoke with a start around two a.m., partly from the irregularity involved in new sleeping habits but more from the high-pitched screech of a car braking on nearby Polk Street.

He felt right away that something was wrong. And then he recollected the urgent nighttime task he had assigned himself: he had to revisit the crash site and make sure no remnants of Marduk stained the ground, remains that could turn . . . troublesome. Will was confident Marduk's soul had gone straight to Babylonian hell— he'd seen fire in Marduk's empty eye sockets, reflected along his skull, after his heart had been annihilated— but Will had learned the hard way over four hundred years lived twice that he didn't know everything about the world of the supernatural. His hybrid state, though liberating in many ways, made him feel a little insecure about his ability to handle Marduk's possible remnants, but he felt obliged to try.

Will had a car in San Francisco and a driver on five minutes' call, but he wanted to drive to the Presidio alone. He retrieved his midnight blue Jaguar XKE from a garage across the street, drove a block west to Larkin and made a right, took Larkin all the way down to Bay Street where he made a left. Bay angled southwest and turned into Cervantes, which went into Marina Boulevard, disrupted by construction even in the middle of the night. Will went west as far as he could go and parked in one of the small lots alongside the harbor. He'd enjoyed cruising the empty streets, the salty harbor air refreshing him when he rolled his window down. Right next to the water, though, the air was foggier and seemed gloomier as he began the long walk toward the crash site. The bridge was invisible. A few blurred searchlights serrated the moonless dimness, one from each shrouded bridge tower and one from Alcatraz.

At first, as he finally approached the crash site, he attributed his inability to make out the wreckage to the night's obscurity. A hundred feet away he slowed, trying not to become agitated. As he came to within twenty feet, reconstructing the crash location by using the bench as a landmark, he could not help but be unnerved: nothing was there. No sentry standing guard, no yellow tape, no charred chassis of a boat, nothing. Just white sand, that empty bench behind him now, and dark waves lapping the shore. As if nothing had happened. No trace of the conflagration: no smear of ash, twist of metal, seared plank, or vampire remains. Between the searchlights and the streetlamps along the Promenade, he could see enough to reach his conclusion, which he augmented with a flashlight. Nothing was there.

Will paced in a fretful circle, gazing out at the fog-sheathed water, as if his motion might unlock the secret of the emptiness. He was a hundred percent certain the mess couldn't have been cleared away this quickly, given the big-city bureaucracies of San Francisco—police and fire inspectors, shore patrol, coroner, district attorney's office, and so on—and he was more than a hundred percent certain the crash had happened: he had a witness in Barnes.

He tried to reassure himself that the disappearance might not mean much, but he knew it hinted at the presence of a supernatural force. And Will couldn't be certain as to what kind of force. He'd heard tales of a colony of ghouls living deep in the cellars of the "Big Rock," Alcatraz, congregating there in anticipation of some great demon returning from the mists of history. They might have been no more than rumors that lifers had made up before the prison was closed, but they had seeped into San Francisco society—at least, into the portion of it aware there was a supernatural—and stayed there for years. Invisible behind the dense fog, Alcatraz gave off a creepy sensation to him. He really wasn't worried about local demons, though, and the thought of them tidying up a harbor crash seemed far-fetched, even if the motive was to eat the sentries. No, he fretted more about the possible intervention of a demon on a grander scale, given Marduk's Babylonian heritage, which transcended Dee's affiliation with warped alchemy and sixteenth-century conjurers. As Will paced the wasteland of sand, he tried to tell himself that such a grand intervention was improbable, and he finally took the first step or two to depart.

Will tripped over a jagged piece of metal lying an inch or so below the sand. As he regained his balance, he felt an electrifying chill go through his body, as if he had brushed up against a current from another world. Electrifying, but not in a good way.

He knelt down, felt cautiously around the metal's edge in the event it could be sharp enough to cut him. It was jagged and uneven, but he was able to grip it delicately enough to pull it up.

Will recognized the artifact the moment he saw it. It was streaked with sand and other less readily identifiable grime, but the original silver gleamed in patches here and there. Each of the bars of the triangle had miniature, grotesque sculptures on it: a scorpion with a human head, a dog with tusks, a man with a monkey's head, a lightning bolt stained scarlet by some unidentifiable substance. It was so cold to the touch that he could barely hold it. This was the five-thousand-year-old Babylonian Triangle, a demonic amulet created by the same wizards who had bred Marduk's bloodline, cross-breeding humans with monsters. The same one the haunted silver box had once held at a New York City auction. The same one that had briefly been shown on the light show screen during the Doors concert.

Nine had been made, but only two had survived from antiquity.

Will had no idea how it had gotten here, or what its connection could be to the wreckage's disappearance, but he was acquainted with its history and knew what he needed to do with it.

Bury it at sea. It required a water burial.

Perhaps he could drive up onto the bridge with it, stop midspan, and—

Despite its coldness, the amulet suddenly burst into silver flames, molten hot. Will had to hurriedly drop it and step away from it. He watched it for a few minutes; there was no sign of the flames diminishing. Even if he had a way of getting it to the car, it didn't seem safe to try to drive it up on the bridge. Impulsively, bracing against the pain, he bent toward it, seized it, and in one continuing motion flung it in a low arc more than a hundred feet offshore, where the water was several feet deep. The flames seared his hand, but he had done it all so quickly that they had barely penetrated his flesh, and he felt only an irritation in his skin afterward.

A silver flash exploded from the triangle as it plunged into the water, so powerful a one that the light splashed off the mists shrouding both Alcatraz and the Bridge.

The triangle was still alive. He could go out in the water and try to retrieve it and bury it in much deeper water, but he sensed that he'd need full vampire capacities to attempt something that dangerous. And it wasn't his priority: Garet was, and for her, the less he was a vampire, the better.

Reluctantly, resignedly, he walked back to his car. Not looking back over his shoulder even once.

Break on Through

The Will who rose with me to face the world that morning was no longer *young* Will. I thought of him as *new* Will as he rallied Annick, Jules, and Kepler to get ready for the concert.

"We must protect Garet above all else," he explained over breakfast. "The Malefactors will try to attack her. She's the focal point. That's why they tried to attack her at Père Lachaise. Now that she has the box, they'll try even harder."

"I will take up the rear and be on the lookout for any Malefactors who might be following her," Kepler gallantly offered.

"Annick and I will take the advance guard," Jules said, falling into line behind Will's lead with surprising alacrity. I would have thought he'd have balked at Will taking charge, but Will radiated such confidence this morning that even Jules seemed compelled to follow him.

"And I will be by her side," Will said, squeezing my

hand. I saw Annick and Jules exchange a look and Kepler raise an eyebrow at our new intimacy, but I didn't care. I'd have to sort out my feelings for the two Wills eventually, but not, I decided, today.

We decided to walk to the Fillmore. Becky, Jay, and Fiona had gone on ahead to set up, but Will felt far too keyed up to go in the van. A brisk walk, we all agreed, would do us good. We set out in our agreed upon formation. I carried the silver box in the laptop case strapped across my chest. We walked west to Fillmore Street and then turned south. The street went up at a steep angle for a few more blocks before reaching the top of the hill. We all turned around at the crest of the hill, as if upon an arranged signal, and looked back at the bay. The fog had lifted—or perhaps moved elsewhere—revealing sparkling blue water, the majestic sweep of the Golden Gate Bridge. The only blot on this pristine landscape was a cloud of what looked like smoke lingering in the area around the marina. It had a faded quality to it that made me think it could be several hours old, as if it was incredibly pernicious or had gotten snagged on some polygonal gap in time (as Kepler might think of it).

"It looks like there's been an explosion," Jules remarked.

"I hope no one was hurt," Annick said, concern creasing her forehead, and then she turned to walk down the hill.

I sniffed the air, smelling smoke and gasoline on the brisk wind. Attuning myself to the currents of air, I listened to what they carried from the marina. At first I heard sirens and screams but faded and faint, as if from several hours earlier. Then, screening those out, I heard a familiar voice. It was also time-lagged, but it came through stronger.

You had the right key word in your first question.

"Is he all right?" an almost identical voice asked from right beside me.

"Yes," I said, meeting his eyes. "And I believe he's destroyed Marduk."

"Excellent!" Will said, grinning, "I couldn't have done it better myself."

I felt a heightened sense of danger as we continued down the hill on Fillmore. Will might have eliminated Marduk, but that would only free the Malefactors to focus on *us*. I scanned the faces on the street anxiously. This part of Fillmore was a fashionable shopping area. Well-dressed men and women strolled along looking in shop windows or lunched at the sidewalk cafés. It was hard to maintain a sense of danger in such a relaxed atmosphere—even Annick was window shopping. She had stopped in front of a boutique and was studying a display of exotic high-heeled boots.

"Really, Annick," Jules was admonishing her. "Someday your love of shoes is going to—" But Jules's voice froze as Annick pointed to something in the window. I looked at the window and saw what Annick was pointing to. Reflected in the glass was the sunny street full of tourists and shoppers *and* a menacing dark figure approaching from the other side of the street. I turned away from the window and the figure vanished. It was only visible in the reflection. I turned back to the glass—and saw that the menacing dark figure was right behind me. I screamed, and shoppers near me stopped in their tracks and stared open-mouthed at me. Then I saw that Will was directly behind the Malefactor. He drew out a slender silver blade and plunged it into the dark creature's back, in a deft and lightning-quick kind of way so that no one near us could see him do it. The Malefactor shrieked and writhed . . . and then vanished. Will stood looking down at his hands.

"Are you all right?" I said, taking hold of his hands and quickly and surreptitiously sliding the dagger back into the sheath in his jacket pocket.

Will nodded. "I am fine. I am only glad I saw the creature before it could attack you."

"How *did* you see it?" Jules asked. "You weren't looking in the glass."

"No," Will admitted. "I was looking at Garet. But as soon as it approached her I saw it."

"Hmm." Kepler, who had caught up with us, studied Will curiously. "I think that's because you yourself are beginning to fade into the time stream. You partly share the same dimension that the Malefactors travel within, and so they are visible to you."

"Ah," Will said with a wistful smile. "Then there's an advantage to my fading. We'd better get a move on, though, before I fade entirely."

He took my hand and we continued down Fillmore Street. I glanced once more into the shop windows to make sure there weren't any more Malefactors about. There weren't, but I saw something else that alarmed me. In the glass Will's reflection had grown as dark and spectral as the Malefactor's.

We reached the Fillmore without any more incidents. When I saw London Dispersion Force featured on the marquee my heart cheered. I hadn't heard the band in a long time. I could hardly wait to hear Jay's new songs.

Annick and Jules presented their tickets at the box office.

"Super!" the girl in the ticket window enthused when she saw the old tickets. "These will get you in, but are you sure you want to use them? I bet you could get a bundle for them on eBay."

Annick and Jules exchanged a look and Jules answered. "I think we'd better use the tickets—just to be sure."

Kepler produced his ticket and I took out the ones I was carrying. "You've got an extra one," the ticket seller pointed out.

"Could you hold it here for Will Hughes?" Will asked, smiling at the girl. "He'll be a handsome fellow who looks just like me—my twin, in fact."

"Wow, there are two of you? Is your brother single?"

"No," Will replied, glancing at me. "We're both taken."

✿   ✿   ✿

"That was nice of you, to leave the ticket for Will," I said as we entered the lobby. "But are you sure he'll be here?"

"Of course," Will replied. "I know I wouldn't miss it, so why would he?"

We found our seats which were in the twelfth row. A Doors song was playing on the sound system—"Twentieth Century Fox."

"A time reference," Jules commented, craning his neck to study the audience. "It looks as though many of our fellow concert-goers are paying homage to the later middle years of the previous century."

I looked around and saw what Jules meant. Men and women wore their hair long, loose or braided; some even, like the song about San Francisco, wore flowers in their hair. I saw tie-dyed shirts, bell-bottom jeans, fringed leather jackets, and loose Indian kurtas. "I guess everyone decided to go retro for the Doors tribute," I said. "Do you think we'll recognize the Malefactors if they've disguised themselves in these clothes?"

"I will," Will said, squeezing my hand. "Don't worry. I won't let anything happen to you. Now, tell me a little about this concert. Will there be madrigals? Hornpipes? Morris dancing?"

Annick giggled and I proceeded to give Will a history of twentieth-century rock. He seemed to be following, but when the curtain went up and the first band—an all-girl group called Vivian Girls—struck a chord, Will nearly jumped out of his seat. Before long, though, he had adjusted to the music, volume and all, and was tapping his foot to the beat. "I say," he shouted in my ear. "These girls are spirited. Especially the red-headed lass playing the shiny lute."

The crowd gave Vivian Girls a standing ovation. The bass player—the red-headed lass—announced London Dispersion Force. Will cheered Jay, Becky, and Fiona's arrival on stage with gusto. The band opened with one of my favorites of theirs—"Troubadour."

"The troubadours wrote songs to salve heartbreak," Fiona sang, "to let beloveds know their endless pain."

"I might as well attempt to scale a tower," Jay crooned along, "a thousand miles in height, its walls slick stone,/ as try to win your heart which by the hour/grows distant and just leaves me so alone."

I glanced at Will and saw that he was sobered by the lyrics, which, I painfully recalled, Jay had written last year about *me*.

The next few songs were lighter fare, a pop tune about silent movie idols and a bittersweet take-off on fairy-tale happy endings called "Beauty and the Beat." Then they launched into a new song called "Out of Time."

I left my home and family
in the seventeenth century
and now I can't get back.

The portal's gone and I'm alone
and all I do is sob and moan
and that's a sorrowful fact.

Someday I hope time opens wide
and I will be right by their side,
get back the love I lack.

For now the sky's so dark at dusk,
and there's no clock that I can trust:
time won't even open a crack!

I looked at Will and saw that his face was wet with tears. I wiped them away and raised his hand to my lips . . . and in that instant felt a cool prickle on the back of my neck . . . as though I were being watched. I turned around, afraid that I'd find a Malefactor lurking behind me, but instead I found myself looking into the silver eyes of Will Hughes—the *other* Will Hughes—eyes that seemed to show the eight hundred years he had lived through. He was a few rows behind me across a crowd of cheering fans, but we might as well have been standing side by side in an empty room.

I started to say his name, but then a look of alarm replaced the look of pain on his face. Something tugged at my laptop case, which I still wore strapped across my chest. I felt ice-cold fingers gripping the strap, and when they couldn't pull it free I felt the sharp edge of a blade digging through the nylon cloth and into my flesh. I turned and looked into the blank hollow eyes of a Malefactor. It was like staring into a bottomless whirlpool. I felt myself being sucked into the maelstrom of time, into the pit of madness, and knew I'd be falling through those eyes forever.

Then something tugged me back. Young Will had tackled the Malefactor down into the narrow space between the rows of seats. Old Will had clambered over to my side, and then he too had thrown himself into the fray. The Malefactor vanished between them. The two men stood up and stared at each other.

"Hey, sit down!" someone shouted from a few rows back.

Will, the older one, nodded and started to leave our row, but young Will reached and took him by the arm.

"There's an extra seat here," he said, pointing to the seat on the other side of me. "Garet will be safer with both of us here."

The older Will looked at his younger self with surprise and then, slowly, a dawning admiration. "Yes, I believe you are right. I should have thought of it myself." The corner of his mouth twitched, and his younger self laughed. They both sat down on either side of me. Looking from one to the other made me feel a little dizzy, so I looked at the stage. Jay was announcing the next song.

"We'd like to pay a tribute today to some of our friends who have traveled a long way and gone through hell and back to get here. This is London Dispersion Force's version of 'Break on Through.'"

The band broke into the old Doors song made new. As Jay sang, something started to happen. At first I thought it was a psychedelic light show . . .

37

Sheer Charisma

The stage and its backdrop began to waver. The backdrop was a huge curtain of alternating red and blue panels, and at first I thought searchlights were playing off it, but then I saw that the texture of the curtain itself was beginning to fluctuate. It would resemble a tall white movie screen on which hallucinatory multicolored images were dancing, then briefly go back to being a curtain again. The screen, which had a title at its bottom in black curving letters, "Joshua Light Show," predominated more and more. Additional colors rushed into the whirling kaleidoscope at the screen's center, while flaming, fire-spitting dragons pranced around its borders. The dragons had the faces of politicians I recalled from my high school history classes: former president Lyndon Johnson, California governor Ronald Reagan, presidential candidate George Wallace. And others I didn't recognize.

For a few seconds the curtain supplanted the screen, for a final time, and then I felt a broad tremor in the concert hall, as if San Francisco had experienced a mild earthquake. Now the screen came back in vivid detail, and I was startled to see an entirely new band on the stage. The song being played was still "Break on Through," but London Dispersion Force wasn't around anymore. Instead, a lithe figure with a mane of long brown hair, clad entirely in black, and the sole subject of a sizzling spotlight, stood to the front of a drummer, a keyboard player, and a guitarist. At the moment he was twining himself around his mike stand as though it were his lover. I'd seen clips of him in concert and I knew this singer was Jim Morrison, risen from the dead, as it were, through the miracle of time travel. The rest of the band played their instruments with great absorption, occasionally looking up and nodding in affirmation of whatever he was doing, while the tremors rocking the building faded away.

I glanced around the audience members, who were staring at the stage with rapt attention, and saw that their general appearance was different from a few moments earlier. Virtually everyone had long hair, so gender could only be determined when there was a beard or moustache, and most had peace symbols dangling around their necks and glitter-bedecked shirts and blouses. Both Wills and the rest of our party were still in our row, but otherwise the crowd was a new one.

It was actually 1967 now, I guessed, with a sense of recognition resembling that of a traveler: as if I had opened my eyes after a nap on a train and found myself in a different landscape. I knew the year only from history books, had read of its legendary "summer of love."

That hadn't arrived yet, but the Doors were going to be big that summer with their mainstream hit "Light My Fire" and Morrison's increasingly singular antics on stage. This was the winter before the summer. It was a much shorter chronological trip than the ones I'd made between the present and 1602 and back, but somehow it jarred me more. Yet I still didn't think we had passed through the portal that could lead directly to the *chronologistes'* Hall of Time. Close, now. But not quite through it. After another minute or two, I thought I detected a thin film, a gauze of some kind, separating our row from the rest of the Fillmore. I reached out to touch it and it would not let my hand pass through it. It was solider than its filmy appearance and exceedingly cold to the touch.

As the Doors went on to "Soul Kitchen" and the haunting song "The Crystal Ship," I puzzled over what to do next. It was great that we had reached 1967, but we still had to pass fully through this mysterious portal of an unknown nature to reach the *chronologistes*. And I was struck by a fresh, if less immediately crucial concern, while observing Morrison's charisma on the stage. He writhed and pranced, crouched then threw his arms up, crooned before shouting, then murmured. Every gyration wasn't necessarily to my taste, but he had a beautiful face, and I was so drawn to him that I understood how late-1940s bobby soxers had thrown themselves at Frank Sinatra, and early-1960s fourteen-year-olds, at the Beatles. When he moved into the rough and jaunty rhythms of "Whiskey Bar," it suddenly hurt me to think

he was going to die in Paris four and a half years from
now. At a young age that no one should die at. I needed
to warn him. I wouldn't be able to get near the stage
with burly security guards standing between it and the
first rows of seats right now, but maybe afterward . . .
Warn him . . .

An impulse took hold of me and I senselessly tried to
leave my seat anyway, past young Will and on down the
aisle. A few others from elsewhere in the auditorium
had preceded me down the aisle, dancing wildly in the
area between front row and stage under the frowning
gazes of the guards, and their numbers were growing.
Young Will looked sharply up at me but then drew his
knees back to let me through. But right past his seat I
came up against the same filmy barrier I had noticed a
few moments before, and had no choice but to return to
my seat. Glumly, feeling trapped, I watched the continuing performance of "Whiskey Bar," resigned to waiting for another clue or signal, which might come in the
next few minutes or might never come. I considered consulting with the others, but the volume of the performance was so great now that I didn't think I could be
heard even at a shout.

The crowd leapt to its feet at the end of "Whiskey
Bar," beside itself with the energy and drama the Doors,
especially Morrison, had generated. There was a tumult
of clapping and shouting that rolled through the auditorium like some sort of primeval wave. I stood myself or I
wouldn't have seen a thing. And then the Doors launched
into "Light My Fire," recently released but not to be a

hit until the next summer, by which time Ray Manza-
rek's extended organ solo and other guitar solos would
be deleted.

At first slowly, then with more momentum, the light
show on the screen behind them began to change again.
It was drifting from an extravaganza of color and shape
to a more specific collage of images. I noted something
that looked like an irradiated amoeba mutating to a
lemon-colored caterpillar, then a sort of blue tangerine.
Then there were many tangerines, and they were trans-
forming without warning to the heads of many demon-
strators at an antiwar rally in Golden Gate Park, followed
by an aerial view of what was captioned as a "love-in" in
New York City's Central Park, followed by scenes from
the 1963 March on Washington, DC, for civil rights.
There was a sort of charm to it, almost that of antiquated
newsreel footage, though of course the causes these
people were gathering for were serious, even tragic.

Then, for the briefest of instants, these political and
historical images began to be interspersed with seemingly unrelated photographs of some vast desert, a few
primitive huts against a great expanse of sand tinted red
by the sunset. By staring closely at the screen I could
make out, on a rough wooden table in the shade of one
of the huts, a glittering, silver, triangular object. A few
villagers were staring at it fearfully. I got a creepy feeling from it, as of evil. It began to fade away intermittently into more snippets of newsreel coverage, but it kept
coming back.

Then I was so startled I nearly fell off my chair. The same triangular object now occupied a much larger portion of the screen, and it seemed to be in modern times, placed in a box on a table on the stage at an auction house. A little spotlight shone on it and an auctioneer could be seen gesturing toward it. The details of the triangular object were mysteriously blurred, but there was no mistaking the box it was being auctioned off in.

It was the silver box in my computer case, the same one John Dee had asked me to open for him in Greenwich Village and that had started all this trouble in the first place. The auctioneer was pounding his gavel on a podium as if there had been a sale, and he came over to the table and closed the box with the silver object in it. As soon as he did so a date appeared at the bottom of the screen in thin white letters like the time stamp you see on a photograph: January 13, 1967, 2:22 p.m. PST. An insight went through me like a thunderbolt, that if I opened the box in my bag and closed it again, we would pass through the portal we were at the threshold of, the one being suggested on the Fillmore screen. I could not tell if I would find that blurry silver object in the box now. But my certainty regarding this insight was definitive, irrational or even surreal though my confidence may have been. I decided to act on it.

The Doors had started to perform "The End," going from its simple opening refrain into a cacophonous and chaotic interlude of various instrumental strains. Jim

Morrison wandered around the stage very much alone, all black in the white spotlight, the other band members making themselves known with their music from the shadows. He looked almost frighteningly solitary, a tremendous, tumultuous energy pouring out of him in all his movements. Every eye in the auditorium was riveted to him, and there would never be a better time to take a chance on opening the box. And closing it.

Immediately.

I did so.

The box itself, which turned out to be empty, seemed inert while being opened and closed. I was nervous about the powers I could be coming into contact with and did these actions very quickly, but not so quickly that they were not discrete motions. As soon as the silver lid touched the silver frame again the entire concert hall suddenly went silent and pitch black. I saw from the corner of my eye Morrison's mouth open in the primal scream at the end of "The End," and that was the last I saw of him; he vanished into oblivion with the rest of the band, the stage, and all the people around me except for my own party.

Then I lurched forward violently in my seat as though I were starting to travel a considerable distance at a high speed—I closed my eyes against this force—though when the sensation of motion ceased and I opened my eyes again there was no sign I had moved even an inch. The interior of the Fillmore remained dark, but sunlight was filtering in from a few high windows and tiny breaks in the walls. The Doors concert had seemed to be at night but now it must have been 2:22 p.m. as the time stamp said, and a glance at a clock over an exit, visible in a sort of shadowy half light, confirmed that. The stage was empty. The others of my group looked all right—a little dazed and struggling to orient themselves in the new surroundings, as I was—but none the worse for wear.

We were all further dazed to see, in the orchestra space between the first row and the empty stage, a stick figure slowly taking shape in the dim air, his sticks quickly turning into limbs. The figure turned to face us with deliberate caution, assessing the scope and nature of his adversaries, then training an apparent weapon on us in one outstretched hand, a winged white rod that resembled the miniature of an ultra sleek plane. I throbbed with dread as I noted him aiming the weapon at me, more specifically at the box in the bag slung across my chest. But what older Will did at almost exactly that instant astonished me, no doubt all of us, even more than the sudden appearance of this Malefactor.

Will's maneuver made his acrobatic window entry to Octavia's dinner party look clumsy. Even as the Malefactor fine-tuned his aim at the box, I saw his eyes swivel away toward Will and heard his breath draw in sharply. His breathing was as angular in its sound as his physique was in its branches, so high-pitched it was almost a whistling. In a blur, Will somersaulted through the air from his seat, reaching a height of at least twenty feet, and then spun dervishlike down toward the Malefactor, who while watching seemed inert with fear. As Will descended, he managed to keep both legs extended scissors-like, menacing the Malefactor even as the rest of his body twirled. Transmigration, the thought occurred to me. His torso and legs were askew, so he might even have been reshaping his inner atomic structure as he went through the air. Magnificent. Full-strength vampire or not, he was like a martial arts savant—one who could lower his pulse to one beat per hour or breathe three times a day—in the realm of combat acrobatics.

The Malefactor was frozen with bewilderment, and then his expression turned panicky, if the creases folding across his ultra-thin, empty-eyed face could be called an expression. The more he exuded panic, the more his limbs began to dwindle. It seemed he was taking flight in time even before Will, who took an extraordinarily long moment to come down from the peak of his somersault, struck him with his perfectly aimed legs. The Malefactor's weapon dropped to the floor with a clatter. He had partly left this dimension, but there was enough of him remaining that I could see a swirl of twigs and branches slide against the front of the stage like the remnants of a wind-cleaved tree. Those sad remains vanished as if tossed off by another gust of wind.

The rest of the Fillmore remained stone-still and quiet. But the light-show screen flickered briefly to life. It showed a poster for an exhibition at the San Francisco Botanical Garden a few miles away:

THE MALEFACTORS—POISONOUS PLANTS—ROGUES

AND ASSASSINS

Despite the menace of the words and the nature of the exhibition, I felt a sense of relief, even confidence, flood through me. All my flesh and nerves tingled with anticipation. We had found the portal! I was sure of it.

38

A Dragonfly's Genes

Because of our transmigration to 1967, we couldn't go back to our rooms in order to safely store the box. But quick-eyed Jules spotted a small post office no more than a block south of the Fillmore. I bought heavy-duty packaging there and mailed the box back, registered and insured, to the address of my father's gallery in New York. The gallery wouldn't have been there yet, but my parents were already living at that location. I'd worry about the box's disrupted time line afterward. I just hoped it didn't put the airplane it was in, or the entire nation, through any time gyrations as it shipped east!

Annick consulted a map and we caught a streetcar. At first I was too distracted by the argument my friends were having—Kepler felt we should try to reason with the Malefactors, both Wills thought they should be killed on sight, and Annick and Jules thought they should be captured for interrogation—to pay attention to the details of 1967 San Francisco, but when we reached Haight Street the differences became apparent. The streets were full of flower children in tie-dyed clothing and long hair. When we got off to change streetcars, a barefoot girl in a long flowered dress gave me a flower and asked for "some bread." I gave her a dollar bill, and she gave me a beatific smile and a peace sign.

We rode down Haight Street and then walked the last few blocks to the Golden Gate Park entrance at Eleventh Avenue and Lincoln Way. From there we walked alongside an interior road to the arboretum, a botanical garden somewhat like the Jardin des Plantes, except it had an even more labyrinthine quality to its winding and circling paths. A variety of flowers and trees from all over the world lined the paths, their identities described on small black placards standing on spindly sticks. The exhibits had more of a botanical than geographical continuity, Argentina adjacent to Italy, Australia bordering India, all thriving in the damp and misty Mediterranean climate of San Francisco.

The fog that shrouded many of the paths we walked along worried me: it was the middle of the afternoon—shouldn't the fog have burned off by now? It seemed to grow thicker the further we walked into the garden. I thought of what Kepler had said about the fog coming through cracks in time. Might we wander into other time periods as easily as we wandered through these disparate geographical planting zones? What if we got lost in time here? Or separated from one another and found ourselves in different time lines? I looked up anxiously and did a head count. Annick and Jules, sensitive to possibilities for an ambush, were peering into the thick shrubbery and luxuriantly leaved groves of trees. My two Wills stood sentinel on either side of me, glaring at the surrounding foliage as if they thought the rhododendron bushes might attack at any moment. Kepler had strayed the furthest, wandering toward a small ornamental pond that was ringed with purple and white iridescent flowers. He knelt beside it, studying its surface. Wondering what he saw in the water's reflection, I joined him. When I knelt down beside him I saw that he was following the flight of dragonflies.

"What is it?" I asked. "Do you see something?"

"Did you know that genetically these creatures are hundreds of millions of years old? I was just thinking that they too are time travelers—in a genetic sense. Perhaps not as dramatic as the kind of time travel performed by the *chronologistes* or the Malefactors, but also not as warlike. Compared to the few centuries I have traversed, their hundreds of millions of years of genetic passage are godlike. Yet I could no more explain their situation to them than I could explain electricity to a bolt of lightning, or molecular structure to water. And look! Their flight describes a distinctive pattern! At first I was concerned that it could be my imagination, as I've long been fascinated by six-cornered polygons, ever since I wrote 'On the Six-Cornered Snowflake' for my friend Johannes Matthäus Wackher von Wackenfels. But I tested predictions of location from this on-the-spot theory, and they work. Their flight is based on the number six. They're tracing hexagons in the air. It may seem unlikely—entomologists would say dragonflies don't even have enough awareness to know who their parents are, so how can they etch complicated geometry? But atoms don't give lectures on physics, either. And recent studies have shown that pigeons, with their 'bird brains,' can do math! My idol, the ancient Greek thinker Pythagoras, believed in animal intelligence. I feel as if they are showing us *something*."

I stared at the flitting dragonflies, but all I noticed was the jewellike quality of their wings. Perhaps we all saw the world through the lens of our own interests and inclinations. I was a jeweler, and so I saw the design for a brooch. Kepler was obsessed with numbers and geometric forms, and so he saw a hexagonal pattern in the dragonflies' flight. Neither observation seemed to have gotten us any closer to finding the entrance to the institute. Perhaps the sign for the Malefactors exhibit had been a false clue and the institute wasn't even in the garden. And if we couldn't find the institute, we might well be stuck in 1967 forever.

"Come on," I said to Kepler, "the others have gone on without us . . ." But as I spoke, I suddenly saw what he saw. The dragonflies *were* sketching hexagons in the air. The pattern they sketched in the air was drawn on the surface of the water—a hexagonal jigsaw puzzle that suddenly cracked open, revealing a flight of stairs leading down into the earth.

"The institute! You found—"

But before I could finish my sentence, it was interrupted by a scream.

39

Many-handed Tree

It was Annick who had screamed. She was standing about twenty feet away, pointing at a tree. I'd noticed the unusual-looking tree on the way to the pond and recalled its plaque now: "the many-handed tree of Myanmar." It was about forty feet high, pitch black in color, with exceptionally slender branches and leaves of a pale green. Now Annick was pointing at one of its highest branches and reaching into her handbag for a weapon.

One branch was narrower than the others, so thin that it looked like a line through the air. But it started to expand as I watched, thickening until it became a black-clad torso extended horizontally from the trunk, growing limbs, then a head, and dropping upright to the ground, a silver rod in its right hand. Malefactor. The body language was not that of consultation or negotiation, but of attack. Annick had not fired her weapon yet; perhaps she was too stunned. But the new arrival felt no such hesitation. He or she fired the thin filament of a laser beam at her. I heard her shriek as she toppled to the ground. She lay still, enveloped in a film of blue glaze. Whether she was seriously harmed or merely incapacitated, I couldn't tell.

Jules fired back with a weapon that appeared to be made of black steel, resembling but different from a gun, launching a bolt of red flame at the aggressor. With a loud crackling noise, the bolt immolated him or her in an instant, leaving nothing but a pile of ashes on the needle-strewn ground. Brutal: but justified, I had no doubt. Next came a few seconds of ominous stillness, during which nobody moved, not even to help Annick. Jules maintained a vigilant pose, scrutinizing the tree where the Malefactor had appeared. I snapped out of my revery and moved to help Annick, and then Jules, who was closer to her, did too. But Will seemed befuddled.

As I approached Annick I noted to my horror that several more of the tree's branches, perhaps a dozen, were beginning to writhe, tremble, and expand. Two or three fully formed into Malefactors, all with a silver rod in their hands, and they dropped to the ground just as Jules and I reached Annick. The "many-handed tree" might have been a real species, but it also appeared to be a demon. We were being ambushed.

The blue film covering Annick was intense ice to the touch, so cold it burned, and neither I nor Jules could comfort her, let alone help her. We formed a four-cornered cordon around her to protect her from further harm and fired away. Jules had removed more weapons from his backpack and tossed them to both Wills and Kepler. I waved away his offer of a weapon. Instead, I rubbed my fingers together, concentrating on the heat in my own skin. I'd only used the firestarting trick that Oberon had taught me a year ago for light, but I thought it might work as a weapon. I was angry enough, certainly, to generate heat. I saw one of the Malefactors aiming at young Will, and I thrust my arm in its direction. A bolt of flame rushed out of my fingertips and struck the Malefactor before he could fire. With an eerie high-pitched shriek, he went up in flames like a Roman candle. Another one took its place and aimed directly at me. I thrust my hand at it, and the creature was instantly engulfed in flames. No fewer than twenty Malefactors had dropped from the tree now; nearly half its branches had turned out to be the insidious creatures! I tried firing flame at the tree itself a couple of times, with the intention of burning it entirely, but it seemed resistant to fire.

The other Malefactors scrambled toward cover everywhere they could find it: behind bushes, boulders, benches, other trees, firing at us as they went. One scored a direct hit on the bench we had vacated, enveloping it in the same blue gloss that shrouded Annick. Once the eye adjusted to the speed of the filaments, it was possible to dodge them to a degree.

The Malefactors nicked us and got near us with some shots but failed to immobilize us as they had Annick. Both Wills wielded their silver rods like swords, against Malefactors who left their cover and tried to approach them, thrusting and parrying like Errol Flynn in *Captain Blood*. Kepler turned out to be an excellent marksman.

And Jules, who remained crouched beside Annick, was relentless in his fury, firing away at any Malefactors who dared to menace her.

Still, I was not sure if we would have been able to stave them off if we hadn't had reinforcements. *Chronologistes* came pouring out of the pond—or where the pond had been: a small army equipped with the same silver rods Jules had given out to us. They fanned out in the clearing, forming a cordon around us and the entrance to the institute. Since my fire-throwing skills were clearly no longer needed, I knelt down beside Annick. Jules was beside her, chafing her cold lifeless hands, tears streaming down his face.

"They've sprayed her with a paralyzing agent. She's still alive, but her pulse is weakening. The same thing happened to a colleague on my first mission. There was nothing I could do to save him . . . I don't know how to remove the agent."

The thin blue glaze coated Annick like a rime of frost, as if she'd been the victim of an ice storm. Her green eyes stared sightless from beneath the ice, her lips slightly parted. I touched my hand to her forehead and was shocked by the intensity of the cold.

"It's the ether of time," Will said, "I can feel it creeping in my own veins." He had come to crouch beside me. I glanced at him and saw he had a line of blood on his cheek from the battle. For a moment I wasn't sure which Will it was, but then I recognized the jacket he'd put on this morning. It was young Will.

The other Will stood, looking down at us. "Yes," he

said, holding up his hand. A thick blue glow surrounded his fingers. "I feel it, too. The stuff of time. It gathers on you when you travel through time, and eventually it freezes your soul. The Malefactors have collected it and turned it into a weapon. God knows what they plan to do with it."

"What can we do for her?" Jules cried. He was still holding Annick's hand. I didn't understand how he could bear the intense cold. Just grazing my fingertips over her skin froze me to the bone. But if he could stand it, so could I. I lay my hand on her forehead, closed my eyes, and listened.

I heard the sound of bells chiming—tiny crystal bells ringing across a vast frozen plain. I was in a snowstorm, Kepler's six-sided snowflakes swirling around me . . . no, not snowflakes—*stars*. I was hurtling through outer space, through the vast reaches of the universe . . . and then I was standing on a spinning atom.

I opened my eyes. "I know what to do," I said, looking up at Will. "She's caught in between times. We have to transmigrate the atoms surrounding her. You've done that before . . ."

Will shook his head a little sadly. "I have, but I fear that just in the past few minutes I may have lost some of my ability to do that. I seem to have . . . er . . . lost something."

He looked down at younger Will. "When I sent my younger self back to the future with you, I didn't realize that, in a certain supernatural sense, I was separating myself into two halves. I thought the ache I felt these last four hundred years was my loneliness for you, Garet, and part of it was that . . ." He smiled ruefully, and I smiled back.

"But it wasn't just that, was it? It's a bit like Good Kirk / Bad Kirk."

Both Wills—my two loves—looked at me as if I'd lost my mind. And Jules scowled at me. "For Heaven's sake! My beloved is dying and you're making analogies to that ridiculous American TV show!"

It's a good thing Jay's not here to hear that, I thought.

"You're right," I said to Jules. "But we do have time to spare . . . or, rather, we have *too much* time on our hands. Annick is frozen in time. The two Wills are split in time. I think—"

I didn't have conventional time to explain my reasoning even if I had been able to. Perhaps Kepler could have. I reached out my left hand to young Will and my right hand to old Will. Together we formed a triangle over Annick. When they took my hands I felt a surge of electricity jolt through me, cold at first, then burning hot. I felt something else. Both these men loved me: young Will with the passion of first love, the thrill of newness and discovery; old Will with the patient endurance of long-lasting love. Was it ever possible to have both? It was an enigma more mysterious than the mechanisms of time travel.

I pulled my hands away and placed them on Annick's chest, directly over her heart. The charge I had gathered thudded through her with the force of a defibrillator. It shattered the blue glaze into a million splinters. I felt Annick's heart slam against my hands. Was the force too strong for her? Would her heart explode? I felt as if mine would, as I waited to see what would happen.

Annick's heart proved to be strong. She gasped as she took in a breath, and her eyes locked on Jules. "*Mon ami,*" she said in a hoarse whisper. "I am quite sure protocol demands that the leader of the mission stay with his troops and not attend to one fallen comrade—"

He silenced her with a kiss.

I stood up to give them some privacy, but my legs, numb from crouching so long—or perhaps the effect of the time-ice—gave way beneath me. As I stumbled, both Wills reaching for me, I looked up and found myself staring into the crazed empty eyes of a Malefactor, his weapon pointed directly at my heart. As he fired, two things happened at once. Old Will threw himself in front of me, and young Will threw himself in front of his older self. The blue flame struck young Will. Old Will tackled the Malefactor, and I fell to young Will's side. The blue glaze was creeping across his face, but it hadn't frozen his lips yet. He smiled at me. "My lady, I seem to be out of time . . . but it's all right." His eyes flicked to his older self, who, having destroyed the Malefactor, knelt beside him. "I will catch up with you anon . . ."

Instead of freezing as Annick had, he began to glow. I looked up at old Will, whose face was stricken with grief as he grasped his younger self's hand in both of his. Young Will turned to his older self.

"Take care of her," he said.

"As well as you would yourself," he replied.

The blue glow enveloped young Will and then exploded in a flash. Weakened as he was, he apparently couldn't hold out against it as Annick had.

When it was gone, only one Will remained.

40

The Boy and the Man he Became

Will put his arms around me and helped me to my feet. I didn't realize until he touched me that I was shaking. Not with cold, but with a sense of absence. My mother told me once that after she gave birth to me she had begun to convulse. The midwife told her that it was because her body was adapting to the loss of heat generated by the baby she'd carried for nine months. I felt that same sense of loss now—as if a part of my flesh had been ripped away.

But then Will put his arms around me, and the warmth from his body took the place of that loss. "He's here," he said to me, "inside me now. You see, I was right; he was my better self."

He steered me toward the opening where the pond had been. Jules and Kepler were helping Annick down through it while the *chronologistes* were finishing cleaning up the battle scene. As I entered the underground entrance I took one glance back. The peaceful grove we had found looked like a tornado had hit it—leaves and branches scattered everywhere. The Malefactors who had attacked us were either dead or had fled.

The flight of stairs down was longer than I'd hoped for and treacherous in places, the moss-slick surfaces suggesting no one used it very often. Twice I started to slip, but Will steadied me with his strong grip. At the bottom we entered a high-ceilinged room that was, at a glance, identical to the one in the institute in Paris, including a pendulum suspended from an oculus, which swept regular circles in a ring of sand. I was struck by the geometric link between these time-evoking circles and the hexagons Kepler had used to unlock time's mystery to get us here, but I didn't linger over this connection, as Monsieur Durant appeared to greet us. He kissed me on both cheeks after enthusiastically embracing both Annick and Will. He shook Kepler's hand so passionately that I realized they must have known each other previously. Only Jules held back from Monsieur Durant's effusive greeting. He drew himself up stiffly and saluted Monsieur Durant.

"Agent Maupassant reporting, sir," he announced in a loud, officious voice. "Dispatched from the Paris institute seventy-three hours and forty-one minutes ago to retrieve two civilians from the catacombs. I regret to inform you that one of our agents, Jean-Luc Moran, was killed in the line of the duty, sir."

Durant's expression, beaming at our arrival, turned sober. "I am very sorry to hear that, Agent Maupassant. Agent Moran will be sorely missed. His name shall be engraved in the Hall of Time and his memory preserved through eternity." Durant bowed his head, and all the *chronologistes* in the hall bowed theirs as well. After a moment Monsieur Durant lifted his head and looked at Jules, who still stood at attention.

"I see that you have brought the rest of your team safely through time. We were afraid you would not be able to locate the San Francisco institute."

"Yes, sir, and as you know, we were followed by the Malefactors, whom, thankfully, your forces have destroyed."

"Would that we had achieved their complete demise," he replied, gazing up toward the oculus as an ancient Roman might have at the one in the Pantheon, beseeching any deity who resided up there and in lieu of one, the sky, for ultimate and total victory. "We believe there are in excess of five hundred Malefactors in this universe alone. And there's no way to tally how many might have slipped off into alternative universes since the organization began, a few decades after the publication of Shakespeare's sonnets in 1609. However, if you had not led this rogue patrol here, they would have caused mayhem elsewhere. I congratulate you all on your bravery and skill." He regarded Jules with a gaze damp with emotion. "You have done well, son." He clamped Jules on the back and drew him in to kiss him on both cheeks. When Jules was released, his face glowed with pride. Monsieur Durant turned to the rest of us and continued.

"Even in San Francisco there would seem to be considerably more than the thirty or so we originally estimated. We are preparing for the worst, for hundreds more to arrive from Europe in the next few days, now that they think they don't have our Paris presence to worry about anymore. But we will be ready for them here, and in fact are also already beginning reconstruction of our hall in Paris while the Malefactors recklessly exult, drunk with victory."

Durant nodded at a corner of the room, and I could see a large stack of weapons there, all resembling the ones Jules and Annick had brought to the arboretum. I guessed there was enough firepower there to win a small war if it came to that, though I hoped it wouldn't. The pile seemed high enough for a force in the thousands.

"Yes, it requires recruiting many new *chronologistes* of military age, hopefully with capabilities like you young people have just displayed," Durant said, following my gaze. "Our librarians and scholars will not be up to it, even in an emergency. But this is a challenge for another day.

"Let me show you around. Our San Francisco establishment was already spectacular when we refugees from Paris got here, and it is more so now!" He began walking toward the door at the other end of the room, and we followed. The next room seemed similar to the one in Paris also, with endless ceiling-high bookcases, long wooden reading tables at which multiple librarians and scholars sat, and stacks of books, journals, and newspapers piled everywhere else, all over the floor. Then my eye caught a spectacular difference.

The far wall of the room was glass and faced the ocean. It didn't have an ocean view; it faced its *depths*, dark green water slowly moving, with streaks of salt and the occasional fish visible. Given the depth of the staircase I understood how we could be below sea level, but it was startling, even shocking, to see. I wondered how a pane of glass could be holding back all that water. An occasional shaft of sunlight as the water shifted suggested we weren't too far down, but the surface was not visible. At intervals some sort of tidal surge sent a crescendo of foam against the window, bubbling and frothing, retreating in a wash of silver.

The longer I looked, the more I noticed living creatures. The head of a seal, eyes wide open, pressed briefly against the glass. The large shadow of something moving just above the window frame: could that be a whale? Then, startlingly, a sand shark about ten feet or so in length glided right along the glass. I knew they weren't man-eaters, but even so I experienced a momentary fear of the glass shattering, the shark spilling in the room alongside us, jaws wide.

We were looking on raptly and Durant was beaming. "We all come from the sea originally, and these creatures are our cousins. What a privilege to be living so close to them. Our living quarters are off a corridor above this hall, many rooms with smaller but similar views."

We nodded in a kind of mystic unison at the breathtaking closeness to the sea. Will came to join me at the window. He put his arm around me. "You're thinking about him, aren't you?" he asked.

Unable to face him, I looked at Will's eyes in the reflection. "I know it's foolish. I know you're the same person . . ."

He shook his head and touched his hand to his chest. "He is inside *here*, but we're not the same. I feel his loss, too, his enthusiasm and passion. I had forgotten how those felt until I met you—then I saw him and I thought I could give you that youthful passion. Now, when I look into your eyes . . ." He turned to me, and I turned away from the reflection to face him. "I see your love for him, and that youthful self comes alive inside me again."

As Will slipped his arm around my shoulders and we stood there looking on and on, gazing into the heart of forever, I thought to myself that it wasn't everybody who got to love the boy and the man he became at the same time.

Lee Carroll is a pseudonym for the writing partnership of award-winning novelist Carol Goodman and her poet husband, Lee Slonimsky. The other two novels they have written together are the acclaimed *Black Swan Rising* and its sequel *The Watchtower*. They live in Red Hook, New York.